MW00622966

Dana:

Thank you so much

for all these years.

Jane

INVISIBLE ORPHANS

INVISIBLE ORPHANS

JADE MOON LE

RARE BIRD
LOS ANGELES, CALIF.

RARE BIRD

This is a Genuine Rare Bird Book

Rare Bird Books
6044 North Figueroa Street
Los Angeles, CA 90042
rarebirdbooks.com

Copyright © 2022 by Jade Moon Le

FIRST HARDCOVER EDITION

All rights reserved, including the right to reproduce this book or portions thereof in any form whatsoever, including but not limited to print, audio, and electronic.

For more information, address:
Rare Bird Books Subsidiary Rights Department
6044 North Figueroa Street
Los Angeles, CA 90042

This is a work of fiction and a product of the author's imagination.
Names, characters, businesses, places, events, and incidents are used in a fictitious manner. Any resemblance to actual persons, living or dead, or actual events is purely coincidental

Set in Minion
Printed in the United States

FIRST HARDCOVER EDITION ISBN: 9781644283141

10 9 8 7 6 5 4 3 2 1

Library of Congress Cataloging-in-Publication Data available upon request

For some of you, to endure means to be alive.
For others, to give up means to be free from torment.

CONTENTS

CONTENTS

PROLOGUE

MEMORY FASCINATES ME. A word, sound, or smell recalls it. I have no control of its coming. My memory plays like a movie making itself as I watch; as if I were walking right onto a set, observing this distinct segment of the story unfold, not worrying about how it fits into the chronological order of the plot.

Memory scares me when I realize I have lost some of it and have no way to bridge what is gone.

Memory is perpetually alive with mental wandering.

Memory lives on its own; all the beauty and experience uniquely mark each of us as individual human beings, a gift and a blessing.

My memories are like a ball of yarn inadvertently cut by scissors with multiple loose strands. For each strand I pull, memory appears like a flashback in a movie: I can see the whole scene before me, filling in the gaps with my mind's eye. As each string is unknotted, my narrative connects like a puzzle being put together, one piece at a time; a chronicle displays, a tale untangles, and a future awaits.

THE ENCOUNTER

HOW DO YOU REACT when you realize that you have lost memories? For me, tears come first without thinking of them. Then I don't know what to do. I try to think, searching for when and what I can remember. Sometimes pieces and pieces of memories gradually surface while I am working in the garden, either tying up the tomatoes; building expansions to hold up the sunflowers; harvesting beans, cucumbers, peas, squashes, different greens; or simply weeding.

The garden has been my retreat. Feeling the serenity of being surrounded by beautiful plants, listening to the leaves susurrate and dance with the wind, and watching branches with waves of shadowy sunlight in early evenings has given me a sense of dreaming, a sense of belonging, and a sense of voicing myself. Most importantly, the garden has brought back memories that I lost years ago, but I do not know if they are in sequence.

The memories contain an unspoken promise, to Matthew. I have a story to tell; a love story evolved by serendipity with a twist of fate.

It is a distant time, back in late January 1984, the winter days just before Chinese New Year.

I was a kindergarten teacher and wanted to go somewhere that I could afford during the holiday break. In fact, I already had a place in mind. When I was in second grade, my geography teacher taught us about Hainan Island in southern China. He told us that Hainan was different than the rest of China, being the top coffee-producing area in the country. For me, growing up amid the Portuguese in Macau, the smell of coffee and the sensation of a scoop of ice cream in a glass of iced coffee on a sweltering day with eighty-seven percent humidity brought incomparable joy. My teacher also told us that in Hainan the locals' first choice of beverage was coffee, second was cocoa, and third was tea, which was a very different preference from that of the Chinese culture I had known. I vowed that someday I would see Hainan for myself.

Hainan had just recently opened for tourism, so I bought my train and plane tickets. Lodging was not in the plan, however. Without any travel agencies servicing the island, I had no information about it. I figured that somehow I would find lodging once I got there.

Tony, my ex-boyfriend, was a calm person. Most of the time, I got my way when we spent time together. But I didn't feel anything special, except appreciation that if I wanted to see him, he would be there at any time, no complaints. I seldom found myself thinking of him. He was merely a useful tool. He didn't bring me excitement or make my heart jump into my throat. Clearly, this was not the romantic relationship I had envisioned.

Tony asked me to marry him in the spring of 1983. I told him that if we weren't married by December, that meant I wouldn't marry him. I broke up with Tony in October 1983.

&

TEN DAYS BEFORE MY trip, Tony called and wanted to know my plans for Chinese New Year. I told him. Two days later, he informed me that he would like to join me. I said okay.

We took the train from Hong Kong across the border into the People's Republic of China and flew from Guangzhou to Haikou, the capital of Hainan. Before boarding the plane, a businessman sat next to us in the waiting area. He told us that he was going to Hainan on behalf of his wife, who was an illegal immigrant and didn't have proper identification and travel documents to leave Hong Kong to visit her parents in Hainan. By the time we landed on the island, the businessman suggested that we have dinner together.

When we entered the dining hall, the businessman was talking to a Caucasian. We went to his table, and he introduced Matthew to us. Matthew had traveled by boat from nearby Zhanjiang and had been guided by a People's Liberation Army officer to the guest house, which turned out to be the designated place for all visitors to Hainan Island.

The next morning around seven o'clock, the lobby was crowded with guests. Apparently, most of the guests were just like the businessman—visiting relatives on the island. Only Matthew, Tony, and I were real tourists. By the time I reached the front desk, I heard the businessman saying to Matthew, "Don't worry, my two friends will travel with you."

"What's the matter?" I asked.

Matthew looked at us. "The service manager told me that I can't travel alone on this island. I can either join a tourist group or have a tour guide with me. Otherwise, I have to leave the island in the next few hours."

The businessman waved his hand to the service manager and without consulting us said, "Comrade, these are my friends. They will all travel together." He pointed to the three of us. Apparently, the service manager didn't speak English. He pointed at Matthew and us and asked in Mandarin, "You know each other?"

I nodded.

He pulled out a form. "Fill in all the information and make sure to report to all local guesthouses with the same information."

After completing the paperwork, we were sent to a minivan with six other guests, all of whom were visiting relatives on the island. We left the guest house around eight o'clock after a small breakfast. We had no food, no water, or any other beverage to bring with us. Along the semi-paved road, there were no vendors. But there was a beautiful blue sky and palm trees as far as the eye could see. The morning was already warm, and soon we heard the sounds of whispering waves in the distance.

After almost three hours of driving, we were thirsty. The other guests asked the driver if we could get some water somewhere.

The driver replied, "No guest houses or shops from Haikou to Sanya."

I couldn't imagine how parched I'd feel by the time we finally reached the other side of the island. Eventually, the driver stopped the van. He took out a machete and some ropes and walked toward a cluster of palm trees. We followed him. The sound of the waves got increasingly louder, and the palm trees seemed to shrink as the road gradually got wider. Before I knew it, we were walking on sand beneath the sun's golden rays. In front of me was a field of coconut trees not far from shore. White flowery waves danced against the rocks, creating a harmonious contrast with the glittering emerald sea.

The driver asked one of the guests to belay him, and he swiftly climbed up a coconut tree. In no time, coconuts whooshed to the ground. Drinking fresh coconut water under the sparkling sun cured my thirst. The clean taste and feeling alive in such a splendid environment elevated my whole being.

We resumed our trip. Gradually, other passengers got off one by one. Now, only three of us, the real tourists, were left. I moved up to the front row and said to the driver, "You were so skillful and at ease climbing the coconut tree. Do you gather coconuts often?"

"Collecting coconuts became very helpful for my family. My mother learned from the natives how to make all sorts of things from the coconuts, which saved our scarce resources for other needs." He stopped talking and looked up at the rearview mirror. I'd been listening so intently that I hadn't realized I was leaning forward into the space above the armrest console. "I was the one to collect the free coconuts. I went to all the nearby places with other kids whose families were in the same situation as mine. Sometimes we got free rides. Most of the time we were on foot. Tianya Cape was one of the places that I frequented and the most comfortable place for me to feel free. The bunch of us would linger until dark and would then drag the coconuts home."

"Is Tian Ya Hai Jiao 天涯海角 (The Edge of the Sky and Corner of the Sea) in Tianya Cape?"

"You will see it yourself."

The van soon stopped again, and we followed the driver as the path gradually expanded to a full view of a sandy beach with different sizes of rocks poking up along the shore near and far. Once I stepped onto the creamy surface, I felt warm and soft as if I were walking groundless but still with a solid feeling of holding myself steady. The horizon got bigger and bigger, and my eyes were filled with blue, white, black, yellow, and glittering sparkles—so gentle with abstract shapes coming and going in white splashes.

"Ah." I thrust my hands upward and yelled, "Tian Ya Hai Jiao 天涯海角, I am here!"

The driver, Tony, and Matthew were laughing. The driver took out a cigarette, then passed the pack to the other two men, who declined. He lit it and walked toward the ocean, standing in the mid distance between land and sea, looking around and back at us. "Isn't it heaven?"

I ran to him and shouted, "I envy you having this in your backyard!"

"Yes, only this saved my childhood and let me feel that life is tolerable."

I looked into his eyes without a word. He stared at me then smiled. "You are too young. Let me take you to the real Tian Ya Hai Jiao." He threw the cigarette butt down, and I watched as he ground it into the solid, creamy sand.

"Huh? Tian Ya Hai Jiao is this beach, isn't it?" I was dumbfounded to hear there was a real Tian Ya Hai Jiao. I thought I was already there.

He raised his head, looked at me as if I were a child not knowing what I was asking, and walked away from me while motioning us to follow him. I went after him without acknowledging my two companions.

We walked along the shore toward some of the rocks near the water. The driver turned around and walked backward. "Come over here."

I hastened to where he stood. A huge boulder was on his right. I walked toward the water and when I turned to face the boulder, I saw blood red writing in Chinese with two characters on the top, Tian Ya 天涯 (The Edge of the Sky), and four on the bottom, Hai Kuo Tian Kong 海闊天空 (Boundless Sea Wide Sky).

"Why here?"

"I don't know. Old people said this is the southernmost point of China."

"Was the writing there when you were growing up?"

"Yes, these are pretty much the first characters I learned. From time to time, my father would mention that we were exiled to the end of the world. Fortunately, we were all together."

I looked at this gigantic boulder. The water hitting it was clear and there were a bunch of much smaller rocks scattered nearby. I took off my shoes for the first time, rolled up my pants, walked toward the boulder, and asked, "Could I touch it?"

The driver laughed and waved his hand. "Go for it. We've climbed on it a thousand times and no one ever goes after us."

The boulder, Tian Ya, was hot. I had put a sweater on when I got out of bed, but now the sun was above my head. I was sweating but I didn't want to take off the sweater among strangers. The driver was wearing a long-sleeve blue jacket with what looked like a wool hat. I thought, if he can tolerate the heat, so can I.

Matthew followed my steps in big strides, the water swirling with his movements. We both leaned against Tian Ya and gazed into the emerald sea.

I wanted to freeze time. I was thirsty and hungry, but I didn't want to go anywhere. I enjoyed the euphonies among the rocks, the sea, and the coconut trees. With the panorama, I understood what the driver had meant by "heaven." There were no structures in sight, not a single building.

Tony waved his hand to get our attention. "Let me take a picture of you two."

Matthew and I looked at each other, deciding how we should position ourselves.

"I want to see all six characters," I said.

"It's hard to get all of them with you. The rock is just too big." Tony adjusted the camera. "How about only the bottom four?"

"Is that the best you can do?"

"If you want to be in the picture."

Matthew said to me, "He's right. Let's squat to get those four characters." He signaled "okay."

Matthew was at least seven inches taller than me. While he squatted, I only half bent my knees to match his height.

Before dark we were dropped off at a guest house, the entrance of which looked like a jungle with different kinds of green trees, vines, and shrubs intertwined with each other. The guest house had a few single-story structures on the premises. We were led to a long building with only two doors along the open corridor. Our room was huge. There were six beds with mosquito nets hung over them. All three of us were in the same room. I tried to persuade the service desk to let me have a room for myself.

"These rooms were built to host six people. Now, you have double the space for only three of you," the person in charge said.

I guessed "gender-specific needs" was not in this manager's vocabulary.

We were ready to devour whatever we could get from the guest house. We were the only guests in the entire dining room. Then I realized that people who visited relatives, like the businessman we met at the airport, would not stay at a guest house.

The server came in quickly with a steaming bowl in her hands. She put it down. It was fish soup. She turned and was about to walk away.

"Excuse me," I said.

She looked at me, and before I could say anything, she said, "The rice and other two dishes will come soon. We serve whatever ingredients we have."

I nodded and said thank you.

Matthew asked, "What did you want to say?"

"I want to see the menu."

Matthew smiled. "My experiences in China have taught me that at some places there is no menu and no choice. This looks like one of those places. But," he took up the ladle, "those no-choice places often serve good and tasty food." He scooped a big spoonful of soup into my bowl.

Small pieces of fish with bones, a few diced scallions, and some kind of greenish-looking sliced gourds with white ground pepper swirled within my bowl. The broth tasted fresh and clean. The gourds were tender and the bones came out in one piece.

The next day we explored the nearest surroundings on foot. To our surprise, we walked into a plantation that was run by a co-op next to the guest house. The entrance of the co-op was crowded with jackfruit trees, and some of the jackfruits were hanging within my reach. As we walked on, I learned that Matthew studied botany. The plantation opened up to him as if it were a botanical garden. Matthew was so excited. He took out a small notepad and began identifying the plants. He held up some peppercorns whose vines were interwoven with some other spreading tropical plants, and pointed to coffee plants with little red fruits and to other vegetation all over the place. He picked up a leaf, looked carefully at one side then turned to the other. He traced the veins and said, "You see, when it's difficult to identify a plant, the veins can tell the subtle differences between species."

In the afternoon, we were up at a high spot with the South China Sea displayed below. There was a massive field of tall pampas grass with dirty white inflorescences swinging in the melody of the ocean breeze. I instantly fell in love with the pampas grass and wanted to pick a few stalks. It was hard to pick them. Fortunately, Matthew had a Swiss Army knife. I was so excited to select the stockiest one to cut. All of a sudden, a soldier emerged from the tall pampas grass and closed in on us.

"Why are you here?"

We looked at each other.

The soldier continued, "Are you all together? Do you know each other?"

"Yes, we're friends, and we just happened to walk by and admire the pampas grass."

The soldier saw that I was holding some pampas grass. He walked around us and said, "You are not supposed to be here. This is an army base, you know?"

"No, we didn't know. We didn't see any signs." I replied.

"Where are you from?"

"Hong Kong."

"Ah, your Mandarin is okay. Are these two men from Hong Kong as well?"

"We're traveling together." I pointed to Matthew. "He is from the US."

The soldier addressed Matthew. "Do you speak Mandarin?"

Matthew raised his right hand, holding his thumb and index finger in parallel. "A little," he replied in Mandarin.

The soldier smiled and gave a thumbs-up. "How long have you been in China?"

"Since last August."

"Doing what?"

17

"I teach English at Shaanxi Normal University."

The soldier gradually became softer as Matthew responded to his questions. Tony appeared nervous. I was astounded by the discovery of Matthew's ability in Mandarin.

The soldier let his guard down and said, "Do you want to see the base?"

I raised my hand and nodded.

"Follow me." The soldier headed back to the pampas grass. In front of us was a meandering footpath that I had not noticed earlier. We went downhill on small switchbacks where there was no pampas grass or any other plants. Soon we were on a narrow pass at the edge of a cliff; one side faced the sea and the other side was a huge open cave. To my astonishment, there were cannons arranged in a semicircle all aimed at the sea.

"Wow," I whispered.

"Hainan is an important military base for guarding South China." The soldier pointed to the sea. "There is Vietnam."

Under the bright sun, I squinted at the sea but only saw small dots above the water. "Are we under the pampas grass field?"

"Not just the pampas grass field, which is only part of the camouflage. The entire peak covers the base. Some areas are restricted, so I cannot bring you there. This is the only area that I can show you."

"Is all the artillery in here?"

"The majority of them."

When the soldier walked us back up to the pampas grass field, he told us, "Hainan is our southernmost frontier to defend against invasion, which is one of the main reasons that this island was not open to the public for a long time, even though other parts of China have been gradually welcoming tourists. You all are lucky to see this. Go home safely."

Matthew extended his hand to shake the soldier's hand, and I bowed slightly with my palms pressed together. Tony was still nervous and speechless.

The next day was the first day of Chinese New Year, but stores were still open and people went on with their daily work lives. I was puzzled why people didn't take the day off.

Matthew said, "The natives are not all Han Chinese," which reminded me that the Li (Hlai), Yao (Miao), and Utsul (Hainan Hui) ethnic groups were also native to this island. Han would celebrate the New Year in mainland China and, of course, in Hong Kong.

We went into a small coffee shop, which was basically a thatch structure. Inside it looked like a bar with wooden seats in front of the long serving counter. There were no tables. We sat down. There were only two servers who wore white shirts and white caps. I saw a long metal pipe with multiple faucets attached to the back wall, opposite to where we sat, approximately at the height of the servers' hips. Steaming water was running, and cups were lined up under those faucets. The servers were busy with rinsing the cups and turning to customers to pour coffee from an aluminum kettle in their hands.

I had never seen any coffee serving system like this. I was so impressed. I asked the most obvious question, "Why are you constantly rinsing the cups with hot water?"

The server said, "Don't know. This is the way we drink our coffee."

The coffee was smooth and strong. The aromatic scent sipped through my taste buds with the silky fluid slowly lighting up other sensors as if it were saying, "Hello there, have a pleasant day."

After coffee, we walked to the center of town, which was only one street away. There were vendors selling vegetables, fruits, small household appliances, coconut-leaf containers, and other things. But there was no meat, no live animals, or slaughtered poultry for that matter. No fish, nor shellfish.

At the end of the town, we saw another thatch structure. In front of it were different sizes of coffins on display. Matthew was interested in talking to the shopkeeper to find out what kinds of wood were used. He needed my help because the townspeople didn't speak Mandarin. I didn't know how to help him, though, because I didn't understand their dialects.

I went in with Matthew, but Tony stood out in the sun. He didn't show any interest in entering the shop.

The shopkeeper was exhilarated when Matthew inquired about what kinds of wood the shop used to make the coffins. The shopkeeper understood our Mandarin and responded effortlessly. He explained, "We use all different kinds of local wood. In general, coffins are often made with more than one type of wood."

He picked up a small piece of wood. "Like this one. We call it *huali*, which is valued for its colors and sturdiness. We craft it for elaborate decoration. We seldom make a complete coffin with only huali. Here is *nanmu*, the most common wood to make coffins with. However, nanmu has different grades. The finest of all the nanmu is *Hongmao nanmu*, which is indigenous to Hainan Island. Smell them."

He held up his hands. Matthew picked up one piece at a time to examine and smelled them. I, on the other hand, had already perceived the pleasant scents of the shop when I first set foot in it. At this point, Tony came into the store and gingerly stood behind Matthew and me. He was dead silent. Tony appeared to be nervous, but that wasn't unusual, particularly when Tony wasn't in a familiar environment with familiar faces. I had seen him acting nervously when we ate at a new restaurant, shopped in a new mall, or anywhere with many strangers.

By late afternoon, we arrived in Sanya City. We were dropped off in front of a guest house that was the tallest building I had seen on Hainan Island. Our room was on the fifth floor. Once again, the room had six beds, but this time without the mosquito nets. Opposite the door were four windows lined up on one side of the room. They were open a little, the beige curtains fluttering slightly. Two beds were next to two end windows, right below the windowsills. I knelt on one bed and peeked out to see the street down below. I picked the first bed of the three in the row next to the door. Matthew picked the farther side below the window, and Tony dropped his bag on the middle bed next to mine. The room was a relatively big rectangle, like a dormitory room, only there was a wide-open space in the middle without any desks. Only two chairs were against the wall in the open space below two center windows. There was no telephone, no television, nor side tables with lamps. The only light was in the center of the ceiling.

The men's and women's bathrooms were in the hallway. After dinner, I went to take a shower while Matthew and Tony were in the room. When I came back to the room, Matthew was reading, sitting on one of the chairs that was close to my side of the room. Tony was fumbling with his bag. Without warning, he ran up on one of the beds by the window and stood on the windowsill yelling "Bruce Lee" and my name.

I shouted, "Grab him!" Matthew reacted quickly and hugged Tony's legs while his upper body was already pushed out of the window. Matthew dropped both of their bodies onto the bed, and they struggled with each other. Matthew was about six feet and a hundred seventy-five pounds, and Tony was five feet ten and a hundred fifty pounds. I tried to hold Tony's hands down and asked Matthew to use his own weight to pin him flat. I don't know how long all three of us were entangled on the bed. Gradually, Tony slowed his fighting, and his yelling faded away.

I managed to stand up and asked Matthew, "Do you have him?"

"Yes, I think so."

I closed all four windows and told Matthew, "I am going down to the lobby to ask for help. Please keep him with you." Matthew nodded.

After I told the front desk manager what had just happened, he went to the room behind the desk, and then came back to tell me that an ambulance was on its way and that I should go back to the room and wait for help to come. I went back to the room. Tony was quiet. Matthew used his hands to flatten Tony's hands onto the hard mattress. His body was half parallel on top of Tony's with his legs diagonally crossing Tony's legs like a scissor leg lift. Tony's body looked crooked.

"Is he sleeping?"

"No, he's just staring into space."

"An ambulance is coming. I'll pack for all of us." I stuffed everything back into each of our bags. I had no clue why Tony had behaved this way. But somehow I knew what to do. I felt bad for Matthew, an outsider being pulled into this situation. I didn't think he knew more than I did in this matter.

A man and a woman, each wearing a white coat, came into the room. The man took Tony's pulse and used a small flashlight to examine his eyes. Tony continued to stare into space and seemed not to know that the paramedics were there. After the brief examination, the man said to the woman, "Give him a shot of tranquilizer, then we can drive through the night to Haikou."

The woman prepared the needle and was about to inject Tony, who violently jerked his body and with both hands extended like a superman who was about to take flight, again shouted "Bruce Lee" and my name. The woman was startled and took a step back.

"You are a nurse. You cannot be afraid of him. Give him the shot!" I demanded.

After Tony was sedated, the paramedics went back to the ambulance to get the stretcher. They strapped him to the stretcher and loaded him into the ambulance and ordered Matthew and me to sit on the bench behind the stretcher.

I trembled from shock next to Matthew on the way to Haikou. We didn't speak. I was mentally exhausted but couldn't sleep for the first three hours of the ride. When we arrived in Haikou, I found my head resting on Matthew's shoulder. We were at the same hotel that we'd stayed in our first night on the island.

The paramedics talked to the people at the front desk and took the stretcher into a room with only two beds and a bathroom with a shower. They didn't remove Tony from the stretcher. They just put the stretcher on top of the bed closest to the bathroom.

The man said, "We gave him another shot of tranquilizer. That should last until this evening. You need to find a doctor at the local hospital, and the doctor will know what to do."

He pulled out a document and handed it to me. "Please sign this to acknowledge you are required to pay for the ride and treatments that we administered." I signed without reading it.

After they left, I asked the hotel staff to give us a cot because I definitely needed Matthew to be in the same room. I was sitting on the cot and thinking about what I should do in this strange place to secure Tony's safety.

Matthew stood in front of me and handed me a piece of paper. "I met this doctor on the boat. This is his address."

I looked at it. "I'll go find this doctor. You stay with Tony. Okay?"

I went to the front desk and asked for a map. There was none. I showed the clerk the address. The young woman took out a piece of paper and started drawing a map. I was thankful that I could read Chinese. It took me about an hour to find the place. A man in his late thirties opened the door. I told him that Matthew had given me his address. He smiled and asked me to come into the house. He spoke Mandarin that was easy for me to understand. I briefly told him the situation.

He said, "I need to arrange someone to come watch my mother before I can leave the house. You go ahead and go back to the hotel and try to find out if your friend had any medications with him."

When I got to the room, I searched all Tony's belongings and the pockets of the clothes he was wearing. I was surprised to find two packs of small light-blue pills in the inner pocket of his windbreaker.

Dr. Wang arrived midafternoon and examined Tony. I showed him the pills.

Dr. Wang said, "Give him one of his pills every four hours. He should be okay in the next forty-eight hours. He doesn't need to stay strapped down. I will come back tomorrow early afternoon to check on him. In the meantime, if you need help, you can ask the front desk to call this number." He handed me a slip of paper.

He and Matthew unfastened the straps and removed the stretcher from the bed. Dr. Wang took it with him and asked the front desk staff to deliver food to our room.

The next day before Dr. Wang's visit, the front desk clerk told me that the authorities wanted to meet with me.

"The authorities?" I asked. "Who and why?"

The clerk replied, "The authorities want to discuss the patient and the current situation."

My short time in Hainan had given me the impression that the island was behind Hong Kong in terms of hospitality, infrastructure, services, and medical professionalism. But news on this primitive island ran secretly and faster than I would have expected. Everything seemed so quiet and not noticeable. Yet, in less than thirty-six hours, from Sanya to Haikou, the authorities already wanted to summon me for an event that I still didn't fully understand. I sensed that this would not be a casual "how do you do" meeting. I told Matthew that I would be meeting with some officials to find out if I could take Tony home as soon as possible, which was indeed my goal for the meeting.

Matthew said, "I would like to go with you to Hong Kong."

The clerk took me to a room near the lobby. Three men who looked to be in their fifties welcomed me with handshakes. After the initial greetings, the eldest of the three asked, "Do you know what kind of illness your friend has?"

"No, I don't."

"According to the paramedic, your friend was violent and loud."

"Violent to whom?"

"The nurse was afraid of him."

"I do not know what the nurse was afraid of. I just know that my friend needs to see his own doctor as soon as possible."

"Well, he is still sedated, right?"

"Not really. He said good morning to me before I came here. He is resting."

The three men looked at each other. The one sitting in the middle said, "We are thinking that for his safety and recovery, he should stay here at our hospital until he gets better."

"What hospital?"

"A mental institution."

"You mean an asylum."

"Yes."

My thoughts were racing. How could I face his mother if I left him here? Once he was locked up in the asylum, how could any of us get him out?

"We do not know what his illness is. I think the best thing to do is to take him back to his doctor as soon as possible," I heard myself saying to them.

"He is too ill to travel."

"Well, you know, in the United States, the local authorities would use an airplane to rush a patient to medical treatment. If they can do that in the US, why not here?"

The three men were astonished at my comments. I looked intently into their eyes and didn't say another word.

"What if he becomes violent while traveling?"

"He won't. We have a doctor friend looking after him now, and he is taking medicine. He just needs some more rest for a day or two. Could you arrange plane and train tickets for us for the day after tomorrow?" I didn't want to give them time to think.

The three men looked at each other again.

The man next to me opened his mouth for the first time, "We want to make sure he is well enough to travel. We want to meet him, by himself."

"Fine. When do you want to meet him?"

"Tomorrow, at this same time, here in this room. By the way, what is your doctor friend's name?"

"He will be here this afternoon. I believe the front desk has his information." I didn't want to be the one to reveal Dr. Wang's identity. Besides, I bet they already knew.

When Dr. Wang arrived, Tony was already awake. I ordered congee for all of us. Dr. Wang took out the blue pills and asked, "How many and how often do you take these?"

"One every four hours."

"Only this, no other pills?"

"I only carry this with me in case of emergency."

"Good. Continue to take these until you see your doctor. You will be fine."

I walked Dr. Wang out to the lobby. He told me that the authorities wanted to speak with him after he examined Tony. I was not surprised but felt dreadful about dragging him into this mess. He seemed to know what I was thinking.

When we parted, he held my hands. "No worries. It's no big deal. I am a doctor, and the officials can check my records."

The next day, I walked Tony to the meeting room and told him that I'd wait for him outside. Five minutes later, he came out and informed me that the officials wanted to see me.

Once I sat down, the eldest man from yesterday spoke. "You can go home with your friend tomorrow. We will get you two sets of plane and train tickets."

"No, I need tickets for three people. We all go together. No one will be left behind."

"What kind of relationship do you have with this foreigner?"

"Foreigner? Matthew is our friend. He helped the paramedics take care of the patient."

The three men looked as if they had never heard anyone talk like me.

The eldest man smiled, looked at the other two men, then nodded. "You are right. The foreigner is your friend. The front desk staff will deliver the tickets to your room. Get some good rest tonight for tomorrow's trip."

The officials did have the power to get things done efficiently. All three of us were sent by official vehicle directly to the seats of a commercial plane before anyone else came on board. Right before we landed at Guangzhou Baiyun International Airport, a flight attendant asked us to be the last ones to get off the plane. A man and a woman wearing army uniforms were waiting for us at the bottom of the stairs of the plane. They checked our travel documents, stamped each document, and accompanied us in an army vehicle to our seats on the train without going through customs. We arrived back in Hong Kong midafternoon, eight days after we had departed.

The next day, Tony called me and told me that his doctor wanted me to go with him to the appointment.

The doctor was a psychiatrist in the psychiatric unit. He asked what had triggered the episode.

Tony said, "First of all, I didn't want to be on Hainan Island. My father told horror stories about being there during the war, then we ran into a military base with many gigantic cannons. Second, we went into a coffin shop on the first day of Chinese New Year. I think that must have triggered my anxiety."

"You didn't want to be in Hainan. Why did you go?" the doctor asked.

"I want to keep her as my girlfriend." He looked at me and lowered his head.

Now the psychiatrist looked at me. "The reason I requested you to be at this appointment is that he does not remember what happened. Could you tell us the whole story?"

"He tried to jump out the hotel room window on the fifth floor." Then, I summarized the event in a few sentences.

"Do you know his condition?"

"No, I have no idea."

The psychiatrist turned to Tony, "Do you want me to tell her?"

He nodded.

The psychiatrist extended his arms by pushing a folder across the desk. "He has schizophrenia."

We had been friends in high school for three years and for three more years after graduation, and then he was my boyfriend for two years. I only learned about his illness after he underwent a life-threatening emergency—how bizarre. A sense of betrayal rushed in. I didn't know how to react.

"Why didn't you tell me?" I asked.

"I have controlled the symptoms. I didn't want to lose you."

When we walked out of the psychiatrist's office, after a few steps, I put my right hand out in front of my chest. "Stop!"

I faced Tony and walked backward toward the elevator. "I saved your life. From now on, please give us both space. Do not disturb my life."

That was the last time I talked to him alone and face to face, in the hallway of a psychiatric unit in a hospital.

The week Matthew stayed in Hong Kong, I was supposed to be in Hainan. My vacation was ruined, and I felt indebted to Matthew. I took him to places that I ordinarily would not go. In a way, being his tour guide gave me a chance to enjoy Hong Kong. We also learned much more about each other.

Matthew was from Indiana. His father, stepmother, and two half-brothers were living in Houston. He was in the process of getting a divorce while taking a winter break from teaching at Shaanxi Normal University. He was a tree doctor, which explained his interest in the wood at the coffin shop and his knowledge of the plants that we saw in the plantation. He explained that he was learning about tropical species since Indiana was not in the same climate zone.

My initial connection with Matthew was much deeper than I thought. We fell in love in just a week. The whole episode of saving Tony's life, the challenge and the process of finding private medical help and getting us out of China, and the time he took to accompany me to take Tony home—all of the unspoken understanding and support accelerated our feelings for each other.

At teatime on the first day, I acted as Matthew's tour guide when he asked, "How did you persuade the officials?"

"I just told them what I thought was best for him."

"Really? What was the best for Tony?"

"I told them that he needed to see his own doctor."

"No, there must be more. What you just said would not be convincing enough for them to go along with it."

"Really, I can't think of anything special." Matthew looked at me with skepticism written all over his face. "I think the officials' interview alone with him did it."

He nodded with a puzzled smile.

Matthew didn't talk a lot, but he didn't seem antisocial either. He just wouldn't talk for the sake of talking. That's how I was too. We were comfortable with each other in silence.

Matthew truly loved all living plants. Everywhere we went, he would examine a leaf or a branch, pick up a fallen seed, a rotten fruit, or a flower from the ground. He was just like a curious child who hasn't explored enough of the plant kingdom. In his eyes, semi-tropical and tropical plants were exotic mysteries whose shapes, colors, and fragrances he had never experienced before. In a way, learning about these beauties expanded his horizons not only in the plant kingdom, but his entire world. I, on the other hand, discovered by observing Matthew that he could be extremely focused for days, beyond anything I'd ever known.

COURTSHIP

THE SECOND TIME MATTHEW and I met up was over Easter break, in China again. This time we took a boat trip from Chongqing downstream to Jiangxi Province to experience the famous Three Gorges.

The boat was a small commercial vessel, and Matthew and I were the only passengers on board. Matthew negotiated with the captain, who told us that the boat would go directly to its destination. We had a cabin to ourselves, a small square box with no windows. Two cot-sized beds stood separately along the two side walls. Straight across from the entrance was the door to the bathroom. We put our bags on the floor.

The Yangtze River looked like any other river, but as we proceeded to Wu Gorge, I was mesmerized by its vastness and the new scenery that suddenly appeared around each bend. Standing on the front deck, I felt as if I were gliding directly on top of the water, and as the boat sharply veered one way or another, the mountainside seemed to slide down into the water, giving the illusion that we were about to crash into a cliff or be abruptly deposited at the shore of a hamlet. These strange, completely unfamiliar impressions hypnotized me all day long. Matthew enjoyed my ecstatic oohs and ahhs and incredulous smiles, but I forbade him from taking any photos of me.

The boat trip to Jiangxi brought the enormity and grandeur of China to life for me. I embraced the authenticity of the ancient poetry describing the beauty that surrounds the Yangtze River. Through those poets' eyes, I saw the misty midday twilight, the fleeting glimpses of obscure structures perched on a rocky pinnacle, the unfathomable sliding mountain terrain with its gloom blissfully shining from far away and gradually illuminating right in front of me.

We arrived in Nanchang, the capital of Jiangxi Province, early in the morning. After breakfast, we wandered around a huge round grassy field in the middle of an intersection, bicycles and moto-bikes like fish swimming between cars in all directions. Four signs, placed evenly around the circle, proclaimed in Chinese: "Grass Field, Do Not Enter."

At first, we walked along the perimeter of the field, but when we saw some people walking on the grass, I wondered if we might walk on the public field too.

In the meantime, people had walked onto the grass without hesitation. Gradually, more and more people were walking across it, playing, or simply sitting down. A few children who looked like fourth graders entered the field.

I asked them, "Why are you walking on the grass?"

A boy touched his own head. "It is a playground."

Matthew and I looked at each other. A playground with a beautiful green lawn surrounded by heavy traffic and "Do Not Enter" signs. We watched the boys who were leapfrogging. There were eight of them. One boy bent his body to an upside-down U. The other seven lined up about ten feet apart from the upside-down U. Once one boy jumped over, another upside-down U formed, and by the time the seven boys finished their jumps, they had formed a straight line of eight upside-down U's. They repeated the same motions and gradually ended up farther away from us.

The atmosphere was friendly and very easy. People of all different ages were doing their own thing. Every once in a while, someone would look at us inquisitively. Someone was brave enough to approach Matthew and ask him in English where he was from. Matthew sometimes answered them in Mandarin. When the locals heard Matthew's Mandarin, they were bewildered. Gradually a small group gathered around us. The elders put up their thumbs to show admiration.

One of the fourth graders looked up at Matthew. "Where did you learn Mandarin?"

"Here, in China."

"How?"

"I have a Mandarin teacher who gives me lessons two hours a day during the week. I listen to tapes and radio, and I watch TV. I practice with my students and strangers, just like now, you and me in a conversation."

The boy smiled and now with a shy voice asked, "What is the fastest way to learn English?"

Matthew looked into the boy's eyes. He could see the eagerness and earnestness on his face. "Practice, practice, practice, whenever you can. If you read, write, listen, and speak it every day, you will be surprised how quickly you have mastered the language. One thing to remember: don't be shy."

The boy's face turned red with a big smile. He nodded, began to run away from us, and turned around. "Thank you," he said in Mandarin.

At dawn we caught the train from Nanchang to Guangzhou, to catch another train to Hong Kong at ten o'clock that night. Our train was caught by torrential rain right at the first few stops of its schedule, and kept on being delayed to let other trains run on time. By the time we got to Guangzhou, it was near midnight. We looked for a hotel room but found none to spend the remaining few hours in before we could board the first train to Hong Kong. We decided to walk the night with a miserable umbrella and a bottle of red wine, which mingled with the rain as we drank. Finally, tired of walking and being drenched, we stumbled into a small hotel lobby. A figure was sleeping in front of the reception area, and a young female desk clerk was trying to get that figure off the floor. Four other Caucasians, two men and two women with camping gear on their backs, were talking in broken Mandarin with a man at the front desk who was just as anguished as they were.

"I don't have a room for any of you. The hotel is full. You cannot stay here. We need to close the door. Please leave," he urged.

A red headed man said, "How could you send us back into that rain? Can't you see that we are all soaking wet?"

"I am sorry, but there is nothing I can do to stop the rain."

The figure on the floor sat up. I saw her Nordic features and light blonde hair. She murmured, "I am too tired," and fell back to the floor intending to sleep there.

The service man and the young woman didn't know what to do. They stood there and looked at us, baffled.

I approached him and quietly said, "Comrade, as you can see, seven of us have no place to go. It would not be to your advantage that we all sleep here on the floor in front of the lobby or get kicked out."

"I really don't have any room, and there are too many of you."

I looked around the lobby and saw some vintage light fixtures that didn't seem to belong to the hallway. A light bulb turned on in my head. "Do you have a conference room? We can all stay in the conference room where the public won't see us. It's after two in the morning. We just need to stay for a few hours until everything is open. We can pay for showers and hot tea."

His frown slowly eased and a thin look of delight surfaced as if he were finding treasure in his predicament. He signaled to the young woman and turned to me. "Let's do that."

The young woman opened the doors of a conference room and some bathrooms a few doors down the hallway from the lobby. The man and the young woman even helped us move chairs to make sleeping platforms. We took turns taking showers, and by the time we all were clean and dry, hot tea was brought to the conference room. The other five of them were so relieved and showed their gratitude with weary smiles, whispering "thank you" from a distance.

"That was how you got the officials to work with you, by guiding them to act from the best of themselves instead of just rigidly following the rules," Matthew said with delight.

I didn't quite comprehend what he was saying, and my face must have been a big question mark. He laid his chin on top of my head. "Get some rest."

CHINA IN THE EIGHTIES

THE SCENARIO OF BEING encircled by locals repeated itself again and again during our trip and the year after we got married and I moved to China with Matthew. People were curious about foreigners, the United States, and what it was like to live abroad. They were more mystified when they found out I was not an interpreter but the wife of a lecturer. From time to time, I also became a foreigner. Most of the Chinese we met thought only non-Chinese or overseas Chinese would marry foreigners. Even at the university where Matthew taught and we lived, the program director of foreign teachers and the interpreter decided that I was Japanese. The interpreter would not respond to me in Mandarin. At first, I thought he didn't understand my Mandarin, but his responses in English demonstrated that he knew what I was saying.

In reality, I didn't know the culture or people of China. I was not born there, didn't grow up there, nor was I educated there, and I didn't have any knowledge of social contacts that related to or impacted my upbringing. I didn't feel discriminated against. But the treatment and subtleness of me being "non-Chinese" was noticeable wherever I went, which was unfamiliar and extraordinary.

I was exhilarated to observe daily life around me. Their methods of doing things, their ways of dealing with life events, and their food fascinated me. The culinary scene in the Northwest Region was like a gold mine, for better or for worse. The ingredients they used for everyday meals were just as amazing as their consumption of preserved foods. Six months of the school year, we had only three fresh vegetables: Chinese napa cabbage, lotus root, and potato. They ate preserved fruits—pears, tangerines, peaches, and several others that I could not make myself eat. Growing up along the coast and being a metropolitan, I had been privileged with fresh produce, fresh seafood, fresh everything under the sun. It didn't occur to me that I could choose to eat preserved fruits. That year living in China, I learned that we do not need much to live on and that we could still be content with life.

Our living quarters had four rooms with no central heat. We had three cast-iron coal-burning stoves, one each in the bedroom, bathroom, and living room.

The school dining hall delivered coal blocks and came in to reignite the stoves every morning around six o'clock without knocking on the door. We had requested the dining hall manager to instruct staff members to knock before coming into our quarters, but knocking was not their custom. Each day there could be a different person and that person would just enter our bedroom and go directly to the stove while we were still sleeping.

One morning, we were making love when a young man came into our bedroom. He definitely knew what was going on and retreated. After that love-making scene, they changed the delivery time to the afternoon around four o'clock, which was yogurt pick-up time, when one of us would line up outside the compound to get our daily yogurt. The dining hall staff also taught us how to reignite the stove. Once we had mastered the ignition, they stopped coming unless we asked them for help.

There were two American guest lecturers. One was Matthew, the other was an entomologist (we called him Dr. Bug), who was our neighbor in the same compound and had decided to share one meal each day with us instead of eating at the dining hall. I could not tolerate the food from the dining hall, which used MSG like salt and put it in every single dish. I even saw a TV commercial saying, "MSG is good for you. It contains glutamic acid, which is easier to digest…" My immediate response was, "But you didn't say what is bad about MSG!" In my family, MSG had never been an ingredient in the kitchen. Both my grandmother and mother would constantly remind us, "Don't eat out every day. The food from a restaurant is loaded with MSG, not good for your health." But we would eat at the dining hall when it was *Jiaozi* 餃子 (dumpling) day, which was two lunches a week.

Our diet consisted mainly of eggs and the three fresh vegetables. We rarely got meat, unless we went to the dining hall kitchen, where I was still reluctant to ask for it as I didn't want to exhaust my credit with the personnel. Instead, I learned to be creative and fed two grown men who were used to having red meat and other rich foods in their daily diet.

Since we had three cast-iron fire stoves, we sometimes made pizza in our living room. I would barter coffee for cheese among the German lecturers, make a sauce of mashed tofu mixed with yogurt, and top the pizzas with thinly sliced lotus root, potatoes, canned olives, or Chinese preserved ingredients that seemed fitting for pizza. If I had enough coffee to trade, I simply made cheese pizza, which would be a luxurious and fancy dinner.

In addition to the two American lecturers there were five Germans, one Scot, one New Zealander, and one Australian, who, like Matthew, had brought his wife with him. At the time, if we wanted to cook, we needed to get permission for provisions from the dining hall kitchen. Basically, we each had our ration card, just like everyone else in the country.

I was a bread snob. Over the seven years growing up and living in Macau, I got used to having fresh bread delivered twice a day to our house, once at six in the morning and once at three in the afternoon. I was so spoiled by freshly baked bread every day that when I went back to Hong Kong, my mother and siblings knew that I would touch the square crustless white bread from the market only if I was starving to death. I could not eat Chinese-style steamed or baked bread. Coincidentally, all the international lecturers at the university had a similar dislike and would not eat the dining hall bread in the morning, except Matthew, who ate anything and loved any food that was Chinese. The Germans would bake, so I asked them to teach me. Maria, one of the two female lecturers, took me as her student, showing me how to prepare the yeast and mix in the milk and flour. Within two weeks, I was baking my basic German bread, which served us well.

At the time, the university hosted a series of weekend outings nearby for all the international lecturers. Sometimes we stayed overnight if we spent the whole day hiking. Most of the time, though, we returned to the university by early evening to have dinner at the dining hall.

When we introduced happy hours on Fridays after four o'clock for all the international lecturers at the university, it was accepted without question, but we didn't get any material support from the university. All the lecturers relied on families sending food packages to keep our sanity. We each assigned ourselves food items. My family was closest to China, so Matthew and I provided yeast and instant coffee, which was a daily necessity for all twelve of us.

Dr. Bug provided whiskey, vodka, and other hard liquors; the Germans: preserved meats, dense dried breads, and cheeses; the Scot: biscuits and shortbread; the Aussies and New Zealander: jams, lamingtons, and their other native specialties.

In addition to our families' supplies, we also kept a lookout for any opportunities to get our hands on fresh produce and meat. Our happy hours were in general on Fridays, but when the university didn't schedule outings for us on Saturdays (which rarely happened), we would all stroll to the University Street Market to search for food, which was the only venue where we could find anything fresh. Otherwise, we had to drive into Xi'an. None of us wanted to ask for a van and a driver just to indulge our taste buds and none of us were willing to take the trip only for grocery shopping.

One Saturday at the University Street Market, I saw a vendor displaying fish in a rattan basket. Other lecturers averred no interest in the fish, but I picked up one that looked fresh, paid a price almost equal to half of Matthew's monthly salary, and happily took it home.

With enthusiasm, I prepared the first fresh fish since our arrival five months before. I acquired spices and other condiments from the dining hall kitchen. We had great expectations for our feast. The fish looked good when I presented it at the table. We all gingerly put a small piece into our mouths. The fish tasted like plastic. I spit it right out. Matthew and Dr. Bug followed my lead. Disconcerted by the fish, we ended up having a bowl of noodles at the dining hall, which was already closed for the weekend, but they made an exception for us.

A few weeks later, we spotted a live goose at the market. I had never killed a bird before and was not interested in killing one now. But Dr. Bug was dreaming of having something like Peking duck and asked if he could use our kitchen to prepare the goose. Dr. Bug had been a hunter back home, killing deer and wild pig and fishing for salmon annually. Killing and cleaning an animal was no big deal for him. We had no reason to refuse since he would be the one doing all the work. So we shared the cost and brought the goose home in a bamboo cage.

The jeans hung to dry in the courtyard were as solid as a baseball bat that I could swing to hit a person dead on this frigid February day. I picked up the glasses and snack dishes when Dr. Bug and Matthew opened the goose's cage. Dr. Bug grabbed the goose by its wings. The goose spun, left Dr. Bug's hands empty, swung around, and rocked out of the cage. Matthew stood behind Dr. Bug, as the slickly quick goose headed directly at him. Mathew bent his knees, with both hands outward. The bird twirled under his hands and continued circling between his legs. I stepped on the threshold of the back door, impressed by the goose's maneuvers, and I wondered how to help.

"Soothe it toward me," Dr. Bug said.

The three of us formed a triangle to drive the goose to the center. The goose obliged. In spite of that, Dr. Bug and Matthew tracked round and round with the goose and could not get hold of it. Each time either one of them had their fingertips on the goose, its agility overtook them. I pulled the jeans off the clothesline and handed them to the men. "Perhaps we can catch it with these and kill it right there."

"Great, one stone to kill two birds," Dr. Bug replied with a smile.

They yanked the jeans toward the goose. The bird did not flinch. It squawked and gyrated like a funicular that progressively advanced in spiral fashion out of the courtyard. The men kept chasing, and at one point the bird ambled back to the courtyard. Dr. Bug and Matthew cornered the bird along the fence, pushed it behind the row of ornamental pomegranates, forced it in front of a wall of twisting kiwi vines, and isolated it on top of the massive wild strawberries on the ground. Dr. Bug held onto the tail of the bird but got caught on a branch and stumbled. To keep his balance, Dr. Bug let go of the goose, and Matthew snatched his coat collar to steady him. The goose gingerly traversed the wild strawberries and ducked itself out of the fence.

By then, the men were exhausted by the stiff jeans. Neither one of them had truly thought about the task and had no idea they would be outdoors for so long in this tussle without gloves. The icy air had no mercy on them. Their hands were red and white. Matthew dropped the jeans to blow air into his cupped hands, but his steaming breath seemed to be terrified by the cold air and evaporated before reaching its destination.

Dr. Bug and Matthew gave up the battle with the goose, and we all went to the dining hall. When the other international lecturers saw us, one of the German teachers asked, "What happened to your goose feast?" Dr. Bug and Matthew just sat down and started to drink the hot soup. They were silent while I told the story of the escaping goose.

Another Saturday, a vendor enticed us with rabbits. The Germans loved rabbit meat and together they bought five skinny rabbits and invited all of us to share the rabbit dinner with them. We took whatever food we had to share to the Germans' quarters. The rabbits were cooked with Tsingtao beer and cut into small pieces with bones. We started eating and within seconds all of us emitted crunching sounds. Stephen, one of the German lecturers, shouted, "*Scheisse, Scheisse!*" We all spat out small round lead buckshot balls into our palms. Some of us had two or three pieces within one bite. We all cracked up laughing and put the bullets on the table. There were about thirty of them. The rabbit stew dinner ended up with us consuming our scarce ration of dry foods.

We didn't have much luck with fresh meat from the University Street Market until May 1985. The Aussies were the first to finish their term and had planned on heading home in early June to enjoy their time off. By May, the university had stopped scheduling outings for us. We had the weekends to ourselves, and our happy hours moved to eleven o'clock on Friday morning and lasted until eleven on Sunday night.

On the third Saturday, we wandered through the University Street Market, scavenging. We discovered goat meat for sale. We all stopped, examined, and discussed whether the goat meat was real. We saw blood, bones, and organs, which all smelled like goat. This time, the Aussies bought the goat meat. The Aussie wife, Rebecca, had her way of getting the dining hall kitchen to assist her. The kitchen staff prepared the meat and cut them into kabobs. By noon, the kabobs were delivered to our place.

Among the twelve of us, ten had their daily meals at the dining hall. Matthew and I were the only ones who cooked most meals on our own and had a kitchen set up in our house during the first month of the school year. Matthew had already started the charcoal in the clay oven on our front porch. Stephen made a screen from mesh wire, and Rebecca produced a paper fan. While five of us took turns tending the kabobs, the rest of the lecturers were in and out to hand us drinks and nibbles, and to chat. That night we feasted on the goat meat kabobs. Stephen was so satisfied that he declared for his remaining weeks he would go to the University Street Market to buy goat meat.

One Sunday in early April, on our way back to the university after an outing led by the interpreter, our van drove along a river. From a window seat as the van proceeded, I saw people washing clothes, taking baths, and doing other things in that murky water.

I turned around and asked the interpreter, "Why are people washing things and themselves in that dirty water?"

The interpreter glanced out of the window, and casually said, "That's the way people clean their belongings."

"Do they have water at home?"

"Some do, some don't. Even if they have water at home, they might still wash things in the river."

"Do they realize that it's not sanitary, that they can get sick from it?"

"Well, for thousands of years that has been the way of life."

I looked back at the river; I saw a dead pig floating no more than thirty feet away; people were still washing and cleaning in the river. Matthew took a picture of the dead pig. After I got back to our compound, I could not help but sit down to write what I had seen and named the article "Dead Pig River," written all in Chinese. The next day, I asked around to discover where I could send the article with the picture. Surprisingly enough, the facilities department read my article and decided to publish it in the district's newspaper. Apparently, the facilities department thought that people in the district needed to be educated about public health. To my amusement, the department asked if I would give a series of lectures about cultural differences. For me, the university's offer was a subtle acknowledgement of me being Chinese.

I ended up creating, designing, and teaching six lectures in six weeks. My students were undergraduates and PhD candidates. I thought they were pressured by the department to attend my class, which I didn't think would count as a credit toward their degrees. But after the first lecture, the subsequent lectures were full of students, and some of them even brought their family members. I tried to get some insights from other lecturers about the overflow classes.

Dr. Bug told me, "You are animated and eager to show them different ways of life outside of this country. Plus, you have colorful slides. I enjoy your class." In fact, most of the slides were provided by Matthew, who loved to take pictures of plants, scenery, and people. Each class was more like a movie with a theme and I, the narrator, voiced the superficial aspects of those lives, which echoed a poem I had read, "Last Words" by Lorna Bennett:

"…Life is a soap bubble caught by the wind
Reflecting rainbows…"

❧

THE YEAR I LIVED IN China was eye opening for me. Although Cantonese was my first language, I could speak Mandarin. But sometimes I didn't understand what the locals were saying. Some of the words, phrases, and sentences were foreign to me. I believe it was the same for the locals, regarding my speech patterns and word choices. I had heard about the Cultural Revolution but didn't know anything about it even though I had traveled to China with my father during those years. The best gift my parents gave me, apart from my siblings, was travel. My parents traveled often. They would start their trips, and then about a week later they would pick us up one or two at a time at the airport, train station, or seaport. But my parents rarely traveled to China, even though I knew my mother had siblings living there. The first time I met my mother's nieces was at the border, where we just walked across a short bridge and went through customs to enter China. My cousins seemed no different than me except they were slightly older. They lived very close to Hong Kong. I didn't know why they couldn't come to visit us until I learned in junior high that I had the privilege of traveling freely because I was born and grew up in Hong Kong.

Ever since, I'd unconsciously sought opportunities to travel. My willingness to go places gave me a taste of life in China. Additionally, my father would take me to visit my uncles in Guangzhou, which was the farthest I went into China during my childhood. Often, I stayed overnight. I had a small suitcase for my linen pajamas, undergarments, a change of clothing, a bath towel, and toiletries. A few times, I traded all my belongings with my cousins for dried longan and lychee fruits, which I loved for their texture and smoky flavor. Whenever my mother saw the suitcase was full of dried fruits, she would say, "You are such a foolish girl." But she was not really mad at me. Later I found out that my mother was pleased by what I had done, because my cousins needed those garments, which were in short supply in China. Other than the dried fruits, I liked to run around the fields and climb to the top of peach, guava, and plumeria trees with my cousins. Since I was the youngest, I could do anything. They took care of me and would never tell on me.

One time, I was using a stick to push some water hyacinths along a pond. I was so excited that I didn't see there was a curve in front of me. I kept running and watching the water hyacinths as I pushed them along until suddenly I found myself in the pond. My elder cousin reacted fast, jumping in and single handedly picking me up. By the time I realized what had happened, I was being dried by my aunt, who declared, "You are not allowed to go near the pond again."

I enjoyed those days I spent in China during the Cultural Revolution, and now, here I was, living in Northwest China, a place more than a thousand miles northwest of Guangzhou. I still saw field after field, but the landscape was completely different. The fields here looked like a sea of tall grass stalks with golden reflections on bright sunny days, versus the low green patches with small grid-like paths in southern China.

I didn't hear anyone talk about the Cultural Revolution at the university. Somehow no one seemed to know or remember. I tried to ask questions, but local professors and students acted like they didn't understand me. So, I gave up asking and chose to believe their pretense.

Geographic location influences the way people live, and this was evident as I considered the northwest, which was very different from southern China. Southerners' diets are based on rice and northerners' diets are based on wheat. In addition to the differences in diet, there were still traveling handymen and salespeople in remote areas. Transportation in the eighties was already well-developed, and merchandise moved freely. But the supply of fresh produce still relied on seasonal growth. People still hung on to their preserved fruits and vegetables even though fresh produce was abundantly displayed in local stores and supermarkets. However, fresh produce remained hard to get to in a small university town. Overall, people were accustomed to the street markets, with produce and other grocery items brought by local farmers and small merchants.

One early evening in October, I rode my bike to the university's co-op to get some soap. At the main gate, I saw a group of adults and children squatting in a small circle next to the entrance of the co-op. I got my soap and went over to see what was happening.

First, I smelled popcorn. I was so excited. In the seven weeks I had lived there, I didn't know that popcorn was available. When I got to the circle, I saw an old man tending a short tri-pot over a fire on the ground. In the open space of the tri-pot, a container that looked like an elongated metal bullet was positioned parallel to the ground. The old man kept rotating the fire-blackened bullet while some of the bystanders held small sacks and watched. Gradually, the old man slowed down the rotation and finally opened the near end of the bullet container. White steam came out with the contents, which flowed into a basket that the old man had placed on the ground. I had grown up with machine-made popcorn and didn't know there were other ways of making it. Children clapped their hands as if the old man had just staged a magic trick. One by one the adults handed over their sacks to get their rice, soy beans, barley, and other grains popped.

This old man came only twice a year with all his tools and gear in a modified tricycle. According to the bystanders, he had been doing this for years in exchange for small payments. There was no appointment or communication. The people somehow knew when he would be there and had all their grain ready for the few hours that the old man was available. No promise, but this tacit understanding was carried on from one generation to the next, the way people learn and pass on traditions. I was lucky to witness such a mundane yet subtle mystical process, which I would not have imagined existing had I not happened to be in this university town at the right time.

ARRIVAL IN INDIANA

I LEFT CHINA BEFORE Matthew because my visa to the States was about to expire. I wanted to extend it, but Matthew feared that the US government might not extend it, and then I wouldn't be able to move to the States. I found it illogical to not take advantage of the option for me to extend my visa.

Matthew got his dissolution decree and gave away all his liquid assets, which included the proceeds of selling a house, bank accounts, and some investments, to his ex-wife. We would temporarily stay with his aunt until we could find our own place. Since he would not be traveling with me, I asked him for his aunt's photo so I could identify her.

Matthew said, "No worries. you'll be able to identify her. She's in a wheelchair."

"What happens if there's more than one woman in a wheelchair?"

"I doubt it. Not many people are in wheelchairs, and it's not likely that more than one will show up at that particular airport at that particular time. Also, my aunt has our wedding pictures. She'll recognize you."

The day I arrived in the United States was the day before my birthday, the day my entrance visa would expire. At the time, the airline was on strike. My flight was diverted to Tokyo, then Seattle, and then Chicago before reaching my destination. On the flight to Tokyo, a tall, big-built man was next to my seat. He smiled at me when I put my backpack with "Fragile" stickers on my seat and looked up at the storage compartment. Without a word, he picked up my backpack and put it in. He said, "You must be carrying gold."

"Yes," I replied. Indeed, I was carrying a gold-plated tea set. One Cantonese tradition is that when a daughter gets married, the mother prepares sleeping clothes (modern-day pajamas) and a tea set to accompany her daughter into the husband's home. For me, growing up with my grandmother and seeing her

Chinese traditions, I didn't care so much for her nonsensical ways of doing things. But I wanted these two things, and I didn't let my mother select them. I shopped with my mother, who ended up paying for a one hundred percent silk nightgown with a matching robe in aquamarine and a tea set with a tray, twelve cups, and a tall dragon and phoenix tea pot all plated in royal yellow gold. I wrapped each of the tea set items and carried them with me to keep them safe. They were heavy.

After my backpack was settled, I went to wash my hands. When I came back, appetizers and a glass of champagne were on my seat tray. He said, "The flight attendant was here, and I took the liberty of ordering these for you."

The appetizers were small pieces of sashimi, fresh edamame, and seaweed.

"I don't drink alcohol on the plane." I held up the champagne. "Do you want it?"

"Sure."

I took a bite of the sashimi and a few bites of the seaweed and then stopped eating.

"You don't like the food?"

"No, I just can't eat on the plane."

"You're one of those high maintenance people." He drew a rainbow shape in front of his forehead.

I nodded. "I don't want any food," I said and put on my eye shade.

When we landed in Tokyo, the guy took my backpack and said, "Follow me."

I walked behind him as we left the aircraft. The rest of the passengers were proceeding to baggage claim. He and I went into another door. He showed the guard his badge, which I could not see the details of. The guard let us through another gate, and after a short walk we were out of the terminal building and on the tarmac. He directly approached a parked plane and signaled me to go up the stairs. We were on our plane to Seattle without going through customs. He put my backpack overhead and winked at me. This time he didn't order any food. He just reclined his seat and slept. I could not sleep. From time to time, I got up to walk around. He slept like a log. We got to Seattle early in the morning.

He carried my backpack to the immigration counter and said to me, "Kiddo, you're on your own now." He waved at the immigration officer and exited. I didn't know who this guy was or why he had taken me under his wing.

When I walked out of the gate at South Bend International Airport, I saw three women in wheelchairs. One was African American, another one looked very sick, and the third one seemed the only possibility, but I didn't know. I stood there, hesitating. The third one called my name.

Matthew's aunt held my hands. "The airline called last night and told us that you disappeared. They only have your luggage and will send it to our address. We were so worried but decided to come to the airport. Now, here you are."

I remembered that after I had gone through customs in Seattle, I pushed my luggage away from the counter and saw someone in a United Airlines uniform holding up a sign with my name. I went to him and he took my luggage, which was the last time I had seen my belongings. He told me to go to the gate, but the flight didn't take off until almost midnight. I had a full day to explore Seattle. I took a cab to Pike Place Market and had my first breakfast on American soil. I spent most of the day walking around the waterfront neighborhoods, where the water was as sparkling and beautiful as usual. Seattle's waterfront didn't seem different from other metropolitan cities. My breakfast was not much different from what I could usually get in Hong Kong. Pike Place Market was smaller than markets in Frankfurt or Sydney. The obvious differences were that people spoke in English and the majority of them were not Asian.

Berenice and Henry, Matthew's aunt and uncle, lived about thirty miles east of South Bend International Airport, and it took about forty-five minutes to drive to their house. Along the highway, I remarked, "No mountains."

"Right, we don't have mountains around here."

We got to the house around mid-morning. Berenice had only one son, Alan, who was two months younger than Matthew and had grown up with Matthew and Matthew's older brother, Jerry. Alan and his wife, Sandy, with their two young sons were there to greet me. They were all very cheerful people. The older boy was three years old, and the younger was fifteen months old, who had a nickname: Mr. No. At his age, whenever adults asked or offered him something, he automatically said "NO" even if it was ice cream. Mr. No seemed to notice that I was different from the rest of the adults around him, but he could not articulate why. He touched my hair and my face and mumbled something that only Sandy would understand. But when Mr. No wouldn't let go of my hair, I didn't think Sandy had any clue what was going on.

The first day at Berenice's house, I learned that Midwestern dinner is at two o'clock, particularly on weekends and holidays. The family welcomed me and celebrated my birthday by setting up a barbecue with hamburger patties and hot dogs. I'd had a cup of coffee and a pastry for breakfast in Seattle and had not had full meal while traveling across two continents. The hamburger patties and hotdogs didn't appeal to me.

I asked, "Could I not eat these?"

Berenice showed concern and patted my hand. "Of course, but we don't have anything else for dinner."

I pointed to the salad made of iceberg lettuce, red bell pepper, and red onion. "I just want vegetables."

"Sure, we have more of that in the refrigerator. Do you want me to cut more?"

"No, I can get it myself."

I opened the refrigerator. I saw half of a red bell pepper and red onion put in individual sandwich bags. I opened the bottom drawer and saw a green-lidded plastic container with clean iceberg lettuce. The refrigerator had only these three fresh vegetables.

I took the plastic container back to my seat at the kitchen table, without taking out a plate or any other serving utensils. I tore the iceberg lettuce and started eating it. Everyone watched me and didn't say a word until Alan came in with the cooked meats that were ready to put onto hamburger or hotdog buns.

He looked at me. "Ah, you like rabbit food."

"Yes," I responded.

"Aren't you going to have a burger or hotdog?"

I shook my head.

"Not even just the meat?"

I shook my head again.

"Are you a vegetarian? Oh, I'm sorry. I didn't think of it."

"No, I'm not a vegetarian. I'm just tired after the long journey and don't feel like eating meat."

"Okay, I understand that. It definitely was a long trip from Asia to here. How many hours did it take you?"

"The usual flight would take about twelve hours to Seattle then another five hours to here. But the airline is on strike, so my journey was about forty hours with extra stops in Tokyo and Chicago."

"Wow." Alan paused and glanced around the kitchen. "We should let you rest."

I slept until ten o'clock the next morning when I heard two women whispering. After I cleaned up and put on a set of fresh clothes that Berenice had given me the night before, I went to the kitchen, where the smell of coffee was very enticing. I saw a new face. A woman who looked close to Aunt's age smiled at me. Berenice said, "This is Aunt Jodie." She greeted me with warmth and geniality. She had also baked me some pastries as a welcome gesture.

I was hungry. I asked if I could have a boiled egg. Berenice said, "Certainly. You don't need to ask me what you can have. This is your home. Eat whatever you want. If we don't have it, let me know and I'll add it to the shopping list. By the way, Aunt Jodie and I are going grocery shopping after we finish breakfast. Would you like to go with us?"

"Sure."

After the egg, I put one of the pastries that Jodie had baked onto a small plate and ate it with my fork and knife. Berenice used her fingers to pick up a pastry and said, "Honey, we eat morning buns with our fingers," and took a bite.

I lifted my head and smiled. "I eat like this," I said, raising my hands with my fork in my left hand and knife in my right.

"My cousin Gabby eats like that." Jodie swung her index finger left to right aiming at my hands.

"Gabby, the one who lives in Bath, in England?" Berenice licked her fingers.

"Yes, that Gabby." Jodie responded.

We all smiled. In fact, eating the morning bun was the starting point of me learning to eat food with my fingers in America. Still, I would use my left hand for the fork and right hand for the knife, working together to cut up my food and eating one morsel at a time, except for pastries, fried chicken, and sometimes pizza.

Berenice, Henry, and the whole family took me in with full, warm hearts as if I was their daughter and sister. I loved to listen to their family history and stories. Matthew would call two or three times a week in the evening. I couldn't wait to tell him what I had heard and learned from his family.

The town consisted of open land and houses, a small strip mall that had a bank, a mini grocery store, and a drug store was within walking distance. For everything else we needed to drive.

Each day, I took a long walk along the roads, which didn't have sidewalks or pedestrian paths. All I saw was moving cars and the landscape. I was the only person walking on the street day after day.

One morning I walked into the mini grocery store with nothing particular in mind. But I felt that eyes were on me. I picked up a quart of milk. At the checkout, the cashier asked, "Is that all?"

"Yes."

When the cashier handed me the change, he had the courage to say, "You're Berenice's nephew's wife."

Other workers were already gathered nearby. I replied, "Yes. How did you know?"

"Everyone in town knows that Berenice's nephew's wife is Asian. You are the only Asian around here. I see you walking every day."

A few days before Matthew headed home, he called. I knew he had started traveling to Beijing and would fly home from there. I asked where he was.

He said, "Qingdao."

"Why are you in Qingdao? You promised that we would go there together."

"I know. But I'm on the way to Beijing and still had time to stop by..."

"Go ahead, take a shower with the beer." I hung up on him. I was mad. I didn't like his impulsive actions. He had done this before when we were traveling with four of his college friends—Glenn, David, Mark, and Spencer—from South Bend early in the spring. We had already discussed the routes and where to visit, and then all of a sudden, he changed his mind without telling me until we got off the train in Shanghai. At that time, I was angry too. I took off, planning to go back to Hong Kong, but I had not been in the habit of carrying things like money and identification. By the time I reached the train station, I discovered that I didn't have money or my travel documents. I turned back, intending to walk back to the hotel and get my belongings and go home. When I walked out of the train station, there was Matthew, sheepishly handing me some money and my passport. "You need to remember to take cash and your ID with you." My anger abated in an instant.

Berenice was amused hearing my side of the phone conversation with Matthew. She asked, "Why beer?"

I explained, "Qingdao is a coastal city in northeastern China. At the end of the Qing dynasty, German settlers started this beer brewing company. Tsingtao beer has been a well-known brand in China and has its share in the domestic and global markets."

"It seems that you're upset with Matthew. What did he do?"

"Matthew promised that we would go to Qingdao together."

"I see. You certainly have reason to be mad. Matthew and his brothers are beer enthusiasts. They love to visit breweries everywhere they go, even before Jerry's death."

Jerry was thirteen months older than Matthew, and their mother, Rachel, died when Jerry was sixteen months and Matthew was three months old. According to Berenice, Matthew's mother was artistic and well-liked by others. Matthew kept a photo of her. Rachel was beautiful and elegant-looking, particularly with her avant-garde eyeglasses.

HONORING RACHEL

I KEPT LOOKING AT the picture, trying to imagine a twenty-two-year-old Rachel who had given birth to two babies in just over a year. How did that impact the body and mind? Immediately, I heard children laughing with a twenty-two-year-old me, a kindergarten teacher.

I had two age groups of students. The morning students were three years old and the afternoon students were five years old. Each day I felt I was playing all day long and I got paid for it—a worry-free three years of my life.

Two other teachers sometimes complained that I had the most mischievous students in the entire student population. They didn't like my students laughing so loud in the classroom or in the hallway. They didn't like my students singing out of tune and making up words to my piano playing. They didn't like it when my students saw them turning off their classroom lights to scare their students when they were not obeying. But some of the mothers of my morning students would come to me saying things like "Could you tell my son this or that? He only listens to you." Or "My daughter always tells me, 'My teacher said this and did that.'" Each time a mother came to me, I would just lower my body to my student's eye level and ask, "What did you do at home that made Mama tell on you?"

The parents would thank me when their three-year-old child changed his or her behavior.

My afternoon students were completely different. They were all forced to do well academically in order to get into the elementary school that the parents wanted. They had to memorize and recite stories in Chinese or English that they had learned in class, do math homework, and copy pages of calligraphy every day.

I regularly said to my headmaster, "How many times will a child be five years old? Why push them so hard this early on?" My headmaster also had a daughter the same age. She looked at me. "Only when you are a mother can you understand the pressures of competing with other kids to get into the best school."

"The best school only means something to you, not the child," I replied.

I didn't think that memorizing words, reciting children's books, and copying calligraphers' work were the best activities for my afternoon students.

One of the books in the syllabus was *Little Red Riding Hood*. In other classes, the teacher would introduce the story and would ask the students to follow her by reading out loud one sentence at a time until the whole story was done. Each day, the teacher would take one student at a time and ask him or her to repeat a part of the story until each student had memorized the whole story.

I told my students, "I am going to tell you a story about a little girl's encounter with a wolf. Listen carefully because I will point to you, and then you will act like one of them, either the girl or the wolf or other characters in the story, to show your classmates if you are paying attention." I told the story a little each day and used a small stick as a magic wand, pointing randomly at different children (but knowing which ones I hadn't pointed at yet) to have them stand up and say the phrases from the book. Each of my students was so eager to be pointed at by the magic wand. When we completed the story, the class was able to tell the story as if we were performing on stage. I, the conductor with a baton; my students, the characters of *Little Red Riding Hood* standing up and down from their little seats.

My headmaster loved my way of teaching, and when she met Matthew for the first time, she sternly told him, "China is not the place for her. She does not belong there. Let her stay with me. Take her only when you are ready to go back to the United States."

Over winter break, Matthew and I went home to visit my family. I had coffee with my former boss, asking her how the new teacher was working out.

"Carmen, who replaced you, is as good as you are and mature. At least she hasn't jumped into the swimming pool yet." My former headmaster replied.

I laughed uncontrollably. Yes, I missed the swimming pool. My afternoon class went to the establishment's rooftop swimming pool once a week. There were lifeguards on duty. Teachers stood around the pool chatting and watching the students, whereas I went in with my students, even though the water was just to my calves. I gently splashed one or two of them at a time. But they ganged up and splashed me top to bottom. One day I brought a huge water gun for revenge. Still, one water gun could not fight off sixteen pairs of five-year-old hands. I usually walked out of the pool soaking wet. Other teachers were dismayed.

So, even with my experience as a teacher of young children, I knew that being a mother at age twenty-two with two little babies to care for around-the-clock would have devastated me. What would I do with another two lives while I myself was still trying to figure out what my life would be? And me being responsible for them?

The thought of these questions reddened my eyes, and I understood Rachel's feelings of being overwhelmed by babies crying and screaming, and help was just not there.

❧

RACHEL'S MOTHER DIED WHEN Rachel was seven and Noelle, Rachel's sister, was ten. Her father, Joseph, a history professor at a private college near the township, married Mariam, a music teacher, when Rachel and Noelle were in their teens. Rachel was rather quiet, like Matthew, and a gifted painter, also like Matthew. When she met Damon, Berenice, and Henry at a dance hall one evening before graduating from high school, she was attracted to Damon's handsome looks, cheerful nature, and the vitality that he brought to the dance floor. At the time, Damon was already working as a hawsepiper on the Great Lakes. He had thirty days off from a freighter after working sixty days straight. Damon was attracted to Rachel's beautiful features and elegant demeanor. When they danced, Damon marveled at Rachel's graceful movements.

Rachel found Berenice as charming as her brother. She was full of wit and was a great storyteller. She could break the ice with any stranger in no time. Rachel wished she could talk as naturally as Berenice. Soon Rachel and Berenice became good friends. Rachel would seek advice from Berenice instead of her own sister, Noelle, who had become very religious and had already started training in an Order to become a nun.

One evening Rachel asked Berenice, "Have you ever thought of going to college?"

"No, what for?" Berenice replied.

"I don't know, I just thought there could be other ways to live than being a housewife."

"I prefer to be a housewife. I like the thought of cooking and organizing a neat household, taking care of a husband and babies."

"Wouldn't it be too boring?"

49

"I don't think so. There's a lot to manage and do. I think running a good household is just like running a good country, which requires great skills that I don't think I can learn in college."

"I just thought that out there there's a lot to see and learn and enjoy. Getting married after high school is just like moving from one household to another where I don't have time and space to be alone, to be by myself."

"I like to be with people. I wouldn't want to live by myself, which would be very lonely and depressing, don't you think?"

"I suppose."

"Are you thinking of attending college?"

"I don't know. None of my classmates are going. My sister didn't go, not to the regular university."

"Have you talked to your father?"

"Yes, he said it's my decision."

"How about your teachers? How about Mariam?"

"Mrs. Thunderberek is an absolutely no-nonsense woman. She said even if I go to college, the end result is still the same: being a housewife. If that's the case, why would I want to waste time going to college? Mariam is a bystander with warmth but without interference or advice. She always keeps her neutral position. Talking to her sometimes is like talking to a wall."

"So, have you talked to Damon?" Berenice tilted her head and looked sideways at Rachel.

Rachel was flushed. "No, why should I?"

"Just thought one more opinion might help you." Berenice shrugged.

Rachel had never thought of talking to Damon about her own future. Even though she liked him, Damon was not the person to give her advice. Damon himself didn't go to college. Rachel didn't want Damon's input to shape her decision.

Rachel had felt very alone growing up without a mother. Her father was a man of few words. Rachel saw him go to work day in and day out, come home to dinner (prepared by a house helper), talk with both daughters about mundane routines or how school was going, and then retreat to his study for the rest of the evening, no goodnights or bedtime stories. Occasionally on weekends or holidays they would go to concerts or chamber music either in the city or at nearby churches. Most of the time, both Noelle and Rachel were left on their own. Rachel went through adolescence by observing Noelle and other girls in school and tried to hang on to

Noelle. They always did things together in the first few years after their mother's death. But when Noelle started junior high, something changed. Rachel didn't know why, but Noelle was gradually pulling away. She spent her time in Bible studies and at church. Noelle didn't try to convert Rachel or talk to her about God, but she seemed possessed by the idea of dedicating herself to religion. That was the purpose of her own existence; nothing else mattered. Even after Mariam joined the family, with music being played in the house and students coming and going, the pleasant melodies and sporadic laughter from the parents of Mariam's youngest students didn't produce a caring atmosphere at home.

In the quiet, unaffectionate household, Rachel found comfort in painting, particularly still lifes. Their noncommunicative stillness had hidden messages to be depicted. Rachel didn't have to verbalize her subject matter. She delighted in using her hands to obscure forms, add colors or shade and shadows, which would reveal the period of their functional and emblematic lives. In fact, her art teacher in high school had commented that Rachel could become a painter. Some of her paintings had been selected for art exhibitions from elementary to high school, and a few that had won awards were hanging at home.

Rachel had dreamt of becoming a famous painter but at the same time was frightened by the thought of it, inhibited by her quiet, reserved nature. She couldn't visualize whether she would be able to handle the pressures of a noisy lifestyle like the one British-Mexican artist Leonora Carrington had led, even though she praised Carrington's works. Carrington's colors and alien-like figures were intimately mingled with real people and things. Rachel wanted to voice her own thinking, exhibit her perspectives about people's lives, and display her own emotions in front of the world. She wanted to boldly show statements of a naked mind and boundless imagination, like Carrington did.

Rachel was accepted to attend New York University starting in the fall of 1950. She didn't tell anyone. When she received the acceptance letter, she was still hesitant about whether she should go because she found herself constantly thinking of Damon, wanting to see him, wanting to know what he was doing when they were apart, wanting to be near him.

They would meet at the dance hall with Berenice and Henry when Damon wasn't out on the ship working. The two sets of lovebirds would dance and go out driving together whenever they could.

Berenice had started working as a clerk in a chemical plant in January 1950, and in March, she fell ill. She had a fever, headache, back pain, and stiffness in the arms and legs. It was the stiffness that alarmed her mother, Dori, enough to take Berenice to the hospital. Sixteen weeks later, Berenice came out of the hospital in a wheelchair. She had contracted polio during an outbreak of the virus, and her legs were paralyzed.

Rachel went to Dori's house every day to visit Berenice. To Rachel's astonishment, Berenice was still jolly and vibrant. Yes, she had been frustrated and sometimes felt sorry for herself, but those wrenching moments were short and gradually disappeared. Berenice quickly adjusted to her new mobilities and to doing things in completely unfamiliar ways. Rachel wondered whether she could cope and live a full life with a disability like Berenice. Rachel was drawn to Berenice's indefatigable spirit. Seeing Berenice every day gave a whole new meaning to life, and Rachel didn't want to leave her friend, the woman she admired and respected. Rachel took Berenice's job, and NYU became history.

Rachel and Damon got married a few months after Berenice and Henry. By their first wedding anniversary, Jerry was born and, soon after, Rachel was pregnant again, which coincided with Berenice's pregnancy. When Matthew was two months old, Alan was born.

I touched the rimless picture frame, tracing the outline of Rachel's face. Matthew had her smiling, elongated eyes. In my mind's eye, the basement was fully lit, and Rachel was trying to soothe Matthew while Jerry was fussing to get attention. No mother to call; no one ever taught her how to be a mother; no helping hands nearby, and Berenice in a wheelchair with Alan to care for. She laid a shrieking Matthew in the bassinet and picked up Jerry to place him in the playpen, with the desire for peace and quiet. Rachel grabbed the bedsheet she had washed in the morning, passed it over a beam, tied a knot above her, and rested her head in the loop in hopes of having a peaceful sleep, without considering the possibility that her children would become motherless.

DORI

Matthew didn't remember his mother. He'd heard stories about his mother from his grandparents and aunts on both sides of the family, but his father, Damon, didn't mention her at all. He remarried and had two more boys, Kurt and Timothy, ten and eleven years younger than Matthew. In the first eight years after their mother's suicide, Jerry, Matthew, and their father lived with Grandma Dori, who didn't approve of Damon's second marriage to Erin. She took Damon out of her will and gave Damon's portion, thirty-two acres of land, to Jerry and Matthew.

Apparently, Jerry didn't get along with his stepmother, Erin. Right after Kurt was born, Grandma Dori took Jerry and Matthew back to her home and continued to raise them. Damon didn't want the family to be separated and didn't want to fight with his stubborn mother, so he purchased a plot from Dori and built a house on the edge of the family's land east of Berenice's house, which allowed the two boys to walk across the field from one home to the other to play with Alan. Berenice's house was approximately halfway between Grandma Dori's and Damon's houses.

Grandma Dori died when Matthew was twenty and attending college at Indiana State University with Jerry and Alan. Dori's death hit Jerry and Matthew hard. For them, Dori was the only real mother they had known. She was austere with them, but she also showed her love and tenderness to the two boys. She considered them orphans because their father had basically left the boys in her care and lived with them like a roommate. Dori was particularly unforgiving of Damon when he got remarried and started a new family just when the boys, at nine and ten years old, needed parental guidance more than ever. As far as Dori was concerned, Damon hadn't considered the boys' welfare. Worst of all, the woman her son had married was not an ideal mother of the two boys. Jerry's reactions to his stepmother proved to Dori that the boys had no home and family except for her. Even though Berenice had been a loving aunt to them, she had her own family to care for.

Berenice and Damon's older brother, Ernest, and his wife were unable to have children, so they adopted three children, two girls and one boy. The two elder daughters left home after they finished college and were infrequently in contact with Ernest and his wife. The boy, Raymond, didn't attend college but stayed and worked at the family dairy farm. But he was not close to Alan, Matthew, and Jerry, who had practically grown up in the same household, whereas Raymond grew up with his two sisters and had been kept at a distance from Dori and Berenice by his parents. The irony was that Ernest was the only one of Dori's children to continue in the family dairy business, and his house was about half a mile away from Dori's house and was right across the street from Berenice. According to Berenice, Grandma Dori didn't like the fact that Raymond and his sisters had been adopted and didn't care about them. Matthew's mother was the only daughter-in-law that Dori had adored.

Berenice was the middle child. Polio had altered her life. She was confined to a wheelchair and relied on Henry or others to drive her places. But the limited mobility didn't keep her from picking up new skills. After she got married, she learned to sew her own clothes and to crochet blankets, dishcloths, and other small items for cleaning the house.

Henry also got an Amish woman, Abigail, to help out and live with them. More than a helper, she became a family member, knowing four generations, from Dori to Alan's two sons. She lived with Berenice until Jerry, Matthew, and Alan were twelve, eleven, and ten, and then she came every two weeks and stayed over the weekends. From time to time, Abigail would say a thing or two about Grandma Dori.

"Berenice is stubborn, but Dori was the most intransigent woman I have ever met. You just did not want to be on her bad side. Luckily, she loved Jerry and Matthew, who could do no wrong, unlike poor Damon, whose family Dori had torn apart. Now, Jerry is dead and has left Matthew by himself. I'm sad for Matthew, losing his mother, Dori, and Jerry, which was just incomprehensible and heartbreaking."

Damon, the youngest son, didn't like dairy farm chores from an early age. He was creative and rebellious and loved to do things that his siblings wouldn't do. He started dating in high school. Right after graduating from high school and starting to work on the Great Lakes, he overheard someone mention that a girl named Rachel was an outstanding art student at a neighboring school. Damon wouldn't miss the chance to introduce himself to her. Old pictures portrayed them dancing, swimming, and fishing with Berenice and Henry while Rachel was still in her last year of high school. Damon didn't like the confinement of working on a ship and being away from Rachel. After they got married and Jerry was born, Damon wanted to find work near home, but the opportunity for him to make the same amount of money onshore didn't arise.

JERRY

DURING COLLEGE SUMMER BREAK, Jerry, Matthew, and Alan went back to South Bend to work at the chemical plant and crashed at Berenice's house. Henry had converted the garage into a sailor's cove decorated as if it were a seaside resort, with an anchor, buoys, and gigantic seashells displayed along the railing of the ramp Berenice used to wheel herself in and out of the house. Inside, there were two long sofas and a mini bar next to a big refrigerator.

Jerry and Matthew would sleep on the sofas and Alan stayed in his own room, where high school graduation photos of all three boys hung. It was only from those pictures that I got a sense of what Jerry looked like. He died young. Everyone believed his death was an accident. He fell approximately thirty feet from a tower platform at the chemical plant minutes after finishing a shift. A few coworkers who had just finished the same shift were walking with him off of the platform. For unknown reasons, he walked behind the rest of the crew. Suddenly, a loud sound startled the guys while they were at the landing off of the platform.

A newspaper report quoted the crew: "At first, we didn't hear a thing, not a cry or any footsteps behind. Then we heard a thud. We looked down, and there was Jerry."

Matthew didn't talk to me about Jerry. The only information I got from him was that Jerry had died and that Matthew didn't believe it was an accident. He thought Jerry killed himself, just like their mother. Mother and son, both dead at age twenty-two.

It was Alan and their friend Glenn who filled me in on more details. Jerry was very meticulous about his appearance, always properly dressed and well-groomed. Girls were attracted to him when he was out with his college teammates in the evenings, but Jerry didn't have an official girlfriend. Glenn said that Jerry was shy when interacting with strangers in public, the same as Matthew. But Alan remembered Jerry as being organized and analytical. He would plan things out before taking action, in contrast to Matthew, who sometimes did things without thinking about the consequences.

Alan said, "One time, three of us finished football practice and walked home through the cemetery. It was getting dark, and Matthew thought it would be fun to run through the rows by hopping over the gravestones."

Jerry stopped him. "Show some respect for the dead. Besides, the heights are different and you could get caught by one of those stones and break your leg."

"How do we know if I don't try?" Matthew protested.

"You don't need to set yourself on fire to see if you'd get burned, stupid!" Jerry smacked Matthew lightly on his temple.

"Another time, we were riding our bikes from Grandma's house to my place. Matthew wanted to ride his bike naked. This time, Jerry agreed and joined in. We threw our clothes off, one piece at a time. When we got to my parents' house, Mom was laughing and Dad was mad. He ordered us to walk back to collect our clothes one by one before allowing Jerry and Matthew to get back on their bikes and ride home," Alan recollected with a smile and added, "Jerry was always the leader and did things the right way but somehow messed up with his life by falling off the platform."

After Jerry's death, Damon decided to leave South Bend, where only Matthew was left from his first family. He accepted a better paying job at a refinery in Texas City, on Galveston Bay. He thought Matthew would eventually leave South Bend once he had graduated from college. For Damon, South Bend held bad and sad memories of his family, and he didn't want to be reminded of them every day. Other than Matthew, his siblings were the only relatives left. In Damon's adult life, he had been apart from them, particularly after Rachel's death. He never talked about it with anyone, not even his two boys throughout the years. With Jerry's death, the feeling of being at fault haunted him. Damon didn't know how to express himself to Matthew, who had become a reminder of his sorrow. Basically, Damon didn't want to face Matthew and didn't want to know how Matthew was dealing with Jerry's death.

INVISIBLE ORPHAN

MATTHEW GOT MARRIED A year after Jerry's death, while starting his master program in college. His wife, Shannon, was working on a master's degree in English. Matthew sold Jerry's ten acres of the land to Berenice, and combined with Jerry's life insurance he bought a house and paid tuition in full for both Shannon's and his graduate degrees. By the time they had finished their degrees, there was no money left.

Apparently, a dislike of wives ran in the family. Berenice, Henry, and Erin didn't like Shannon. They all thought that she loved to spend money, and Matthew allowed it. Shannon didn't care for them either. Only the first year they were married did she show up for Thanksgiving and Christmas gatherings. After that, they only heard her voice over the phone when she called Berenice's house demanding to know when Matthew would be home. Every once in a while, Berenice would ask how Shannon was doing. Matthew always gave a short, unclear response. As time went by, no one seemed to remember her existence until Matthew announced that he would be going to China with Shannon.

"Why China?" Berenice asked.

"Shannon got a teaching job at a university in China."

"Do you have a job in China too?"

"Not yet, but once I get there, I'll find a teaching job as well."

"Is that what you want?"

"I think it is a great opportunity for me to travel."

"You can travel in different ways." Berenice was a bit hesitant to continue. She knew that once Matthew had decided to do something, no one could stop him. She understood so well that stubbornness ran in the family—her mother, Damon, Matthew, and herself.

It was summer 1983 when Matthew and Shannon went to Northwest China. They taught at the university in Xi'an, about a forty-five-minute ride to the site of the Terracotta Army. For Matthew, the thousands of Terracotta Warriors, completed around 200 BC, were the epitome of Chinese history. The crafting, the individual expressions, and the sheer number of them illustrated political, economic, scientific, and artistic development long before the United States had come into existence, which was unimaginable in his mind. As he traveled in nearby towns and outside of the province, Matthew gradually absorbed the locals' lives and got a sense of Chinese culture through time and space. The people he met evoked gratitude within him and made him realize that the world was larger than his corner of it. Yet, life and death phenomena were universal in various circumstances. He met grieving parents whose children had died at young ages; elderly, middle-age, and young people who had lost loved ones during the Cultural Revolution; and ordinary people who had become widows, widowers, and orphans, just like him.

The first year he spent in China inspired him to stay away from the US, so he decided to continue teaching in China for a second year despite the fact that by then his wife was having an affair with a Chinese PhD candidate who was also married. Before the winter break, he had landed a lecturer position at an agriculture university ninety kilometers northwest of Xi'an.

Life happened so fast that none of the family members, including Matthew himself, would have thought that by August 1984 he would have dissolved his first marriage and remarried. With me, he spent another year in Northwest China, and by the fall of 1985, we were living in Indiana.

I learned the family history in my first two months living with Berenice and Henry. Berenice was eager to inform me about every one of the tragic events that seemed like a curse that had been invoked on Damon's first marriage and weighed on the family continuously for twenty-some years. With only Matthew still alive, and Damon and his second family living far away, there was sorrow in each person, and I sensed that Matthew was the glue keeping the two generations together in a family that hardly expressed their feelings about the tragic deaths. Only Berenice was willing to share her thoughts about the events. Matthew, Damon, Kurt, Timothy, and the other family members had been silent, and no one knew how they felt.

I gradually became the catalyst that allowed them to channel their anguish and concerns about each other. Matthew's stepmother (I followed Matthew and called her mom) said that I was a godsend and asked Matthew if I had sisters to introduce to her two sons.

Matthew was not a talkative person and was hard to read, but he was very open and at ease with his college roommates, who happened to be all guys. Matthew told me that there were ten of them, including Alan, Jerry, and himself. Gradually, I met all seven of their friends; four of them had visited and traveled with us while we lived in China. They all stayed in South Bend except one who moved to Scotland with his wife. We visited him in Aberdeen, and he and his wife came to California to camp with us at Yosemite National Park. Only among these friends did I see an absolutely cheerful and totally comfortable Matthew, who was wide open in talking, laughing, being sarcastic and charming. I enjoyed watching his interactions with his college roommates. I realized that it was only among these friends that Matthew didn't need to hide his emotions, didn't need to explain, didn't need to please, didn't need to guard himself, and didn't need to be afraid of the world that he had to face every day.

MATTHEW

Two months after Matthew came back from China, he got a job at Notre Dame, and we moved to our apartment near the land he had inherited, where we started cultivating the soil and wanted to convert it into an organic farm. We would work the land on the weekends and stayed overnight with Henry and Berenice, who was particularly pleased with the arrangement. For Berenice, Matthew was home again. She could chat with him often. Alan got to spend time with Matthew again and his children got to know Matthew, who was actually their father's cousin but whom they called Uncle Matthew. They had heard stories about Uncle Matthew continuously throughout their young lives.

Matthew used to take care of things like buying bread, doing laundry, planning trips, managing our finances, and reminding me to check expenses. I was practically free of these tedious chores. I went grocery shopping with him. I cooked, kept the place clean and organized, and was Matthew's assistant for other things when he asked for help. We traveled back to Hong Kong a few times, took trips to Mexico, and drove across the country a couple times to visit most of the California national and regional parks. Life was easy and pleasant. I was pampered for years, until Matthew got sick. Then everything changed. We changed.

One winter afternoon, I came home after my classes. I found Matthew sitting against the wall on the floor in the corner of our living room. At first, he didn't notice the sound of the door opening. I walked through the kitchen as usual to the dining room when I saw from the corner of my eye a curved silhouette on the floor. I stood there to get my eyes used to the dark room. Gradually, a body with its head buried between two knees and wearing Matthew's clothes clearly emerged. I wondered why at three o'clock Matthew was not at work. I went to him; he raised his head and saw me kneeling in front of him next to the couch. He smiled.

"What's the matter?" I looked into his eyes.

He said, "Nothing, I'm just tired."

I held his gaze, putting out my hand. "Take a nap. I'll wake you when dinner is ready." He took my hand, and we both depended on each other's weight to lift our bodies up.

At the time, I was focused on my postgraduate in architecture at the University of Notre Dame, where Matthew worked as the director of the landscaping department. At lunch time, I would walk over to the maintenance building to find him with his crew having lunch together. Sometimes a crew member would shout out, "Mrs. Becareful, how are you doing?" They were referring to the daily Post-it note I stuck on Matthew's brown bag, which ended with "becareful" by itself. There were about fifteen of them, but not all of them were ever at the same place at the same time. The manager, Connor, who was very fond of Matthew and considered Matthew his mentor, often teased us about my notes. When we lived in China, we had developed a habit of using Post-its. We would post: "Don't burn the rice," "Becareful on the snow," "Pick up yogurt at 4" on all the doors and the kitchen walls. Sometimes I posted "坏蛋" (Bad Egg/Bad Person), and then Matthew would post "I'm sorry" with a sad face without asking why I was mad. A few hours later, he would wave that note in front of me and want to talk. We seldom quarreled verbally. I would walk away from disagreeable situations and, worst of all, I would give Matthew the silent treatment, which he hated. Matthew would try everything he knew to initiate communication. We also wrote letters and notes to each other, whether we were living under the same roof or thousands of miles apart.

Despite my bad temper, Matthew never got angry at me or raised his voice. He was gentle and patient, which I was not. But I learned by observing Matthew that my temperament had slowly changed. When I was a fifth grader, teachers would walk students home to ensure no one skipped lunch. One day, I can't recall why I was so angry, but I took out my notebook and started tearing pages and throwing them while I was walking. When I got home, my teacher handed all the pages that I had torn out to my grandmother and said, "I don't know why she was doing this."

I told Matthew this story before we got married. I wanted him to know in advance and think over what I was lacking and what I would not be able to accept, such as, if he got fat not due to illness, smoked marijuana before retirement, or had any extramarital affairs.

When I failed my first driving exam, I was furious at Matthew because he hadn't taught me how to do a three-point turn. I tore stacks of newspapers to pieces, took out the chipped gold-plated teacups and other dishes from a drawer where Matthew had stored them and dropped them one by one on the kitchen floor. The sounds of porcelain shattering and pieces flying all over the place relieved my anger. After breaking all of them, I went to a movie by myself. By the time I got home, the kitchen floor was clean, and I didn't see any trace of the broken pieces in the trash can. But the next Saturday, I was out in the backyard and discovered a new small colorful tile path to the chairs. Matthew had built the path with the pieces of china that I broke and presented them beautifully, like a small broken dragon flying away to escape an atrocity without a word. After that, I never deliberately broke another dish, and that incident was the worst forty-eight hours of silent treatment that Matthew had ever received.

Matthew had his way of defusing my irate moments. On snowy nights, Matthew and I would read or listen to his music, and he taught me chess, which I became obsessed with from my first move on the chess board. In less than three weeks, I ruled the board and massacred his troops until no one was left. He often smiled and said, "You are the chess player in the family."

"How come you're not even agitated by my brutal attacks?"

"You played much better than me. I deserved that."

Suddenly, I was disturbed by his calm, cool-as-a-cucumber attitude. I couldn't understand that while I was bloodthirsty, he just took it in without being upset by my pride and arrogant manner.

"I don't love you anymore!" I burst out in frustration.

He put his face close to mine. "Sure you do."

That melted me.

TURNING POINT

BUSY WITH MY COURSEWORK, I didn't really notice the changes in Matthew until one January morning in 1992. I answered a call, which was for Matthew, and passed the phone to him. After he hung up, he went back to bed and sat upright, which was unusual. Neither one of us liked sitting in bed. I was in and out of the bathroom getting dressed and brushing my teeth. When I saw him sitting there, I knew something was wrong. I asked him who had called. He closed his eyes and didn't respond.

I walked to the bedside. "Matthew, what's wrong?"

He opened his eyes. I saw sadness in them. He searched my face, and slowly he said, "Mrs. Hunter. I missed my appointment with her."

Mrs. Hunter was an attorney representing a plaintiff, who wanted to have a white pine tree cut down. Matthew had served as an expert witness in court three days before.

I looked at him. "What was the verdict?"

"I killed the three-hundred-year-old tree."

"Was that your recommendation?"

"Yes."

"Then the tree should go. You know it will kill someone if it's not taken down."

"But the tree was here before any of us. We don't have the right to cut it down."

"Matthew, unfortunately humans have the privilege of making that decision. As long as we are dominant and live in an environment where trees may threaten us, we will make the decision to protect human lives."

Matthew looked at me with tears filling his eyes. "I don't want to be that decision maker."

"You aren't. You only gave your professional opinion."

"I have killed the white pine. The court took my advice as an authorization to order cutting it down."

Matthew had forgotten that he had also saved numerous ancient trees. He had been an expert witness for a few years and defended many of them. One of them was right on the southeast corner of University Avenue and White Pine Street, a residential street. The tree was already leaning at a thirty-degree angle, and the big slab of concrete sidewalk had broken into three pieces with an arch shape poking up around the bottom of the trunk and some exposed roots. Two-thirds of the oversize white pine was hovering over the one-story home on the southeast corner. Whenever we stopped at the traffic light before turning right onto University Avenue, I looked up at that tree, mumbling, "Someday this tree will hurt someone if the city doesn't take care of it."

Apparently, I was not the only person who noticed the danger of that tree. Someone wanted to take it down and the case went to court. Matthew was called to the witness stand to defend the existence of that old white pine. He also recommended how the city could prevent the tree from continuing to lean. As a result, from one-third of the height, cables and gigantic stainless-steel buckles were symmetrically crossed over, as if they were multilayer scissors caught in the trunk, the branches, and nearby light poles. Regardless of the city's preventive measures, one morning in early June, on one of the heaviest days of rain, the aging white pine tree on the southeast corner of University Avenue and White Pine Street fell across the southwest corner of the street, smashing a pickup truck that was just turning right at the green traffic light, killing the driver instantly. When I learned about the accident on the local evening news, tears of pain ran down my cheeks. I silently looked into the sky. "Matthew, this morning, your buddy the old white pine, fell and took a man in his forties with it."

The white pine tree came down a year after Matthew's death.

The day Matthew missed the appointment with Mrs. Hunter was the beginning of his withdrawal. He stayed in bed longer and some days just didn't get up or didn't go to work. I called Connor and met him at the Danish pastry coffee shop near the entrance to the university. Connor was in his thirties; had a five-year-old son, Sam; and had just gotten divorced.

He asked, "How is Matthew doing?"

"Not good. Is there anything that I have neglected?"

"I don't know. Lately, he has been quieter than ever. He has been searching geographic locations for white pine trees. He has often said that they're native here. Why would we want to destroy them?"

"Connor, do you know why he is so obsessed with the white pine trees?"

"Well, we all know that he loves trees. He's a tree doctor and tree whisperer. With the population growth and regional development, he foresees more white pines being cut down to meet the demands of growth. That stressed him a lot."

Matthew was caught in between the life and death of the white pine trees. Over time, even with his subject matter expert credential, he would not be able to save many of them in the region. I decided that it was time for us to move away from that environment and to seek treatment for his apparent depression.

When I mentioned this idea to Matthew, he said, "No, you haven't finished your studies."

"My studies can wait. Let's just move back to the land and focus on the farm."

ABSCOTA

ABSCOTA ORGANIC FARM, NAMED after a type of soil in the upper Midwest, took seven years to become certified. Each year we needed to provide soil samples to test its organic matter as part of the criteria for certification. We had talked about starting an organic farm when Matthew came back from China. Each year we had planted mixed cover crops, such as winter wheat, rye grass, and hairy vetch and turned them into the soil. We also planted white pine trees from seedlings and expected to have a grove of all white pine trees.

At the beginning of 1991, Abscota had about a year to become completely organic.

We moved into an old stone house next to a small creek in November 1992. The house belonged to a distant uncle, John, who the townspeople thought was eccentric. I didn't know much about him, and even Berenice couldn't tell me who he was, but he and Matthew seemed to speak the same language. When John heard from Berenice that Matthew was planning on moving back to town, he offered his house to us, rent free. We only paid utilities, water, and other charges from the township. We lived in that house for a year before moving into our own place.

Matthew drew a planting map and showed me where the plants would be. He planted black locust trees to generate cash as poles along the adjacent line with Berenice's land on the west side of the farm, built a shed that was about half an acre away from the road on the north side by salvaging materials from old barns in nearby towns, and excavated a well in front of the west-facing shed. Vegetable and flower fields extended from the road three acres to the south. In the southeast corner of the property, we planted ten acres of cluster white pine trees. The rest of the east side was a marshy area that we decided to reserve for Canadian geese and other birds to take refuge in on their yearly migrations. Most of the central land to the west would grow hops with a divider of currants, elderberries, and persimmon trees for the birds between the vegetable garden and the drive to the end of the south side of the farm.

In the area, including us, there were only eight organic farms established, sized from an acre to thirty-two acres. We met throughout the winter to learn from each other. We discussed topics, such as what vegetables would be best in each of our locations. One farm only grew potatoes and flowers. Other farms grew root vegetables the best.

We started spinach, chard, lettuce, and pea seedlings in the basement while cleaning up the field in the winter. I also got a part-time teaching assistant post to teach AutoCAD drawing at the local community college. My classes were in the evenings from Monday to Thursday.

In 1993, we first harvested spinach, all kinds of lettuce, and peas—the only farm that could produce greens in early spring—and sold them at the farmer's market on Saturdays. On Friday afternoons, I started harvesting the vegetables. Harvesting peas was just like racing. The more I picked, the faster they grew. I could hardly keep up with the rows and rows of peas. I often laughed between the rows of peas, and around seven in the evening I would call out to Matthew, "Stop them from growing!"

The Saturday farmer's market was a place that reminded me of my time in China. The major differences were that I was under a roof and many of our customers were immigrants from eastern Europe.

Besides greens, we also had bachelor's buttons and Achillea (pearl yarrow), along with different herbs. We dug the herbs with roots and soil and put them into individual cartons so they would be easier for people to transplant at their own places. Those herbs were the first things to sell out.

An older woman's eyes lit up when she saw my bachelor's buttons. Slowly, she approached me and asked how much they would cost her. I told her, and then she asked, "Do you accept food stamps?" At first I didn't know how to respond since we hadn't established anything with the market organizer regarding food stamps. But I could see that this woman wanted the bachelor's buttons more than food. The flowers must have meant a lot to her. Without waiting for Matthew, I said, "Sure." She picked a bunch, held them near her chest, and talking mostly to herself said, "When I was growing up, my mother grew blue cornflowers in the field. The war…" Then she looked at me. "Do you know this is my native country's flower? I have a set of china that is decorated with blue cornflowers. I haven't seen the fresh flowers for years. Now, I find them here. Thank you!" She walked away without waiting for my reply. When Matthew came back to our stall, I handed him the food stamps and told him what I learned from this woman. Matthew looked at me with a smile and turned to find the organizer. A few minutes later, he came back. "The organizer said we can exchange dollar for dollar with him at the close of the market."

From that day on throughout the flower season, I reserved a double size of the bachelor's buttons in my bucket behind the counter for this woman at the same price. She often carried the flowers away with her big smiles and missed the bouquet only twice.

Matthew had been seeing a psychologist and a psychiatrist, who prescribed Prozac. Matthew didn't like it. He complained that Prozac made him feel drowsy. Yet, he could not sleep. In addition, Prozac didn't settle his anxiety. I encouraged him to talk to both of his doctors. The psychiatrist only adjusted his dosage and continued the Prozac.

At times, Matthew was busy planning the garden and seemed happier. But despite the hard work we put in, financially, the garden could not support us. With my salary as a TA, we barely got by, which distressed Matthew.

Matthew got a job as an arborist at a local landscaping company. Every evening when I got home, I saw him sitting in the armchair with his eyes closed, not knowing I was there. He'd started losing weight, and strands of long, white hairs dangled on each side of his temples. He seemed to have lost interest in the garden and everything else, including me. I often squatted down beside the armchair and asked how he was doing. He put on a smile and just said, "I'm tired."

One Friday evening, I was cooking dinner.

Matthew asked, "Why do people think suicide is a bad thing?"

I replied, "It's a social stigma. People don't understand what it takes for a person to do that."

"Do you understand?"

"No, I don't. But do you remember I wrote an essay regarding euthanasia? I think it takes a lot of courage to act on suicide despite the state of the person's mind. Each of us should have the right to determine whether to live or to die."

"Thank you," he replied.

GOODBYE

December 1994, a few days before Christmas, Matthew didn't come home for dinner. When he woke that morning, he was already tired and didn't get up. I massaged his temples and whispered, "It's okay to stay home."

He held my hands to his chest. "What good can life be if I can't think, can't function, can't fuck…"

"Shh…" I tried to comfort him by kissing his forehead, his face, and lips. Tears came from his closed eyes and wet my lips. He eventually got up, dressed, took a cup of coffee and a banana, and got into his truck. He sat there for a while.

I went to the driver's side. "Keep up your spirits," I said and then headed to my car.

He said, "Goodbye."

I turned my head, smiled, and told him, "Jiaozi 餃子(dumplings) for dinner. Don't be late."

I'd made jiaozi on his birthday, which was in late November. I learned to make the traditional northwestern jiaozi the year I lived in China. Jiaozi was a staple meal throughout northern China, but northwestern jiaozi had its own fame. In Xi'an, you could go to a restaurant that served only jiaozi, hundreds of different varieties of them. Matthew just loved them, and he could easily devour sixty of them in no time. When we were at the university, his students organized a jiaozi party at our house in the spring. I watched the women working with flour to form wrappers, chopping veggies, stirring meat, rolling dough, boiling a few big pots of water, and then I joined in to learn how to wrap the dumplings. Matthew and the men rolled up their sleeves to clean the yard, cut down dead branches, repair walking paths, and wash all the doors and windows. Around three o'clock, we all sat down on makeshift benches and tables with his students' families, ate jiaozi, listened to stories, and drank until nightfall. That Matthew was the happiest man on earth.

After we came back to South Bend, he requested jiaozi for his official birthday dinner. He knew that making jiaozi was time-consuming. Otherwise, he would want it as a daily meal like people in Xi'an. I made them a few times a year, and that December day, I thought it would uplift him.

Matthew was late for his favorite food. I called Alan around seven o'clock. He came with Ian, his chief deputy friend from the town's police station. I wanted to file a missing person report.

Ian said, "A missing person report can only be filed after a person has been gone for twenty-four hours, but we'll look for Matthew without a report."

The police department knew Matthew came from a long-time local family and knew of the family's tragic events through two generations.

At 1:49 a.m., on December 21, 1994, the first day of winter, I heard steps while I was knitting an almost-finished vest for Matthew. I jumped out of the armchair and ran barefoot to the front door. I opened it just as Ian was about to knock.

"Are you by yourself?"

"Yes. Did you find Matthew?"

"Let me call Alan first. Go get your shoes."

I changed out of my pajamas, put on my shoes and a jacket. When I went back to the living room, Alan, Henry, and Berenice were there.

I was puzzled and looked at Ian.

He said, "I didn't want you to be alone. We found Matthew on Cleveland Avenue. He's dead."

Thirteen hours later, when I woke up and went to the living room, Damon (I called him Dad), Kurt, and Timothy had already flown in. Dad was on the phone with the coroner's office. Dad finished talking, walked over, and hugged me very tight. I let Dad hold onto me. I was full of sorrow for this old man with thin layers of white hair. In forty years, he had lost his entire first family. First, he buried his twenty-two-year-old wife, carrying three-month-old Matthew in one arm and with the other hand holding the little palm of sixteen-month-old Jerry, who was hardly standing steadily on his own. The second time, he buried a twenty-two-year-old Jerry, with twenty-one-year-old Matthew, eleven-year-old Kurt, and ten-year-old Timothy standing by his side.

This time, we would bury his second son, less than a month past his forty-first birthday.

We went to the coroner's office. Pictures of Mathew as they found him evinced in front of me, and I identified him. I asked to see his body, but they refused. I asked to go to Cleveland Avenue. They refused and said they were still investigating the scene. Two days later, the coroner's office instructed us to claim Matthew at a mortuary, which was 3.7 miles away in the next township, and to pick up the death certificate.

The certificate stated: male, forty-one, cause of death: suicide by carbon monoxide poisoning.

"Could any of his organs be donated?" I told the coroner that Matthew was an organ donor.

"Unfortunately, we needed to perform an autopsy to determine the cause of death. Since it was carbon monoxide poisoning, we could not harvest any organs."

Four of us went to the mortuary to see Matthew. He looked peacefully asleep. I placed my lips on his cool forehead and murmured, "Someday, I will forget you."

Dad and the two brothers took off the same afternoon, after Matthew was cremated. Dad expressed that he would like Matthew to stay beside his mother and brother. He ordered a plaque from the crematory. Kurt and Timothy suggested putting a pinecone in the upper right corner with *The Tree Man* below, indented three inches to the left.

I didn't tell Dad that Matthew and I had made a promise to each other, that if either one of us died before the other, he would like to be part of Mount Huangshan in Anhui Province in China, where the Huangshan pine trees (*Pinus hwangshanensis,* Hayata) can live thousands of years when undisturbed, standing tall and proud.

When the mortuary informed me that I could pick up Matthew's ashes, I walked the 3.7-miles there and back. To my surprise, Matthew was heavy. The pieces of him were not all ashes. The majority of them were like minute pebbles mixed with various shapes of miniature arrows and sticks. The mortuary put him in a plastic bag with a knot and placed the plastic bag in a square cardboard box. I walked home by holding him in both of my hands, perpendicularly in front of my pelvis. I divided Matthew into two sacks. One would go to the cemetery, the other would go to Huangshan.

EXPERIENCES OF DEATH

I DON'T REMEMBER HOW the days went. Sometimes there seemed to be a void all around me. I didn't remember what had happened or what was missing or the sequences of the pieces of missing memories. I only knew that Matthew was not there. I could not feel him, and I could not touch him.

I called Dad and asked him how he handled the grief caused by death. Dad told me, "Just deny it. If you deny it long enough, you believe it isn't true."

Dad's answer brought Uncle Mike back to life. My uncle was always cheerful, loved to laugh, and each time he came to visit I saw sunshine come with him.

When I felt something poke my back and heard, "Don't move—police," I knew that was Uncle Mike. He would look for me before he took off. Each time he saw me with a book, he confiscated it and said, "You little bookworm, what are you reading?"

When I read *War and Peace*, my uncle said, "You're too young to read that." When I read *Dream of the Red Chamber*, he said, "You're too young to read that." When I read *Persuasion*, Uncle Mike said, "You're too young to read that."

One summer afternoon, my mother sat all of us down and started sobbing. "Your uncle Mike was killed this morning in a car accident. The police are still trying to find out who else was involved."

Later the police report stated that Uncle Mike was on his motorcycle. Possibly he was too close to a truck, or a truck had slowed down suddenly, and Uncle Mike's bike got caught by the chain that was attached to the bottom of the truck bed. He and the motorcycle were both dragged under the truck. But when other drivers found Uncle Mike on the highway, no other vehicle was around. Uncle Mike's skull was cracked and half of his face was gone.

I loved to ride motorcycles. Whenever we got a chance, Uncle Mike would take me for a ride with his friend on the race routes of the Macau Grand Prix. He would let me ride the motorcycle alone from the top of Fishermen's Curve all the way down the slope to Black Sands and then into the Melco hairpin, while he and his friend rode parallel with me, the wind so intimately brushing each millimeter of my skin, so sharp yet affectionately gentle. I was free of all boundaries, as if I were flying naked and controlling the speeds with my fingertips.

On the day of Uncle Mike's death, mother declared that no one in our family, whether marrying in or marrying out, could ever ride on a motorcycle as long as she lived. When my sister got married, my brother-in-law had to give up his motorcycle.

I simply rejected that Uncle Mike was gone. I thought the adults were playing a sick joke. I refused to go to his funeral or to visit his grave all those years. Uncle Mike died at twenty-one. I was eleven.

Years later when I reread the books in English that Uncle Mike had gently snatched from my hands, I could see my twenty-one-year-old uncle with the sun's rays shining on him, and he smiled and said, "Now you can read them."

When I read *Lolita* at age thirty-one, I could not put the book down. It was past midnight in my study, and I saw Uncle Mike through the reflection in the window, standing there with a serene twenty-one-year-old face. "Now you understand why I kept telling you that you were too young to read those books."

Denial was the way I plowed through Uncle Mike's death, which was the way Dad handled his losses. Dad's denial allowed me to realize that turning a blind eye would not take me far with Matthew's death. I just didn't know how to deal with grief, despite having experienced a second death when I was twenty-one.

I love reading and writing. Reading is like an invitation to enter an imaginary world, where unimaginable scenes unfold with familiar sensations and feelings associated with seemingly real people and events. Hand in hand with reading, writing is more like a sacred ritual. A person's innermost self can be accurately stark naked with honesty without worrying that someone else might steal away his or her cognitive capacity and emotional process, which is stated in black and white.

At the beginning of high school, I started taking teen writing workshops, transitioning after graduation to youth writing workshops. Most of the mentors in the writing workshops were university students and postdoctoral fellows in Chinese and world literature.

Zi Meng had been my literature mentor since I was a junior in high school. He served as my counselor in literature appreciation summer camps for three years. In the last year of his graduate studies, the literature mentors started a youth literature publication to encourage young people to submit their writing. I volunteered to work with the publication, and the group met five to seven nights a week. We had heated discussions about how to use the limited funds to award which writers, what theme we would focus on each month, and who would negotiate with the landlord to extend our meetings. Night after night we were dog-tired, walking out of the little rent-free office awash in laughter and sometimes swearing. When it was a Saturday or a holiday evening, we would cruise the streets to feel the residual fiesta. Often, we ended up on the helical stairs outside of Admiralty Station on Hong Kong Island after midnight. Five or six of us sat at each step to form a spiral. Those times, we passed around marijuana. I was the youngest among them. I actually passed it to the next person up the step, listening to one of the member's experiences in a study-abroad program on a ship around the world (he also smuggled in a small sack of fresh figs, the first fresh fig that I'd ever had). Others described their experiences at UC Berkeley, which was also the first time I had heard details about that magnificent institution. I thought, "Someday I will go there."

Zi Meng took a trip to Mongolia to celebrate graduating with a master's degree in Chinese literature. He had already secured a teaching assistant post at a Chinese university the following semester in September. He started his journey in the middle of May. Six weeks later, he came home. After a week at home, he was admitted to a hospital and shortly after that, he went into a coma.

Zi Meng had contracted hepatitis B while he was traveling in Mongolia. He died in a coma at age twenty-five, the third week of August. He was an only child. I felt so wretched for his parents. There was a bright future in front of Zi Meng and for no reason at all, he was taken.

Zi Meng was stern with his upright posture, as if he were the ultimate authority in our subject discussions at camp. We teenage campers joked about envisaging him standing out from the brightest scholars, because he took himself so seriously, no others would want to be next to him. He seldom smiled, but I had seen him laughing wholeheartedly when the publication group suggested that he play the role of a young timid woman from one of the plays that we had selected to publish. He picked up a Hello Kitty from the sofa, placed it to his cheek, swung his head left and right, blinked his eyes with a bashful smile. "Would this work?"

he asked and then aimed the Hello Kitty at the proposer in all his mighty power. I just adored him at that moment and discovered the comical Zi Meng, who had not yielded to conventional wisdom.

When we discussed *Dream of the Red Chamber*, Zi Meng said, "Some critics have suggested that the novel is a cookbook. Do you agree with that?"

I raised my hand. No one else did.

"Could you give an example and tell us why?"

"The soup made with fresh bamboo and ham. Descriptions of food or eating were in each chapter, some of them with details and some with brief introductions. There were at least 180 dishes with main courses, side dishes, soups, snacks, desserts, fruits, seeds and nuts, spices, drinks, and different kinds of dumplings, cookies, cakes, teatime items, and imported exotic foods. All of those dishes were not purely imaginary. We could reproduce all of them today by following the instructions with the exact ingredients and cooking methods."

Zi Meng looked at me, "Ah, you do your homework. True, the novel is not merely talking about a love triangle. It also illustrates the culture of eating, the intricate and delicate chemical reactions of each ingredient, which evoke all of our five senses. We all know that's a big part of traditional Chinese life today. It may be a bit of a generalization to say that this novel is a cookbook. But the essence of the plot does tell us that without the recipes and dishes, *Dream of the Red Chamber* would lose its color and liveliness. This also would dispel the feeling that all is like a dream; in other words, a duplication of the feeling that we treasure as long as we are human."

One time we were discussing a poem that described homosexuality in the fifth century. One of the campers asked, "If homosexuality was so common through time, why in our twentieth-century society have people resisted it?"

Zi Meng looked around the group. "Anyone have any thoughts?"

The majority of us were so stung and unfamiliar with the topic that no one was willing to say anything except the one who had asked the question.

"I thought it's not normal for people of the same sex to have a sexual relationship. A man and a woman are designed as a pair to have sex," the camper said.

Zi Meng's eyes were beaming, "Does that mean it's okay for people of the same sex to love each other without sex?"

"No. How do we know they don't have sex?"

"Is having sex the only issue here?"

"I don't know. It doesn't seem right for two men or two women to have romantic and physical affections toward each other…What do you think?"

Zi Meng looked around again. "Homosexuality is part of human nature regardless of whether society accepts it or not. The characters in the poem were paragons, who had the privilege of exhibiting their inner calamity or joy. As an imperial society, when the top power could do that, the general population would not object publicly, which does not prove society's point of view. But today we are interpreting this record, and we know the genuine feeling was coming from a human being, like you, like me. That person's passion was no less than ours. Yes, the descriptions of sexual longing did indicate sexual activities were a big part of the love that one man had for the other man. Was anything wrong with that?" He searched our reactions. No one said a word. "Having sex was their private sharing, just like we want to make love to our boyfriends or girlfriends. We don't announce this desire to the whole world, do we? If today someone you love, such as your brothers, sisters, or dear friends tell you that they are homosexuals, does that change who they were yesterday?"

Zi Meng's sharp critiques of historical literature and uncompromising views of the current state of the world had initiated my own critical thinking of social and humanistic impacts on us. He persuaded us to believe that authority, money, or power couldn't overtake, couldn't control, and couldn't direct us. Nevertheless, he advised, "We are very fragile in front of these enticements and materialistic temptations. We so easily succumb to them without reflecting that they may have taken our souls."

But Zi Meng was gone. I would not be enlightened by him anymore.

EMOTIONAL AWAKENING

I STARTED TO LOOK for Zi Meng at coffee shops and places and streets we frequented. I walked days and nights, searching each passerby's face in hopes of spotting him. I thought if I was careful and looked closely, I would find him again.

The group carried woe no less than mine. In the cooler evenings with the solacing autumn breezes at our tiny publishing office, whenever we touched on topics that Zi Meng had left behind, we didn't hear chortles or ardent debates. In a still way, we surveyed each other as if we were petrified of waking the elephant in the room.

One member, Chris, forced me to see a counselor. He made an appointment with his friend, a psychologist, and he seized me in his arms and hauled me in to sit in front of this friend in the psychiatric unit at Kwong Wah Hospital in Kowloon.

Chris was eight years older than me. He had graduated from Hong Kong University a few years before Zi Meng. He was a key player of the group. Chris had singlehandedly negotiated the office space for the existence of the publication. His connection to performing artists, social elites, and international cultural exchange personnel was vast and widespread because of his post as an administrator in the culture center. At the time, he was my idol. I read many of his poems and verses, particularly the ones that described his encounters with, courtship of, and eventually loss of his girlfriend, which tugged at my heartstrings. I never met her, but through the poems and verses, I learned that she was a dancer.

At age twenty, I had not really fallen in love yet. I felt heartbroken for Chris, for his loyal love for his ex-girlfriend. The idea of his love toward her had formed such a fancy in my mind that I wanted him to love her for eternity. It was not merely my phantom idea of his romance. It was through his way of writing, waiting patiently for her in the alley of the dance studio, watching her from a distance, protecting her even though there was another man next to her, and remembering her by smelling the *Michelia alba* flowers on rainy summer nights on the street that paralleled the Kowloon Tong Station. All of this emerged lucidly like the changing images at the beginning of a movie whenever I smelled the intense fragrance of *Michelia alba*. On hot August days, I loved to float five or six of them in a tiny white porcelain *ochoko* cup stamped in blue with the word 酒 (wine). How could she leave him?

Chris and I lived in the same apartment compound, so we were just a few blocks away from each other's apartment. On those late nights after working at the publication, he would see me into the secured door of my apartment building before walking home alone. I shared a flat with a roommate while I was teaching at the nearby kindergarten. On Friday nights, my roommate's girlfriend would show up and stay over the weekend with her. Our space was crowded on Saturday mornings when her girlfriend tried to make breakfast while I was already in the kitchen. When I mentioned it to Chris, he just handed me his apartment key and said anytime I wanted to stay at his place, I could go without asking him. He often worked at odd hours. Sometimes he had to welcome international groups, and he would stay in the same hotel where the performers stayed. His unusual times away from home gave me a lot of freedom to roam his apartment. I could practice piano, I could read all his books, and I could write with or without him being there. When he was there, he was occupied in his room, and I would be in another. We didn't interrupt each other until it was time to eat or to meet with the group to work on the publication. After Zi Meng died, I was in a constant perturbed state, and Chris took the liberty of taking charge of my mental well-being.

I went through weekly counseling without any medication until the end of the year. One day my psychologist said to me, "You are okay. Go out there to face the world. We all experience sadness, which is imprinted in our lives, something enigmatic and acute to appreciate. Your sessions with me end today. I suggest that you destroy your record of seeing me here. Society is still not fully accepting of people who have visited a psychiatric ward."

New Year's Eve of the year Zi Meng died, we all went out to celebrate his life. I brought some white roses; we went to Stanley Village on Hong Kong Island to have a late dinner, and then we walked to the beach near midnight. Villagers were already shooting up fireworks for the new year.

Standing with my feet in the water, I placed one of the white roses on the water, looked into the darkness of the sea, which occasionally glowed with blue light as the waves were breaking, and uttered: "Zi Meng, remember a verse from *Dream of the Red Chamber*:

Today, laughing as I am a fool to embed falling petals to a flower tomb. Pondering, in the coming years, who will be burying me?

Here is a white rose for you, with the pureness of your spirit, please watch over me."

We recited poetry, shouted at the spectacular fireworks, sang, cried, laughed, and drank too much that evening. Another member, Wei Tung, who was just two years older than me, was too drunk to go home. Chris and I took him back to Chris's apartment. I was not drunk but exhausted by the emotions, plus it was too late to go back to my apartment, knowing that my roommate's girlfriend would be spending the night. I crashed in the living room because by then Chris had made his two bedrooms into one big room. After Chris put Wei Tung to bed, he came out of the bedroom. I was sitting on the floor next to the coffee table, thinking of Zi Meng's parents, feeling that there was no justice. I was very tired, and when Chris sat down next to me, I rested myself into his lap. He stroked my hair like I was a little kitty. Then he pulled me up, and I just hung my head on his shoulder, about to fall to sleep. I felt that his hands slowly moved from my head to my back. Delicately, one of his hands was under my shirt. When his hand reached to the back of my bra, I stood up and went to the bathroom. When I came out, he was not there and the bedroom door was closed. I slumped myself onto the loveseat, huddling.

Around five in the morning, Wai Tung came out of the bedroom and said, "Sleep in the bed. I'm leaving."

I went to the bedroom and slept next to Chris. Around 11 o'clock, I woke up. Chris was still next to me. I got out of the bed and shook him, "Do you want to go get breakfast?"

He held onto my hand; eyes still closed, said, "Return my tears…"

I let go of his hand and walked out of his apartment. After that first day of the new year, I only went to his apartment when I was sure that he wouldn't be there, and I continued to dig into his writings, published or not, leaving him notes on what I had read. Sometimes I wrote corresponding verses or poems on the other side of his writing and never mentioned that to him.

I could not return his tears, which should belong to his ex-girlfriend, the dancer, whose slender figure I could see with those precise, graceful, and dazzling movements with the fluttering, translucent ribbon-like white tunic weaving with her body before the audience's attentive gaze. The love Chris had to offer, written in thousands of words exhibited to the world, was not for me. I was not that person. I just wanted to be the person to feel his longing and to crystalize the "forever missing her"—she who was so close, yet out of reach.

A lot of supportive friends came to Matthew's memorial service, although my family and the people I wanted to see were not there. One of the people I really wanted to see was Chris. After Matthew's death, Chris showed up in my head. I just wanted his hugs, his soothing voice. I thought he would be the only person who could perceive my pain, who could save my sin. I didn't know why Chris, why I trusted him that much. I always felt that he understood even though he didn't ask questions. He could feel my emotional turmoil and intellectual keenness. We had experienced Zi Meng's death together. He knew how hard it was to accept. When his girlfriend left him, I was there mutely easing his pain. Maybe he would do the same for me, albeit our situations were completely different. One thing I knew, parts of us had died at different times.

REDISCOVERED SUICIDE

IN JANUARY 1993, MATTHEW and I spent almost a month driving around the United Kingdom. We visited Chris in London, where he had been living for over four years. Chris was working on his PhD and had become an activist for Chinese immigrants. I was particularly interested in his research for his academic thesis. He was studying a twentieth-century poet who I was not familiar with, but who was well-known in scholarly circles.

The trip to England was the only time Matthew had set foot on his forefathers' land. Well, partially. His mother was French. Matthew and I had set up rules and preferences for our adventures. When we were driving, the driver would not argue with the navigator, who had the map or directions in hand, even though the navigator could be wrong. Each of us had a "must do" list, and we would fulfill both lists in a given area before undertaking anything else. We drove out of Heathrow and headed directly to Cambridge for lunch. I wanted to show Matthew the setting of "Goodbye, Cambridge" by the early twentieth-century poet Xu Zhimo, which was on my to-do list.

It was a cold morning. The river and buildings had not changed since my last visit. The bicycle riders along the river and crews on the water had all gone without a trace. Canoes were covered with a thin frost and were cleated with short ropes. The rich summer foliage of the trees was withered. The famous weeping willows along the River Cam in the poem were aging and colored in salt and pepper with grayish brown. Yet, the winter bitterness with the cloudy sky added to the sentimental beauty of this apparently deserted campus. We walked carefully on the white powdery stones while I recited: "Soundlessly I took my leave, as inaudibly as I came, quietly I waved goodbye, to the rosy cloud in the western sky...the golden willows by the riverside, are the new brides in the dusking sun, their reflections on the mirroring waves, always pull the strings of my heart." I could hear the wind brushing past my ears—*whoosh, whoosh, whoosh.*

Matthew took a deep breath. "We're seeing the winter Cambridge instead of the poet's autumn view."

"Yes, but I love these chilly and tranquil moments." I walked backward facing him and smiled.

After lunch, we went to the Botanic Garden, which was on Matthew's list. Even on this chilly winter day, Matthew was elated with this research garden, emphasizing biodiversity, cross-pollination, and plants that were collected from all over the world. He headed directly to the Woodland Garden; he wanted to see the dogwood, Scots pine, and Cambridge oak. The way he turned the pine needles, looked at the seed cones upside down, touched the yellowish-brown frangible oak leaves, and his curious expressions were no different from the lively Matthew I had first met nine years before. I watched him while he reviewed each piece of nature's wonder.

"At home, where was Matthew?" I almost spoke my thoughts out loud.

When we got to the huge glasshouse, he was like a little boy finding treasures that he had expected all along. The alpine and tropical specimens were the first two destinations. The contrast of them wowed Matthew as much as me. "It is a beautiful world," Matthew marveled.

"How much has changed in these nine years?" I asked myself. I traced our footsteps. The first year we were in Indiana, Matthew got the job at the university and I enrolled and took English classes. Two years later, I was accepted into the architecture program. Tuition was free because I was the spouse of an employee. I also worked for hours as an interpreter for local community colleges and social services agencies. My colleagues told me, "We've seen other Asians walking down the street or on TV but didn't know any real person as a friend or coworker. You're the first Asian we've gotten to know." The income was enough for my own expenses. We were doing fine and traveled across North America and back to Hong Kong a few times until that afternoon, in the dark living room, when I found Matthew sitting there alone. Matthew had changed overnight. It was hard for me to believe a mental illness could spin up at the snap of a finger without any forewarning. Or was I not paying attention? I revisited the question again and again and still, to the day Matthew died, I was so shocked and so disbelieving that he tried the second time and succeeded.

We drove to the Highlands through the cold rain. At first, Matthew had some difficulty maneuvering the right-hand-drive car on the left side of the road. When he came to a roundabout, I needed to make sure if the first, second, third, or fourth exit would take us in the correct direction. At one point, we were driving round and round on the circle. I knew we were on the right road, but somehow as we exited and drove farther away from the circle, I got the sense that we were heading the opposite direction. We backtracked and tried again. Finally, on the third try, we got the hang of the roundabout, and we took flight from that point, proud of our hard-won experience.

A few times as we were driving along, I blurted out, "Stop, stop, stop." Matthew would park the car half uplifted on the narrow, stony footpath.

"Look, what's that?" I pointed upward to a wall, where a cluster of gigantic creamy yellow flowers were dangling.

We got out of the car and crossed the curving road. Standing next to the wall, which was shorter than I had first perceived, Matthew tip-toed to grab a branch, and the flowers tumbled downward.

"Rhododendron." Matthew held the branch with one hand and lightly touched the flower petal between two fingers.

"Wow, I have not seen such huge rhododendrons with this rare color." I stood on my toes and stuck my head close to the flowers.

"Yes, I've read about them, but this is the first time I've seen them. This must be one of the hardy hybrids that bloom in January."

Before we reached the Highlands, we saw more enormous rhododendrons in white and light yellow. Matthew was whistling. I had almost forgotten that he could whistle. I had not seen vitality and excitement in him for almost three years. I thought we had made the right decision to take this trip, even though we were worried about our finances.

We hiked up the expansive Ben Nevis, the highest peak in Britain. The air was fresh and the vastness of the mountain range was exhibited around us wherever we turned. No rain, no blue sky, but a fair day for hiking. On our way back, we saw hundreds of sheep all across the moors moving downward. In less than a hundred meters, a man in a Scottish kilt slowly approached us. His hands were in front of his waist and busy with something.

"He's knitting," I whispered to Matthew. I had never seen a man knitting while walking.

"Halo." The man looked to be in his forties, tall and big built, with a friendly smile.

"How do you do?" I replied, and Matthew nodded.

"A fine day, isn't it?" He looked up at the gray sky and looked back at us. "No rain."

"Yes, it is a fine day. May I take a look at your knitting?" I asked.

"Sure." As he walked closer to me, I noticed he was working in three or four different colors. He wore a tool belt that had six or more pockets in front of his waist. I saw that at least four of them contained the yarn. In the others were different sizes of safety pins, needles, and crochet hooks. "Do you knit?"

"Yes, but I'm not as skillful and professional as you." I touched the piece, which was about eight inches wide and eighteen inches long. Three of the diamonds that were bordered with double cables were already completed, one above the other, forming a straight line. In the center of each diamond, a leaf in green, butterscotch, and crimson red, the tip pointing upward with eyelet holes and knit stitches.

"What is this for?"

"Ah, it's the central panel of a girl's sweater. As you see, I cannot hold the whole piece while herding these creatures."

"Is it more work to sew them together?"

He smiled. "It is, but it takes less time to finish when I can knit at my day job."

"Is it common to walk and knit at the same time?"

"It was, but no more nowadays. Many people have abandoned this craft and left the Highlands for other opportunities. Now it's only fools like me with no skills other than accompanying these bloody sheep." He cackled at his own humor.

"You have the finest job in this beautiful natural environment. Your knitting, wow, that's a skill not many people have," Matthew commented.

"I think so. I love to walk around and see the hills and feel the sun, the rain, the wind, and all the changing weather of the different seasons on the moors." He turned around with shining eyes and smiled at us. "Cannot imagine life without them."

In a split second, I understood why Matthew was so distraught by the slaughtering of the white pine. The two men in front of me had the same passion for nature, for the elements of the environment. All they wanted was to maintain the reciprocal relationship with a wider ecological consciousness, to keep their respect of other living things, to give back the gifts that nature has given by nourishing its existence, guarding and stewarding its place to sustain its own rights. Now, I could feel that passion, bigger than life.

"Where do you get your yarn?" I asked the shepherd.

"We color and spin our own. You can find good yarn in Glasgow, where textiles have been one of the major industries. Even though the textile industry is at the end of its heyday, the residuals of its products, such as yarn, are still fine materials."

"Could I buy some yarn like yours in this region? I love the colors and the feel of it."

"If you mean the homemade yarn, no. You see, our population is very small and scattered in these vast Highlands. Shepherding is diminishing as we speak. We keep these as a self-sustaining livelihood, not for commercial use."

"I admire you." Matthew raised his hand to his right temple in salute.

He smiled and scanned the mountain range. "It's time to go. Enjoy your visit."

"Good day." We waved goodbye.

On the way to Wales, we stopped in the picturesque Lake District. We got to the village before dusk, as the sun was going down.

Through connections of Aunt Jodie, we were able to stay in a four-hundred-year-old barn, just a hundred meters from the homestead owner's house, in the Lake District National Park. Inside the barn, there was no toilet, no electricity, and no water. Outside the barn was a row of three outhouses running only cold water. Fortunately, the temperature was milder than in the Highlands and there was no rain.

When we walked into the barn, the setting was just like a featured piece in an architecture magazine. The windows were four big circles, located above the entrance and the exit, and one each in the middle of the two long walls just below the ceiling. We could see the ceiling with two open balconies running from one end of the barn to the other. Stairs to the left and right of the entrance went up to the half-open second floor. Two wooden plates, labeled "Ladies" and "Gentlemen," were hammered at the first step of each stair. The ladies' sleeping area was a row of military-style platforms. At the edge of the platform, blankets and pillows were set at each sleeping slot, the size of a small cot. On the wall, a name was hanging for the bed that each person was assigned. Between the assigned beds, there was a single built-in drawer at the bottom of the platform, approximately a one foot square. I walked all the way to the end, finding another set of identical stairs. I went down and up to the gentlemen's section, and sure enough, the layout was the same as the ladies'. The ground floor was like a study hall of a university research library. The center of the hall was occupied by two long rectangular tables set apart from each other, creating an open space for people to walk. The two long walls had built-in bookshelves. In front of every other section of the shelves were stationed two armchairs with a small stand between them for placing a cup and a book. There were vintage oil lamps: one on each stand, four on each table, and one hanging on each side of the stairs.

There were no other guests. Matthew and I owned the whole barn.

"There's only one tavern nearby. In the summertime, it would be a lovely walk there but now it's cold and gets dark early. You should drive there to get yourself supper," the farm owner told us.

The farm owner didn't assign us a bed. I picked the slot next to the gigantic round window, hoping to see sunrise from the barn. Matthew did the same on his side. We could see and talk to each other by standing against the balcony railing, which reminded me of my middle school years and living away from home.

My parents sent me to boarding school the first year I started middle school. The dormitory room was designed for six girls, with three sets of bunk beds and wardrobes. Each room had girls from the same grade. Most of us were classmates and roommates at the same time. Every night the night governor would check on each room to make sure we were all accounted for and went to bed at lights out. Many nights, we invented a million ways to deceive the governor and partied on, the whole floor, sometimes the whole building. We had pillow fights. Feathers, roasted dry rice, tea leaves, cotton stuffing, and whatever materials each child's family had given, the contents of the pillows were dispersed all over the room. We would have pillow fights with the next room or next floor in the gathering hall. If people walked down the corridor, they could see the silhouettes of shades being yanked up and down when the bright moonlight shone in. We also did blanket wrestling. When we needed to leverage the pull of the blanket, we would use our mouths to strengthen the pulls. Every corner of the blankets had bites and tears. But we were very efficient and after each fight we cleaned the place spotless. The day governor never discovered anything unusual in our war rooms.

Our room was on the top floor, so I had easy access to the rooftop, which was my favorite place to read, to look around the city at sunrise and sunset, to see the glittering lights at night, and to hide from all the girl talk about pop singers, movie stars, and school gossip. We started with six girls. When the second semester started, we only had five. Qin Ning was gone, and we didn't know why.

Qin Ning was my best roommate. She didn't talk incessantly like the other girls. Sometimes I thought she was quiet because something was wrong. I asked, and one time she said, "My mother is in the hospital."

Qin Ning and I together would fend off the boys when they offered Vietnamese chili hot peppers soaked in soy sauce, while the other girls would giggle with them in the dining hall. We played basketball in the hours right after class and did homework together at the library, where I caught her staring out the window a few times at nothing in particular. On the weekends, when we all went home, she would be the last person to leave. From time to time, I wondered if she ever went home.

One late September evening after dinner, I went to the rooftop. I saw the night governor standing there smoking. I didn't want to get her attention or be noticed by her. The night governor was a serious, strong-headed, and diligent middle-aged woman. Even though we had tricked her many times for our party nights, she caught us a few times. When we got caught, she would punish us with a list of chores and Chinese calligraphy assignments, which we needed to complete within forty-eight hours, leaving no time to play. I turned and walked back where I'd come from. She called my name. I turned around and looked at her hand with the cigarette. She pressed the cigarette to the above-waist-height wall then dropped the butt. "Am I in your way?" she asked.

"No, I don't want to disturb you."

"You aren't disturbing. Are you one of Qin Ning's roommates?"

"Yes, do you know where Qin Ning is?" I dared to ask.

The governor looked directly at me. Apparently, she was crying. The tears were still hanging near the lines beside her mouth. I stood near the stair landing, not knowing what to say or do.

"Qin Ning won't be coming back," she said, keeping her place.

"Do you know why?"

"She moved with her father to England."

"What happened to her mother?"

She gazed at me; tears just naturally came out from under her eyelids. She didn't seem to be able to control it. She covered her mouth and squatted down. I saw the shaking movements of her shoulders but only faintly heard her sobs.

"Qin Ning's mother committed suicide two months ago. I am Qin Ning's aunt."

I was stunned and froze in place.

"My sister was depressed. She had been in and out of mental health services for a few years. She suffered so much. I could see her pain and could not... " Her crying interrupted her talking.

"She was only thirty-five. So much life in front of her. I wish I could have helped. She was my only sister. I am the only one left. What will I do without her?" She just spilled all this out in front of an almost-thirteen-year-old.

As a teenager, I wasn't aware of the existence of depression. I saw the shadow and felt the anxiety of it in Qin Ning. Suicide was not part of my vocabulary or my association with family and school. But I knew the pain of death because I had not seen Uncle Mike for almost two years.

"Let's go have a bite," Matthew called out from his side.

I looked across the open balconies. There stood Matthew, vibrant and elated by the primitive and rustic surroundings. I realized that the illness of depression and suicide were introduced to me in my teens, not by Matthew's attempt eleven months before.

We arrived at the tavern without incident. The roof of the tavern looked like a South African hut with layers of thatch, but the building itself was a small ordinary-looking cottage. Matthew had to duck his head to enter. The space was a twenty-foot by fifteen-foot room with a low ceiling and six wooden beams straight across the room to support the roof. There were about seven men in the room.

The bar attendant looked at us. "Well, well, well, what do we have here?"

"Hello." Matthew nodded his head to everyone, and we stood in front of the counter. Everyone was looking at us and ready to listen.

"What can I get for you?"

"What's on the menu?" I asked.

"We have mutton and fish and chips."

I'd had mutton with frozen or canned peas and pearl onions all week. I didn't want another piece of mutton. I didn't want fish and chips either. I contemplated silently and looked at the attendant, hoping that he'd give me a menu. He seemed to be reading my mind. "We normally don't have visitors in the winter, and we don't prepare much food. Tell me what you'd like, and I'll find out if we can accommodate you. Want a hamburger?"

Matthew nodded and asked for an IPA. The attendant looked at me. "What about you, lady?"

"A pint of stout." I didn't like beer but I would drink stout, which I'd started drinking at age sixteen.

The attendant raised his eyebrow. "That's my gal. Want to eat?"

"Besides what you have mentioned, do you have anything else?" I was hopeful.

"I have my mum's homemade chicken pie. I can spare one for you."

"Definitely. I appreciate it." Thank God that he had chicken pie, which was my teatime favorite. My mother knew each of her children's favorite food. At teatime, she would save one for me if I ran home late, unlike my grandmother, who wouldn't allow us to have anything if we didn't get home by three thirty for tea.

One of the men asked, "Where are you folks from?"

"The States," Matthew replied.

"Ah, the big brother. Where are you staying?"

"The old barn."

"Ooh, I didn't think it was open in the winter." He looked around, and the other men shook their heads. The bar attendant came back with our food. He'd obviously heard the conversation.

"That's right. It's not open. Old Robert said that a relative's friends would be staying for a day or two."

"Well, we should drink on that to welcome our friends here. Let's have a round on me," one man said.

Everyone cheered for the free drink, and I was surprised by the warmth of the welcome. The British are well-known for being polite but reserved. From the Highlands to here, we had been greeted by friendly people and nothing like the snobby Brits that I'd had in mind. We chatted about what we'd seen. Matthew was particularly talkative and asked a lot of questions.

"I want to see the Ring Garth and the stone walls that were built around individual farmsteads. Where should I start?"

"Ah, that will take you a day or two. Here's a bit of the history. From the fifteenth century, the population grew and the demand for food consumption was increasing. Farmers had enclosed the farmlands above the Ring Garth—a stone wall—but they could graze their animals on the fells. Still, that was not good enough for the farmers to ensure their animals and crops were protected. In around the eighteenth century, farmers as the landowners began to express their concerns to Parliament. As a result, landowners could apply to enclose their farmlands under an Act of Parliament. Today, you can see the large and square or rectangular enclosures on the fells. They're almost everywhere you look."

"You're saying that the stone walls are common places that I can just walk around without a particular destination?" Matthew looked around.

The men nodded. "They're basically property lines for us."

The land and the powerful history starting in the late-ninth century with the building of ring garths and smaller stone walls that this man described in such a casual manner was realistic. Our idyllic notion that the stone walls were a natural phenomenon was erased at the moment when history was told by a local in this tiny, lonely tavern.

I started to sense Matthew's nostalgia. He seemed not to belong to the twentieth century. With the exponential growth of the world population and our waste, and nations speeding up everywhere, I had no doubt that we would exhaust our natural resources in a flash. Matthew's intentions of saving the trees and protecting the natural environment were fading away, gradually out of his reach because of the demand for land development. With that insight, I felt that Matthew was losing hope about guarding the earth. I didn't know how to help him overcome this enormous burden.

Despite the beauty of the Lake District, Matthew's mood had changed. We walked in silence, which was not unusual, but something was clearly not quite right. He seemed to have lost interest in the stone walls. We walked in the morning, seeing rows and rows of stone walls on the hillsides, a minimum of four feet high and enclosing each property. The walls were made with stones of odd colors and configurations but constructed in a way that looked like uniformly unruffled planes. We spent less than half a day walking around, and Matthew didn't bother to go up to see the origin of the Ring Garth. By noon, we had left for Southampton to stay with another cousin of Jodie's: Meredith and her son Jacob.

Meredith was a fourth-generation dairy farmer. According to Jodie, the farm was more than two hundred acres and she used to ride a horse with Meredith down the hill to the property line just next to Southampton Water before she moved to the United States.

We arrived at twilight, and the weather was unexpectedly colder than in the Lake District. Meredith, maybe a couple of years older than Jodie, welcomed us with warm affection as if she had known us for a long time. We entered a compound that was built of stone. The small inner courtyard led us into a huge kitchen on the ground floor. To the right side of the kitchen door was a bench about three feet long and two feet wide. One side cleated to the stone wall and the other was against a white stove. The space underneath the bench was completely filled with wood. The stove was unlike the ones I'd seen in the States. Two burners were on the left side, and a rectangular opening to put wood in on the right. Under that wood burning area, a compartment extended from the main body. A big rectangular door horizontally dominated half of the range and two same-size square doors stood vertically next to their bigger component. A sturdy wooden table, just a bit smaller than a ping-pong table, was situated in the center of the front room. No less than half of it was full of jars and other containers holding I didn't know what. Behind the table, in the dark, was a space set up like a living room. On the left side of the kitchen, a door led us to the food storage unit, a half-underground rectangular cellar we had to walk down two steps to enter. The storage room was bigger than the kitchen. Huge, tall freezers were lined up along the walls and rectangular coolers stood side by side in the open space. Meredith opened one of the freezers by sliding the door. Packages and packages of meat, labeled and dated were clustered neatly together.

"Wow, you don't have to leave the house for food! You have enough food for at least a year." I said to Meredith.

"At least three years or more. This is a dairy farmer's life." Meredith looked around the room with a smile.

When we went back to the kitchen, Jacob was there and offered us tea.

Meredith, again with a smile, said, "I worked late today at the farm with some helpers, so I didn't have time to cook. Tonight we're going to have pizza, which Jacob has just brought in."

"Where did you drive from?" Jacob asked, handing me a piece of pizza.

"The Lake District," Matthew replied.

"Ah, did you stay at the old barn?"

"Yes, we did," I said after my first bite of pizza.

"That old Robert, we visit them in the summer. Did you like it?"

"Yes, we liked it very much," I replied, to help Matthew out before his agitation kicked in.

After eating the pizza, Jacob sat on the stove right on top of the rectangular opening and leaned against the wall.

"This is the warmest place in the whole freaking house—the only heating system for the entire structure."

Jacob's remarks brought back memories of the cast-iron stoves the winter we lived in Northwest China. "Do you keep it going all day and night?"

"Yes, otherwise, we'd freeze to death." He looked at Meredith.

"Don't be so bloody dramatic." Meredith squinted at Jacob and went on, "You see, this stone house was built more than six hundred years ago. The way it's built isn't compatible with today's heating systems. We'd need to modify some of the structure and replace the stones with other materials to install a heating system, so I am not interested in making the changes. We have portable heaters in each room but I rarely use them."

Indeed, the architectural style of this compound was unusual in contemporary England. The exterior stone walls were as tall as the second floor of the structure. Even when I walked from the kitchen to the opposite side of the bottom of the stairs to the second floor under the sky, I felt like I was walking indoors. There were five rooms plus a bathroom, which was slightly on the right side of the upstairs landing. Our room was just next to the bathroom on the right, and Meredith's room was above the kitchen at the end of the far right. Jacob's room faced the entrance. The open hallway encompassed a bracket-shaped veranda, from which we could see the others if they happened to walk out of their rooms. This type of architectural design is common in southern China, built with different kinds of materials, and seeing it here in southeastern England was intriguing.

The next morning when I walked into the kitchen, I saw Matthew sitting at the table with tears in his eyes. In front of him was a small glass filled with white foam. He was holding a small spoon, and one bite at a time, he was eating the top layer of the fresh milk that forms the white cream before pasteurizing.

Matthew had told me that when he was growing up, Grandma Dori would save him the lactoderm from freshly milked cows because he loved the taste of the creamy raw milk. I thought only family members knew of Grandma Dori's endearment to Matthew. Now Meredith, who we had met less than twenty-four hours before, acting openhandedly with familiar benevolence, must have triggered feelings that were deeply rooted in Matthew's heart.

"I haven't had this for many years. Thank you," he said to Meredith.

"Don't mention it. Jodie told me that you like the milk skin. I just scooped you a tiny bit. The workers are getting the milk now. If you want more, we can get more," Meredith said while frying the eggs.

After breakfast, we walked to the barn where the cows were being milked. There had been some talk of horses but riding a horse to the seaside was not advisable due to the cold wind and short winter days.

"We milk them twice a day, once in the morning and once in the afternoon around three or four o'clock. The afternoon is a lighter milking," Meredith explained.

The milking parlor was modernized with a milking machine. Each cow had four teat cups attached to their teats with a tube on each, through which the milk traveled down to the claws and then, using vacuum pressure, the milk was channeled to the milk tank.

"Do you want to try?" Meredith asked.

Matthew shook his head. "I've done that."

"I want to try," I said.

Meredith led us to a worker who was about to attach the teat cups to a cow. He asked me to wash my hands, demonstrated how to clean the udder, and used his thumb and index finger to pull the teat and then squeezed. I put my hands to work. One hand I rested on the edge of the bucket, and with the other I milked the cow for the first time. I didn't like the feeling of touching the cow's teats. The pulling and squeezing were just not pleasant to me. I stopped after a few pulls and smiled at Meredith. "Interesting."

The farm had six or seven structures in the field. In the winter, only a few long-term workers stayed on, monitoring the milking and doing maintenance to prepare for the spring. Seasonal workers would come back after Easter.

While we were walking the farm, Meredith proposed, "I heard that you're a great cook. Jacob and I enjoy Chinese food, particularly sweet and sour pork. Would you mind making that dish tonight?"

"No, not at all. It would be my pleasure."

Next to the kitchen, outside the stone wall, Meredith kept a small vegetable garden. Beets and cauliflower were vigorously showing their full bodies, trying to get attention as if they were saying, "Pick me, pick me." In late afternoon, I took a four-tine spading fork, dug out three grapefruit-size beets, and cut a head of cauliflower as big as a size two soccer ball, twenty to twenty-two inches.

Meredith had already taken out some pork chops from the freezer the night before. I found a can of pineapple and made a thin paste with ground coriander, ground mixed yellow and black mustards, paprika, scotch, soy sauce, brown sugar, garlic, and apple cider and rubbed it on the pork chops and let them rest for forty-five minutes. In the meantime, I mixed the pineapple juice with ketchup, white wine vinegar, and sugar, and added that to the pineapple and onion that I was cooking in a saucepan. Besides making the sweet and sour sauce with pineapple and onion, I sautéed the beet greens with garlic, steamed the cauliflower florets, dressed them in tahini vinaigrette and garnished them with parsley, shredded carrot, and red onion. After I'd boiled and drained the red beets, I squeezed in half an orange to marinate for ten minutes, and then added balsamic vinegar, olive oil, salt, and pepper. Next, I roasted baby potatoes simply with a slab of butter and some salt and pepper.

By the time I had finished the other dishes, I'd seared the pork chops five minutes on one side and five minutes on the other side. After they were browned, I baked them in the oven for fifteen minutes at 220 degrees Celsius. Then, I transferred the tray from the baking rack to the broiler on high for five minutes, flipped the pork chops to the other side for another four minutes until they were caramelized and golden. I turned off the broiler and kept the pork chops in for another five minutes before taking them out from the oven.

I presented the dishes in red, white, yellow, orange, purple, and green. The aroma of the spices and meat filled the whole room at a comfortable temperature, which created an atmosphere of an exquisitely prepared dinner. When Meredith and Jacob took their first few bites of the pork chop, I could see their delighted smiling eyes beaming around the dining table. My version of sweet and sour pork had won over our hosts' taste buds.

"How do you make the smoky aftertaste? Meredith asked.

"Mustard and paprika do the trick."

"Hmmm, they're bloody tasty. You can stay as long as you want," Jacob added.

Meredith and I laughed at Jacob's comments. Matthew smiled at the enjoyment of our eating and chatting.

The rest of the trip, I was traveling with a somber and melancholy Matthew. His enthusiasm for seeing his ancestral home had dissipated. Instead, I saw "anxious to go home" inscribed all over his face. Not even Kew Gardens could make him relax. He walked past those big trees without turning any leaves over, examining any cones, or inspecting seed pods. Going to Kew was just something on the list for him to do. The only time I saw him with vague smiles was the time we spent with Chris in London. Matthew was happy to see Chris, which I suspected was because Chris brought back happy memories from eight years before when they'd first met.

Chris met Matthew in February 1985, when we spent our first winter break in Hong Kong. They clicked right away. With Matthew, I still used the key to enter Chris's apartment unannounced, knowing that he would be there. They would have drinks, and I would play the piano or flip through Chris's books and read his poems. Sometimes, I thought they forgot I was there listening to their conversations. Chris was very interested in life in China, and hearing from a non-Chinese person fascinated him. Matthew was delighted to share his fondness for China with Chris, whose volumes of published poems Matthew had seen even though he didn't read Chinese well.

THE MYTH OF MENTAL ILLNESS

I HAD LOST THIRTEEN pounds in the first two weeks after Matthew was gone. I could not sleep, and my mind ran a million miles a second. I kept asking how come I couldn't save him?

Matthew was labeled as having chronic depressive disorder. He had been suffering from depression for at least four years when it was officially diagnosed. I informed Matthew's psychologist and canceled his appointments. His psychiatrist called me and wanted to see me three weeks after Matthew died.

He said, "A few months ago, Matthew signed a release of information that has given me permission to disclose his medical conditions to you."

The psychiatrist took a pause, pushed up his eyeglasses, and looked at me, "Matthew's psychological and mental illness was terminal."

I didn't believe what I was hearing. "I have never heard such terms. Do you believe what you just said?"

"In Matthew's case, yes."

"On what basis?"

"Matthew believed that he'd accelerated his mother's death. He also believed that his brother and he had both inherited the same mental illness from their mother. He said it wasn't right that he had outlived his mother and brother to almost twice their age."

"Matthew never mentioned that to me," I muttered.

"No, he didn't tell me either. He said this to his psychologist, my colleague. I wanted you to know that there was nothing you could have done to prevent his action. No one could have."

"I don't care. If I could have saved him on that day, he would still be here."

"You couldn't watch him every hour of the day and night. You know—and I know—this was not his first try."

"Yes, Matthew's death was his second attempt in less than three years," I said to myself.

I asked, "Since he had a history of trying to kill himself, does Prozac treat any suicidal-ideation behavior?"

"No, Prozac is an antidepressant, which is in the class of selective serotonin reuptake inhibitor that helps to stabilize and regulate mood."

"Are there any drugs that could have prevented this type of behavior?"

"Researchers are still working on the best drug candidate to treat acute suicidal-ideation behavior. But acute suicidal-ideation behavior can't be isolated from resistant depression or other psychiatric disorders. Currently, there is no specifically approved treatment for it. Treatment options are dispersed. Keep in mind that suicidality is not an illness by itself."

The psychiatrist didn't provide any relief. For me, one more day was one more day. That's how life is, the passing of every day would take us closer to getting old together, of which Matthew had said: "I want to grow old with you. You are my home."

THE PROMISE

IN MAY 1995, I TOOK the summer break from the community college and went back to Hong Kong and planned to take Matthew to Huangshan. I contacted Ethan, my college buddy, who at the time was working at the *Wall Street Journal* in Shenzhen, just across the border from Hong Kong.

I met Ethan when we were both in our second year at Notre Dame and he was studying Asian languages. He was born in Japan when his father was stationed at the US military base on Okinawa. The family moved with the father's assignments, and after years of being away from Japan, Ethan went back alone to finish high school in Tokyo. His parents thought it would be better for him to complete college back home in the United States. We met in our first course of Classical Chinese, which is a dead language. There were only eight of us in those courses, and I was the only Asian and the only woman. From the beginning, Ethan followed me to the library and studied as long as I stayed.

If another classmate was looking for me, he would tell him, "Go to the Asian Studies library. When you see columns of books stacked up high in a circle, you'll find her inside."

Ethan and I had endless discussions of those mystical verses, lyrics, poems, and stanzas with thousands of interpretations and documents to support each of our arguments. We reveled in backing up our discoveries with proof. We would double, sometimes triple, our findings with evidence for a single literary artifact. Sometimes we worked to forget time until his girlfriend, Bora, or Matthew came to find us.

Ethan and Bora's families were in California, and they both were vegetarians. At the time, it was hard for vegetarians to get good food in South Bend, unlike in California, where they could just walk to a neighborhood restaurant. Matthew and I started feeding them. They came over for a meal three or four times a week.

The four of us loved nature. We hiked and camped whenever we could get away from our busy lives. They both loved to dig potatoes on our land when it was still in transition to becoming an organic farm. In those late August to early October weekends, Ethan would find any excuse to go to the land and search for potatoes.

"It's like digging gold." He sweated while tilling, then knelt down with both hands plunged into the soil. "I find one after the other and the discovery of them seems to have no end." When he lifted his head up, his smiling face with dark little particles decorating his upper lip, and with a few new potatoes in his hands, Ethan could not hide his bemusement over the potatoes that just kept coming.

Ethan and Bora didn't shy away from food or shelter at our place. Even at school, when we finished one class and stood in front of the building for a moment before going to separate classes, I would open my messenger bag and delve into my sandwich bag full of carrot and celery sticks and different colored bell peppers. Ethan, standing six-foot-four next to my barely five-foot frame, would lean over and help himself without asking. Other classmates would see it and say, "Don't let Ethan steal your veggies!" Ethan would wave a carrot stick, holding it up high like a middle finger at them with a sly grin.

In return, each time when they came back from visiting Bora's family in LA, there would be three decks of prepared Korean food standing fifteen inches high with different containers on our dining table. One deck had Bora on each container, the other had Ethan, and the third had my name. Bora's mother, who I had not met, prepared the most authentic and delicious Korean food for her daughter and for Ethan, and now included me. Each time I got the food, she had put a note to me in one of those containers, "Thank you for taking care of my daughter."

A year before Matthew's death, Ethan and Bora had broken up. Ethan went to Asia, and Bora was about to finish her graduate studies at UC Berkeley. When Bora learned about Matthew's passing, she flew in to stay with me. Bora was very angry at Matthew, while at the same time lamenting that she should have visited us at Thanksgiving, which she and Ethan had done for years when we all were studying at college. In the mornings, she would bring me Korean scallion pancakes and sautéed lotus root slices (my favorite from her mother). I'd heard her asking her mom over the phone how to make them when I didn't want to get out of bed. She stayed with me until late January and then went to Hong Kong for her Fulbright Scholar Program. Ethan, on the other hand, was in the middle of climbing his career ladder at the newspaper and asked what he could do. I told him that he could accompany me to Huangshan.

Early one morning in July, I met Ethan at his office at the *Wall Street Journal* bureau in Shenzhen. He just needed to submit his last story before taking a few days off from work. We went to the Shenzhen Airport to catch an 11:45 a.m. flight to Tunxi Airport in Huangshan City.

The security checkpoint was about fifty steps away from the twenty-passenger aircraft that we were about to board.

When they checked my backpack, a security guard asked, "Are you bringing stones?"

"No."

He searched my bag and took out a sack that I had wrapped in a blue paisley bandana.

"What is this?" he inquired.

"Ashes."

"Do you have the document?"

"What document?"

"If you are bringing ashes, you need to have a government document to prove you can legally carry it in China."

"I didn't know that requirement. I went through US, Hong Kong, and China security and customs. No one ever asked for the document."

"If you don't have it, I cannot let you board the plane."

"How absurd! I came through Shenzhen security and customs this morning without any hassle, and now you are saying that I cannot get on a domestic flight?"

The security guard just kept me at the spot. Ethan chatted in Mandarin and said that the guard should let me go. The guard was surprised to hear a Caucasian speaking Mandarin so fluently. But he didn't budge. It was about eleven thirty, and I was the last passenger being questioned by this headstrong guard. All of a sudden, Ethan ran to the bottom stairs of the aircraft, spread his arms and legs across the stairs as far as he could stretch and raised his voice, "If you don't let her in, the plane cannot leave."

His action and loud voice caught the attention of other security personnel. A man in his forties, dressed in a tailored People's Liberation Army suit in garish dark blue, walked in my direction and asked the guard what was the matter and inspected my travel documents. Ethan saw that and ran back to my side. He handed his badge to this man and asked his permission to let us board the plane, all in his eloquently articulated Mandarin.

The man was very pleased to see this young, tall foreigner behaving with such respectful manners. He nodded and said, "You know, the country has its rules that we all need to follow. But I understand you may not know any of that since you are not a resident of China. With respect for the deceased, I will make an exception for you this time."

Ethan bowed, said thank you, hurried to put Matthew back in my bag, took my hand, and walked toward the plane. He just didn't want this man to change his mind. Once the plane took off, Ethan said, "We made it."

"Thank you. I couldn't have gotten on the plane without you. You did great with the commander."

"Ah, I've lived in China long enough to learn a few tricks in dealing with the authorities."

I smiled and thought of how I'd dealt with the three Chinese officials eleven years before, except that I'd played hardball with them. In retrospect, seeing Ethan at ease and humble before this commander, I felt that I had been extremely lucky to get Matthew, Tony, and myself out of Hainan Island with the officials' assistance. How strange life events had turned out. Now it was Matthew who'd gotten me into trouble with the officials, and here was Ethan, another foreigner, who'd played soft to defuse an unwanted issue. I wondered, if similar events were to happen again, would I alone be able to successfully contend with the Chinese authorities and officials?

The next morning it was raining. According to Ethan's research, the hike to the top of Huangshan would take at least eight hours. We started early and planned to reach the top before nightfall. The hike was not as bad as I thought. Most of the time we were climbing on big even stone steps that the local tourist office had ordered to be installed in order to attract tourists. There was also a cable car that could take people up to past the mid-level of the mountain. With the rain, Ethan and I were the only two fools climbing up. Along the hike, we saw workers carrying supplies, tons of weight on their shoulders, moving upward. From time to time, Ethan and I stopped to rest and looked at each other, wondering when we would reach our destination. It was past noon, and we were totally wet despite our ponchos, when we heard someone calling out to us. We turned around, and there were two men below us, looking up and shouting, "Do you want a ride?"

They had a bamboo and wood sedan chair on top of their shoulders. "For two hundred yuan we'll carry you to the top."

Ethan looked at me. I was puzzled. Was I in twentieth-century China?

We moved aside to give room for them to pass. I shook my head. The guy at the back turned around and said, "You still have three to four hours to go. Come on, let us take you. Make it easy on yourselves."

I still shook my head. He said, "How about 180 yuan each?" Ethan gestured for him to go away. "Go ahead, we want to walk."

After they were in the distance, I asked Ethan, "Is that a common practice?"

"Yes, they do hard labor for a living. They seemed physically strong."

"How could I sit there and let them do the walking for me?"

"Some people think that's a fun thing to do."

Sure enough, right after Ethan said that, we saw a huge woman swinging left and right just behind us. The two men carrying her apparently had difficulty inching their way up the steps. We took a lunch break and witnessed the scene as it gradually disappeared from view.

Around six o'clock, we arrived at the only hotel at the top of the cliff. We didn't have the energy to scout the surroundings. We took hot showers and had a bowl of soup, then crashed in bed by eight o'clock.

Around four thirty in the morning, I was woken by the sound of birds tweeting, which was like a long tune wavering with slightly different melodies that were rather pleasant. I went out and walked to the edge of the cliff with a flashlight. In front of me, the whiteness swam among dark shadows of trees and irregular rocks, reproducing scenes from the nights that I visited Matthew at the mental health facility. Then I drove through the thickness of dense fog, but now I was not in the middle of it. Magically, the whiteness gingerly became a sea of clouds sprawling without any concern about where it was heading. The birds continued their singing, the air was sharply fresh and cool, and a sliver of light popped up, as elusive as the clouds.

By six o'clock it was raining again. Ethan and I each devoured a big bowl of noodles and, for Ethan, two additional *baozi* (buns).

We checked out and started back down the mountain. Trembling, not able to tell if it was rain or tears on my cheeks, I took out the sack and tried to steady myself to open the bandana. Ethan stopped me and held out his hands with a compassionate look.

I passed the sack to him.

I grabbed a handful of Matthew. "Here you are. My promise to you."

Going down the mountain was much harder than hiking up the day before. With the rain and treacherous winds, we could hardly move in the first three hours on the open terrain. We were beaten by the winds from all directions. Some sandy pieces of Matthew blew back to cover my face. I might have swallowed little pieces of him. While we tried to shelter in between two huge boulders, a vendor came down toward us. He could see we were badly hampered by the weather. He offered us hot soup from his carriage. When we tried to pay, he said, "Don't bother. It's not for sale. Do you see on your right?" He pointed. "There's a narrow passage that will lead you to the cable car station. It will take you about two hours to get there. Once you get to that point, you can take the cable car or continue to find an extension of the stone steps to the other entrance."

The narrow passage was not a road but had become a trail by the locals' constant use, no flat stepping-stones. Yet, the rugged footpath was relatively sturdy. Once we put our feet on the trail, slowly we realized that the winds had become less pounding, although it was still raining. Steadily, the terrain turned into a valley surrounded at a distance by enormous peaks. The serpentine trail was a series of switchbacks that kept us zigzagging lower and lower. About an hour into the trail, the wind died down and we were only skirmishing with the rain, which had turned into sun showers. The steep descent was taxing, and we were sweating under the July sun, grateful for the cooling rain. By the time we reached the cable car station, Ethan signaled with one hand pointing to the cable car, the other to the stone steps.

"I carried Matthew up the mountain on foot. I want to carry myself down the mountain on foot as well."

We arrived in town before six o'clock, and Ethan and I found a small eatery in an alley. We ordered twenty-some dishes, which were small portions, but I had never had so many dishes at once. We finished them all—dumplings, beef noodles, scallion pancakes, varieties of vegetables, and a big bowl of fish and tofu soup. After dinner, Ethan and I sat down on the long steps of a riverbank. The sun was coming down like a gigantic egg yolk. I rested my head on Ethan's shoulder; tears and exhaustion enfolded me.

The next day we went back to Guangzhou. Ethan had a story to investigate, and I would take the train back to Hong Kong. Before we parted at the train station, I wanted to repay Ethan for all the expenses. He just waved his hand and said, "Take care of yourself. I'll see you in Hong Kong in two weeks." Ethan arranged everything for the four-day trip to Huangshan and would not accept my payment.

THE FARM

I WENT BACK TO teaching and interpreting in late August after taking Matthew to Huangshan. The farm had been neglected for eight months. Numerous new shoots were circling the rows of black locust trees. Burdock leaves were three times bigger than my face. Blackberries, like renegades, were spreading all over the place. Residual rye patches were wobbling flowerless. Weeds were two feet tall, casting out the chinooks, nuggets, and cascades in their infancy. Some of them were dead on the bottom of the hops poles. The well's red handle was rusted by the bitter winter snow. The disastrous look of the farm drove me half mad and half desperate.

"How can I do this alone?" I asked Matthew.

I called Connor, Matthew's former colleague at Notre Dame, and asked for help. He drove Sam, his five-year-old son, to the farm on Saturday morning to meet with me and Alan. The three of us stood there, but I couldn't concentrate on what Connor and Alan were saying about their plans for rebuilding the farm. All I knew was that Connor would come on the weekends while Alan would look for migrant farm workers to clean up the mess.

I reviewed the map and tried to locate the plants that Matthew had started. He had studied permaculture and believed that was the only way to make our small farm work. Matthew had started implementing the principles by stages.

I could still picture the look of the farm when it was in full operation. In the spring, I could see fields of *Achillea* (pearl yarrow) intermingling with seas of royal blue bachelor's buttons, beds of spinach under the poles of snow peas and sugar peas. Borage with tomatoes were side by side in early summer, and then squashes would be flowering before the tomatoes were at the peak of harvesting in late August. Brown-eyed Susans, in a split second, would blanket field after field with their golden yellow petals edging their dark brown centers, dancing with the gentle north breeze in the evening from summer to fall. Red oak arrow lettuces were between the pale greenish buttercrunch, with dark green kale shooting up in the middle of September. Wheat and hairy vetch would cover most of the property by late October.

But right now, all of that was a blur in front of me. With Connor's help, could I restore permaculture to the land? What did Matthew want? Is that what I wanted to do? I pondered these questions day in and day out. My sleep patterns went haywire. I wouldn't sleep for two or three days, then on the fourth day I'd just slam into a coma-like state, which very soon created a vicious cycle. My doctor asked me to take sleeping pills. "Your sleep pattern is not good. You need to sleep regularly. These pills will help you to get back to a normal sleep cycle."

I refused.

My mind raged with the memories of working with Matthew and picking up farming techniques from him. I wanted to remember each thing he had said—which plant to plant and where to plant it, when to plant them and when to harvest them; when winter came, what kinds of maintenance needed to be in place. I was so afraid of not remembering all of these tasks and missing the seasons. I was panicking.

Matthew had had his own pace on the farm. He ordered and sowed seeds, plowed the soil, divided rows and beds, put in irrigation systems, and planted trees one by one. I never saw him in a hurry. Occasionally, Alan and Connor would come on the weekends to give him a hand erecting poles for the hops and other heavy lifting tasks. By the sixth month we had worked at the farm, the whole property was transformed to an amazing beauty. We would work into the evening in the summer months when the sun didn't go down before nine o'clock. There was always a lot to do. The weeding between vegetable rows could take me days; tidying up plants and guiding them to climb required the skills of making surgeon's knots and engineering expansions for the stability of head-heavy sunflowers and bottom-heavy beefsteak tomatoes. Harvesting took even longer when I insisted on getting all of them, not leaving one behind. The races between my speed in picking them and their growth rates were neck and neck from late March to early October. Matthew watered, cut branches, cleared the swamp, checked the white pine grove, and cleared the rock piles, which he and Alan had hauled from a distant cousin's abandoned farm. They loved to sit there to have a beer and talk. By the time we finished our chores for the day, Berenice would have dinner ready for us. We, including Alan and sometimes Connor, just walked across the field to the steps where Berenice could see us through the screen door of her kitchen. Those were serene and happy days. Yet, the darkness of Matthew's mind deceived us all.

After his first attempt, I didn't have any thoughts other than that he would be fine. I was so shocked and so unbelieving that he did it the second time and succeeded.

The nights when Matthew just sat in the armchair and closed his eyes, I sensed the despondency of his being. He seemed far away and remote, which was so ironic in comparison with those months when we were physically thousands of miles apart yet felt so close. Each time I squatted down beside the armchair, at first, he would open his eyes and try to give me a smile. Later on, he didn't respond at all, as if I were not there. He didn't see or hear me. Apparently, he communicated with his own mind, which I had failed to reach, to hold on to, to understand.

As Matthew drifted farther away, sometimes I didn't see him in the fields when we were supposed to be working together. When I first noticed his disappearance from the farm, my initial thought was that he'd gone over to Berenice's house for a bathroom break or something. As time went by, I wondered why he would take such a long break. I walked over to Berenice's a few times, and each time Berenice said she had not seen Matthew at all. I started to search the land and found him taking refuge in the white pine grove. He just sat there motionless and stared into the air.

"What is it, Matthew?" I asked.

He turned to my voice and reacted as if he didn't see me. From his downcast eyes, the brightness of the greenish hazel was simply diminished. With a slumped posture, he raised his head. "What?"

"What are you thinking?"

"Nothing."

The increasing quietness and one-word responses startled me. I could not talk to his doctors due to patient privacy. I phoned Dad, asked Berenice, Alan, and Connor, and sought his college friends' advice. They all tried to communicate with Matthew in person by showing up at the farm. Matthew would chat with them at the rock piles. When Dad, Kurt, and Timothy popped in together or at different times, we all went to the nearby towns and local breweries as a family ritual. All of that didn't change the relentlessness of Matthew's dull expression. He had entered a void, the depths of which not even he was aware.

Connor had been coming to the farm more often to help me. He and Alan restored most of the plants that Matthew had put on the map. My mind was restless most of the time, particularly from midnight to four in the morning. I usually didn't get out of bed until eleven o'clock. Most days, I didn't want to wake or get up. Berenice was very concerned. She and Henry would first call me around nine o'clock. After Matthew died, I would unplug the landline and turn off my cell phone at night, and at nine in the morning, I was sleeping. After the phone call didn't work, Berenice and Henry would knock on my door. My appearance evidenced that I was sleepy, so they stopped coming. I made an effort to show up at lunchtime at their house and then worked at the farm. This new routine made them feel a bit more at ease. But I didn't want to continue to show up or to work at the farm.

I just could not farm the land by myself, even with regular help. I hadn't studied agriculture or permaculture. I farmed because of Matthew and the prolific beauty of nature's gift. But that alone could not keep me farming the land without Matthew, who was so dedicated to giving back the nutrients in order to sustain the earth, who felt that taking and giving should be reciprocated.

I signed a ten-year agreement with Connor that he could live on and use the land to grow organic produce free of rent. He just needed to provide receipts for one thousand dollars of proceeds from selling the fresh produce each year to qualify the land as farmland for tax purposes. Connor was happy with the arrangement for himself, seven-year-old Sam, and the girlfriend who had been living with Connor for almost a year. They ordered a prefab log house and settled it south of the rock pile. By the time the agreement ended, Sam would be gone to college. If we didn't renew the agreement, they could always lift the log house and move to somewhere else in a farming community along the Great Lakes, maybe even in Ohio or Pennsylvania.

LETTERS, 1985

GLENN, ONE OF THE four guys who'd visited us in China and who was in the same class as Jerry, had mentioned, "Since Jerry's death, Matthew has changed. In the first year, Matthew walked away from all of us. The only way we could get to him was through his wife, Shannon, who at the time, didn't really know any of us. It was difficult to know how Matthew felt. He was not talking. The obvious change in him was that he used to hang out with us every weekend. Every once in a while, we all cruised out of town with camping gear and visited different microbreweries. But after Jerry's death, he stayed home. We all sensed that there were other facets of Matthew that we didn't know."

After I came back from Huangshan, Glenn met me at the cemetery. He knelt there, clearing the scattered late summer leaves on top of Rachel's and Jerry's gravestones and Matthew's "The Tree Man" plaque. He squinted at the horizon and pointed to the sunrays. "Matthew is out there. He is watching us. We should give you a medal for keeping him as long as he was able to bear."

A medal? Who wanted it? Glenn didn't know that I was a "godsend" in the family. I was the daughter and sister that Dad, Kurt, and Timothy didn't have—a fairy whose magic the family wished to be everlasting.

All of the harmony of the past ten years was an illusion. If I were a godsend, how could Matthew abandon me? I kept reading his letters and notes to me and still could not find any solace.

XXXX, 1985
Dear Vivi,
Tonight, Dr. Bug and our interpreter are staying in Qishan County near Baoji. Good weather but a lot of driving between temples. We saw a performance tonight

in town that really made me feel how great China is. Some old men played about six large drums and six cymbals, very loud and lively. I could imagine in the past men listening to the drums before going to war, excellent! Then we saw a play with shadow puppets and opera music, also good.

During lunch today, I thought how you would have enjoyed the noodles, but tonight you would have had intestinal infection.

What do you think of Berenice and Henry? Alan and Sandy? I hope you are comfortable until I arrive. Ask my aunt to show you where my grandmother's house is. That's where my brother and I would ride our bicycles without clothes.

I think about you all the time. I miss you, my love. I will write again tomorrow. Good night.

XXXX, 1985   6 a.m., Baoji City

We saw a lot of things yesterday but now all I can think about is your flight to South Bend. You should be arriving soon but I don't know. Your telegram said everything changed. I am worried about it but I can't do anything.

We saw a children's program last night, lovely children. I want our child to have your hair, nose, and eyes, OK?

China would be a good place for him/her to grow up. What do you think?

You know why I love you? Because you are like a child sometimes. You know why I love children? Because they make me feel young and alive with energy.

Say hello to everyone for me. Don't be lonely, I love you so much. How much? You know.

Love,

Matthew

XXXX, 1985

Dear Vivi,

Happy Birthday! I am celebrating by drinking Nescafé! [This note was written on the back of the Nescafé label] *Got your telegram today from South Bend, what a relief!*

The film Ren Sheng (Life) was on TV tonight, good. Have you seen any good films in South Bend?

Try not to feel lonely. When I begin to feel lonely, I think about our reunion next month, then I feel good.

I got a haircut and shave today, 0.5 元 (Chinese currency)

Time goes by so slowly and time can do so much, BUT I know you are still mine!!!!

See you soon

Love,

坏蛋 (Bad Egg/person)

XXXX, 1985

My lovely girl,

Thank you for your frank letter #3. You are thinking a lot about life. You are right, I am different from my family. That is why I have not been living in my birthplace, I guess. Don't worry, you will be busy after I arrive.

I know you would not be happy at home in a big house all day waiting for Fat-Boy to return from work. Don't think about this, we can do ANYTHING! Live ANYWHERE! I will live in the city if you will be happy because you make me happy, give me life and hope. I am always thinking about California and San Francisco, but first we have to make some money.

Where you are is a very quiet small place, especially if you have lived in Hong Kong for a long time. You cannot compare the two places. Remember, you are only seeing a very, very small part of the US.

To me, the quiet is not terrible, only boring.

You have taught me to be frank with you and myself. Thanks.

Give my love to everyone. They all helped in making me what I am today. I will see you in a few days so sleep sweetly.

Love,

Matthew

XXXX, 1985

Dear Mrs. Gandhi,

Are you ready to return to China?

I am in room 606 at the University of Xi'an by myself. I came to visit Jiao Chang Xue my artist friend for the day. I didn't bother to call Shannon this time, no reason to. I did some shopping today. I miss your touch, your voice, your thoughts. I am really glad you married me, forever! You are my home because you know my thoughts and you accept me with all the mistakes I have made in the past. I can tell you everything about my thoughts. Only you and I know my thoughts.

I am beginning to feel like Gandhi. I don't like it. But I am patient.

Have you made any cookies yet? I don't care if you learn any cooking or not. I like the way you cook, Chinese food, Hong Kong food. I don't need anything else. You are a good cook!

My friend at An Kong #2 Middle School came to visit me Thursday. I showed him your photo. He said you looked "so-so for a Chinese girl." He's very frank. I thought about what he said, and I decided I don't care what anyone thinks, I am biased. Besides, I am in love with a person with a mind and emotions and character. I am not in love with a photo. No one can feel you like I do. No one can feel me like you do. My life is linked to yours forever. You are in my heart and mind every day every night.

Time to sleep. I hope you will touch me in my dreams until we meet again.

Love,

G.A.N.DH.i

XXXX, 1985

Dear Lover my Vivi,

Two things happened inside my brain when I heard you on the telephone Thursday night.

1st, you touched my heart deeply. You took the world away from in between us. I was once again one with you. I knew exactly why you called, and I knew what I had to do.

2nd, I suddenly became very angry at the Foreign Affairs Office because of all the time they waste. I am still angry now, and very impatient. I cannot relax until I am together with you.

I can still not explain how much I love you but I can explain the pain I feel when you are not here. It's a deep intense feeling that is with me all the time. People will surround me but I still feel it. People talk to me but I still feel it. It's as if something is missing inside my body, part of my brain gone, only memories remain.

Listen, next time I suggest that we go somewhere at two different times, FIGHT ME!!!! HIT ME!!! OK? Thanks.

Next time, we stay together. We work very good together, we live very good together, we quarrel very good together.

KISS ME!! HOLD ME!! LOVE ME!!

P.S. No more Mrs. and Mr. Gandhi.

Love,

Your Bad Guy

Matthew wrote one or two letters each day during our first separation in 1985, when I had to enter the US before my entry visa expired. I initially wanted to extend the visa and leave China with him when his semester ended in late July, but he was worried that asking for an extension might imply to the US government that I didn't care to go, so he preferred me to leave first. I didn't insist, because I knew if I extended the visa, he would have been worried until I could put my feet on US soil.

I supposed when people are young and happy with their lives, a month of time wouldn't be a concern. Yet, with the inefficiency of the Foreign Affairs Office and whatever other reasons, Matthew could not get his plane ticket home for an additional three weeks. His decision to have me travel alone to the US was the seven weeks that he regretted the most.

SEPARATIONS, 1991–1992

OUR SECOND SEPARATION WAS in 1991, when Matthew took a six-month sabbatical to study permaculture eighty miles away. The program required apprentices to live on the farm and they went home on the weekends. For that period, we took turns. I went to the farm for one weekend and Matthew came home for another. I learned permaculture by visiting the farm on the weekends and working side by side with Matthew and a few of the other apprentices who didn't go home.

The six-month, full-time residential program was based at a thirty-acre organic farm. The program trained adults in the concepts and practices of organic gardening and small-scale sustainable farming. The apprenticeship blended experiential learning with traditional classroom studies on topics that included soil management, composting, pest and weed control, crop planning, irrigation, farm equipment, direct marketing techniques, business planning, farm labor issues, food policy, equity, and other social and environmental issues in the food system. The apprentices accepted into the program each year came from all regions of the US and abroad, and represented a wide spectrum of ages, backgrounds, and interests.

The cohort consisted of about forty people. There was a huge community hall with a kitchen, eating and studying areas, and four solar shower structures. Everyone put up his or her tent along the edge of the farm. Each day, two apprentices were assigned to cook for the cohort.

On the weekends, most of them left, except for those who came from far away, including out of state or other countries. The remaining apprentices loved my visits because I would cook for them and sometimes brought extra goodies to satisfy their cravings. I enjoyed their company. They taught me how to examine the soil for bacteria, when to pick fruits before other animals got them, what to look for when vegetables were sick. They also had all different kinds of humor from all over the world. Some were very funny, and some told jokes I never got. Yet, none of them were offensive. On August days, evenings, and nights, we would listen to tree crickets and katydids. They were loud. We watched the stars and moonlight above our heads. When autumn came, we moved close to the steps of the community hall and listened to stories from far away homes. The experience on the farm brought back memories of China, when all the foreign teachers would gather together during happy hour. We talked about home, about activities we missed the most, and about life in China. Matthew was content during those days on the farm and visualized someday transforming our farm into a place like this commune.

3/10/91

Dear Vivi,

I thought it would be a good idea to write more often in order to improve my communication skills. And REACHABLE…you might enjoy reading a letter from me. I just finished doing some volunteer work over at the arboretum. A beautiful young bald cypress was being damaged by a small steel wire cage that should have been removed years ago. It took me about an hour to cut away sections of the cage that would have eventually killed the entire tree.

That is all for today. The ball is in your court.

Love,

Matthew

July 20, 1991

Dear Vivi,

It is strange being at home alone today while you are at work. I feel quite useless because I am not making any money today. The longer I am in the Horticulture Program, the more desperate I feel even though I know we will survive. I realize that we are in fact quite fortunate to be able to live together.

I never would have imagined that I would find someone I love so much on the opposite side of the Earth. You are as fascinating to me today as you were Feb. 1984. Our journey has just begun. I believe we have the creativity and strength to hold each other up for many years to come. I will do the best I can.

Love,

Matthew

Matthew completed his apprenticeship at the end of September 1991.

In late January 1992, less than a week after Matthew missed the appointment with Mrs. Hunter, when he was working as an individual consultant and received notifications for court appearances, attorneys' briefings, people calling for advice regarding whether they should or should not take down old trees in their backyards, he drove all the way to Indiana Dunes National Park. When a park ranger found him unconscious in his truck with a whiskey bottle at his side and locked windows with the engine running, the ranger broke the window and called an ambulance. I got the call from the emergency room at noon. I drove to visit him at a mental health facility where he stayed for recovery. Matthew spent the next four weeks in a psychiatric ward, and I visited him every day.

I would drive thirty-two miles home after ten o'clock, some nights in dense fog. All of a sudden, I would see only a vast smoky veil of fine, colorless strands twisting in front of the windshield. The increasingly obscuring mists swayed in various forms and shapes to seduce me to go along with them. With mind numbing and physical fatigue, I fought to concentrate and not be tempted and lured into the unknown whiteness.

Monday, Feb 17, 1992
10:25 p.m. Eastern Standard Time
The steel gray Indiana wind
Howls
through the bare limbs
of my woody friends
I constantly remind myself
they're only sleeping
Dear Vivi,

I realized today another reason why I love you. For the last eight years, your presence has distracted me from the loneliness that haunts me now. You are right, loneliness is a part of us. Sometimes we can ignore it but it will always return. I wish I could hold you close to me so I could feel your vitality and energy, your happiness and anger, your frustration and satisfaction, your raw emotions, which flow from you like a fountain.

I walked around a cemetery that is within the facility's property. I wondered why there was a cemetery, and I openly questioned why was I here. Why do I stand here breathing in the cold winter wind, talking to a landscape of grass and trees and stones?

I can't help but to continue to ask why. It's an obsession lately. At this moment in time, I feel as if everything I have done in my life was just a distraction so I would not have to confront the question, why. And now I realize there is no answer within me, but the question will not leave my brain.

I could be happy living with you, growing food, building a home, watching a thunderstorm from the porch, drinking strong coffee after making love to you and just enjoying a peaceful moment if the why would leave some of my mind.

So much has entered my mind within the last week, and I have survived. It can only make us stronger.

Take care my love. I will return to you as soon as I am well.

Love,

Matthew

Friday night, 2/21/92,

10:15 p.m.

Thanks for kicking my butt over the phone tonight. I am well and optimistic.

You have done more for me than you can ever imagine. I thank you; the trees thank you, and the future thanks you.

P.S. I better write more often. I really need the practice.

Saturday, 3/7/92

12:30 p.m.

Dear Vivi,

Since the white pine tree incident in January, I discovered that I cannot consciously contribute to the dismemberment of the earth's natural systems. I can never return to chemical pest control or indiscriminate removal of woody plants. So, where to from here?

I am very impatient at this moment. I want clarity of thinking now. I want the answers to our future now. I want a sense of security now. All very unrealistic requests but they occupy my mind with an intensity I cannot ignore. I must learn to accept the moment at hand and realize who I am and what my strengths and weaknesses are. I have learned much more over the last month and a half. I have begun to accept the frailty of the mind. One can harden many facets of their minds over time, but there will always be seams between these facets that can open up and reveal how delicate the threads are that keep us sane. If any one person really comprehended the horror that can be printed in a daily newspaper, they would lose their minds. So, the question is, do we comprehend what is happening here and ignore it, or do we try to confront the destruction and try to change the future at our own expense.

I am at the crossroads where I want to try to change the world for the better, but as of yet I am afraid to lose sight of the path of indifference, the easy road. The Beatles wrote a line in a song, "Strawberry Fields": "Living is easy with eyes closed"

The more I open my eyes, the harder it gets, but in order to continue I must face and understand our world.

March 10, '92
12:50 p.m.
Dear Vivi,

As I review the above writing, I feel as if I am a painter who is painting himself into the corner of a room. I must face my work and let it dry before I can leave the room. As I stand in the corner waiting for the paint to dry, my old enemy, Claustrophobia begins to emerge, and I prepare to run over the fresh paint with only one thing in mind: escape.

The concept of escaping fear has been a recurring theme throughout my life, but I have never succeeded in winning the race. I think mainly because I have not accepted the fact that I cannot escape from myself. But it is time to acknowledge this simple fact.

Vivi, I truly appreciate the love you have shown me. You have seen my faults and fears and you still show me love. Thank you.

Love,
Matthew

We planned to move back to the farm in the winter of 1992 after I finished my three-month training at University of California San Francisco (UCSF). I was accepted into a worldwide experimental program to become a mental health counselor for people with developmental disabilities, particularly in the deaf population. The program paid for everything with a monthly stipend.

One day when I was seven years old, my father was holding my hand, waiting for the traffic light so we could cross the street. There were two men standing next to me. I looked up. Their hands were dancing beautifully, and I saw smiles on their faces. I pulled my father's hand. "What are they doing?"

"Oh, they're using hand language. They can't hear."

I thought, "Wow, they are so smart that they don't need to use their voices to communicate."

Years later when I was in my graduate studies, I saw a woman who was arranging a chair next to the podium when I entered the lecture hall. Somehow, I knew this woman was an interpreter and she would be using hand language. When class was over, I went to the interpreter and asked, "Where can I learn the hand language?"

"It is not a hand language. The language is American Sign Language, ASL." She corrected me.

The same evening, I went to the community college to register and enroll in ASL. Subsequently, I started to volunteer in the deaf community and service agencies since I already knew two other languages, which would help me work with families where there could be generations of deaf, hard of hearing, and speaking members all in the same household. Soon, I was hired as a case-by-case interpreter for the tri-counties social services agencies.

During that period, Matthew's symptoms had already been present for over a year. I decided to change my course of studies and focus on mental health, which was a mistake. I was so involved with Matthew's illness that I blinded myself and became a subjective mental health supervisor instead of a spouse.

Eight of us were selected for the UCSF program. One person was from Maine, one from South Africa, one from India, and me from Indiana. The other four people were Californians. The program arranged that we four out-of-state students would lodge at a bed-and-breakfast in the Ashbury Heights neighborhood, which was close enough to walk to campus and to Langley Porter Psychiatric Clinic, where we would fulfill our internship hours with outpatients. Among the eight of us, I was the one who had the least academic study in mental health. I had more hands-on experience working with the deaf community. I had worked as an interpreter with social workers and judges in family court. One of the most memorable cases left me wishing deep down that no mothers, able or disabled should experience separation from their children for life.

A social worker wanted to take away a hearing infant boy from a young single mother who was deaf with a developmental disability and who lived with her hearing father. I worked on that case for nine months with the court, social workers, rehabilitation counselors, doctors, and the young woman's father to keep the boy with her. Two of the measures to determine her eligibility were a month of intensive daily two-hour observations and weekly unannounced visits that sometimes coincided with hospital appointments related to the child's health and development.

The young woman and her father lived in a low-income neighborhood and were on government assistance. The father used to work in a meat packing plant and had become permanently disabled when his index and adjacent fingers were cut off by a meat slicer. Soon after the accident, his wife left him and their ten-year-old daughter. The father didn't know sign language, but he was able to keep the household going and continued obtaining limited social services for his daughter, who got pregnant at age seventeen. No one, including the social workers and staff at an activity center where the daughter went daily, knew how this happened or who the father was.

In those daily two-hour observations, the young woman tried very hard to comprehend how to change the diapers, feed the baby, and keep him clean. Sometimes, she just stared at her father and could not repeat the same tasks that he had just done. Her eyes expressed frustration and desperation.

In one of the unannounced visits, the social worker caught her giving a piece of hard candy to the boy while her father was washing the bottles. The social worker quickly seized the candy from her. She retreated to the floor, curled her body into a ball, and started rocking.

I'll never forget the look in this young woman's eyes as she asked for help, for support, for mercy that would allow her child to live with her. She had tried her best to protect the child with her father's aid; she had worked with all of these professionals in her management team in order to become a capable mother. All her genuine desires were lost in translation. The social worker focused on her clinical knowledge. The judge concentrated on practical and moral obligations. They weren't able to look in her eyes and imagine her potential.

I was screaming at the top of my lungs on the platform outside the courthouse, watching the young woman walk away from the courthouse without her soul. In the end, she lost her child to the legal system. The judge ruled that social services would place the child in foster care for one single reason: the mother could not rely on her father's help to take care of the child.

The training at UCSF was intense. We started at seven in the morning, and two or three days a week, we wouldn't finish until nine in the evening. We were able to take an hour lunch break, at all different hours, depending on how the day's activities went. I loved the moment around four o'clock when I was able to sit in the library with very few others around and look out the window and see San Francesco gradually descending in front of me. I would sit still for ten or fifteen minutes and then I'd start writing to Matthew.

The days working at Langley Porter were the hardest. I saw exasperation, heard shrieks, felt the pain of the voiceless, knew their inability to communicate their need for comfort, for knowledge, for nourishment of their beings. I observed them. Every once in a while, I linked them to Matthew, whose mind had seemed to function well for a long time, but something had been missing, something had been hidden—something intangible that I couldn't discern.

September 2, 1992

Dear Vivi,

Life here is busy but quiet. In a way, it's very peaceful mixed with the element of emptiness.

I try to crowd out the emptiness with various projects, cleaning flowers, designing the shed, reading, planting seeds for a fall harvest, etc. I am sure some people spend their whole lives with a hole in their hearts.

There are advantages and disadvantages with every situation especially when two individuals try to mold their lives in a mutual relationship. I hope when we get together again, we can learn each other's tolerances and live within these limits. I would in fact like to grow old with you. Talk to you soon.

Love,

Matthew

9/8/1992

Dear Matthew,

It is very interesting how our relationship has shifted. I am not that angry any more. Instead, full of concerns. On the other hand, I miss the time in which we shared our daily routines. I also miss talking with you. I find loneliness surrounding me despite a crazy busy day at Langley Porter. I think the feeling of loneliness is the enemy of all of us. Some people manage to get over that feeling. Some cannot and are restless in their lives. Right now, I am the latter.

I will be home before you know it. Keep talking.

Love,

Vivi

September 24, 1992

Dear Vivi,

I miss your presence here very much. Lately my mind has gone back to the moment we were in the ambulance in Hainan Island and you returned my kiss with a passion I had never experienced before. That is one of the greatest moments in my life, and I shall always remember it. Now, as I think of that time my joy is mixed with the emptiness of the present. Will we ever be able to live together in peace and harmony?

I anxiously anticipate your return to Indiana. Three months seem like a long time, but we have survived separation in the past, and we shall do so again.

I hope you are feeling better. It's interesting, physically you are the weaker of us two but mentally, you are the stronger. I suppose that occasionally the balance tips both ways but generally this is true.

Last night about 10:00 p.m., a fever came upon me. I was sweating and my muscles ached even though I took Tylenol. I wasn't until after I called work this morning and told them I wouldn't be in that I was able to get to sleep. I got up about noon today but even now (2:45 p.m.) my head is heavy and I feel dull. I also don't like staying at the house alone. Time moves so slowly. For some reason I can spend hours at the farm without feeling lonely, but when I come back to the house time slows down.

Autumn has arrived with a couple of clear days and cool nights. I was planting butternut seeds (white walnut) in the field last night and the sunset was spectacular. Shades of oranges and golds blanketed the field as I went about my business of digging small holes and depositing a nut in each one. Occasionally, I would come upon a small butternut, walnut, or oak tree I planted from seeds last fall and I would relocate the new seed about ten feet from the others.

I hope you are not jealous of my woody children. If it were not for them, I would probably be with you in California right now.

I am going to the post office now and also do a bit of shopping. I will talk to you this evening.

Take good care of yourself.

Love,

Matthew

10/12/1992

Dear Matthew,

I know what you mean about "dwelling upon" life. I have the same feeling every once in a while. But, don't let it depress you. Take it as the process of life. On this *matter, just be patient and let things take their course. I am impatient with many things, but not with life. I question it.*

This is a terrible period for both of us. But look at the bright side, it could be helpful for you and me to define our relationship. At least, I know I am still in love with you, and I don't want to divorce you.

Take care and time will go fast.

Love,

Vivi

October 27, 1992

Hi Girl,

I just finished watching Dan Rather. He had a segment of Eye on America where he talked to three different families that were all working hard but were making less now than they were five years ago. This situation is not uncommon in this country where jobs are being restructured and downgraded.

The American Dream will only be achieved while the masses sleep. For many it will never be more than just a dream. Speaking of dreams, my brother Jerry joined me at some long-forgotten seashore during my sleep last night. I forget the specifics of my dreams, but the landscapes and the feelings of being with my brother again will stay with me for a day or so. I don't even remember any dialogue but I felt comfortable being with someone who shared a mutual experience of growing up in a divided home.

October 29, 1992

I had another dream last night. There was a girl and I walking along the frozen edge of a body of water. It was near dark. I did not recognize the girl (age twenty-forty?) and I don't recall any conversation. As we walked on, the shore became a steep slope to the edge of the water. Suddenly the girl slipped quickly and went under the water and disappeared. I reached out my arm in the hope that she would return to the surface but she didn't. I was afraid to dive into the water because I was sure if I did, I would also not return alive. So, I stood there frozen in fear as darkness enveloped the landscape. Then I woke up. The scene haunts me now as I write this. Many years ago, when Timothy was a baby, I dreamt that he fell off a harbor pier and disappeared below the water as I stood by in horror, and now thirty years later a similar dream returns.

10/31/92 Sat, a.m.

It was great to talk to you last night even though you sounded agitated and upset with me at times. I don't really know what the future holds, but today I am optimistic. I am still not sure what I heard you say last night on the phone, but I thought I heard you say we are going to have a child in 1993 and you said it with conviction in your voice. After eight years of knowing you, you still amaze me at times. I love you deeply. I am even beginning to love myself. Anyway, we will continue this conversation at a later date, as I have to go and plant the rest of the ginseng seed.

Life, what a wild ride through time.

Love,

Matthew

November 3, 1992

Dear Vivi,

How is the girl I love so much today? It's lunch time during my busy day of fertilizing trees in Mishawaka. I didn't have any paper except a donut bag from your favorite store, but I feel the need to write to you, so here it is. In the world of small achievements, I finished the bookcase last night and emptied out most of the boxes. It felt good to accomplish this task.

While putting some photo albums on a shelf, I glanced at some of the pictures of us together in different places in the States, Mexico, Hong Kong, and China. I feel very fortunate to have been able to experience these places with you. I would like to experience many more places with you in the future. The biggest conflict I have at this moment is that I want a cake and to eat it too. I want to build a home and be able to roam the world with you. Mentally, it has been a hard year for both of us. Coming back here has been very difficult for me, but it forced me to examine reality.

I have put long term investments on hold such as apple trees and blueberry bushes, which would not start to yield fruit for four to eight years because the reality of the economics depends on a lifetime commitment. What I am feeling right now is the "right" place for us to grow together. It may be too early for me to come to a conclusion but it is what I am feeling right now. Some people spend their whole lives in one spot unable or unwilling to move to another location. I had initially thought that returning here would be like coming back home, but I have been extremely selfish in that sense. I want you to feel that where we live is home. For me, I feel somewhat of an alien here so far. I can ignore it when I am working the farm but that's only part-time.

Well, it's time to go back to work. I love you Vivi, and I am trying to open up, especially to you. I will talk to you soon.

Love,

Matthew

EXPECTATION

I KNEW THAT IF a person had a heart disease, one of the symptoms is chest pain that might feel like pressure or a squeezing sensation. I didn't know whether strong physical pain could happen to a healthy heart, which I had, but sometimes my heart was tightly squeezed and I needed to bend at a ninety-degree angle to reposition the smallest coronary arteries as if something were blocking them or there wasn't enough blood flowing to bring oxygen-rich blood to my heart. The pain of losing Matthew was as vivid as if I were holding my own beating heart, witnessing the slowly dissipating blood red color.

I started writing to Dad the summer after Matthew's death.

Dear Dad,

I have planned to write you this letter long before today. Procrastination is my problem. Summer is almost over. But the sun is still very bright. Most evenings, I walk round and round on the farm. I smell autumn and see the leaves falling.

We are not able to talk about Matthew over the phone because I don't know how to express myself. I am at a loss. My memories start getting blurry from the day Matthew died. I have been very confused for the past nine months. I don't know who I was, who I am, or who I will be.

The other night, I was in the kitchen; I held an onion. At the time, I didn't know what it was, why I was holding it, and what I should do with it. I was in tremendous agony of not knowing what to do with it. I sat next to the dinner table with pouring tears.

One thing I want you to know is that I loved your son, and he knew that. We both were too consumed by his illness, which pushed us to the edge. I remember Matthew asked if it was OK to die. I said what I believe, that each person has the

125

right to decide. In retrospect, Matthew was asking for permission. How could I be so blind? I know it was not my fault that Matthew made his decision. But I don't know how to live with the feeling of guilt.

You have gone through this again and again in the past forty-some years. I have a lot to learn from your wisdom. At the same time, I want you to know that I have constantly thought of you and shared the pain with you. I hope someday I also can share your joy in life. It does not matter who I will be. Matthew, you, and other family members are my family, which is staying with me.

Keep in touch and stay healthy.

P.S. If Mom doesn't get the chance to read this letter, please say hello for me.

Love,

Vivi

Dad and I corresponded with sporadic letters, phone calls, visits, and trips. Despite how life had unfairly mistreated him, he didn't lose his cheerful nature. Years after Matthew's death, he was still that delightful old man who talked and danced around life as if he himself were in different plays performing different roles at different times with different emotions. He was really into those roles. On multiple occasions, I could not trace any signs of grief in him. I observed Dad with Kurt, Timothy, and Mom in many instances. He was a macho man and in control of his environment, even though Mom and my two brothers-in-law might protest what he was saying or doing at the time. He was just being who he was and didn't allow anything to interrupt whatever fun he was having in the moment. After Kurt got married, his wife, Dana, was a bit of a fanatic about cleanliness and diseases spreading, which prevented Dad visiting Kurt and his son, Jaxon, at their home. Dad didn't have a word of complaint but worked around it by staying in their hometown at a hotel, making restaurant reservations, or booking events where Kurt and Jaxon would meet with him for a few days. I truly admired Dad for living his life so fully. His whole life, Dad kept telling me, "I deny it, and if I deny it long enough, I will believe that Matthew is traveling somewhere else, like the years he spent in China."

The morning I learned that John F. Kennedy Jr.'s plane had crashed, I was so shaken. I called Dad. I was inconsolable. In between crying and breathing, I asked Dad, "If there is a god, how could it be so cruel as to take two daughters' lives from their parents at once?"

Dad held the phone, heard my choking, and whispered, "It's life. A lot of the time, we just don't know when life plays tricks on us."

This old man taught me that sadness is part of being human, which echoes what the psychologist had told me years ago when Zi Meng died. Five years had passed since Matthew's death, and I hadn't mastered the idea that being sorrowful is okay. I found myself in Matthew's shoes—every day was repeating yesterday's misery. There was no light showing when that would end. The feelings of helplessness and hopelessness were invisible and kinesthetically put down roots to drastically blur all other senses. It seemed that my heart had a hole; blood was rushing out. I tried to fill the hole with something. Yet, I didn't know what I could put in it. A feeling of despair would run up to my throat by crushing my stomach with empty air—headache, and muscle pains, my body seemed to be breaking down, piece by piece of it aimlessly dropping here and there. Even so, I felt extremely heavy, like I had been dragging the weight of the world with me.

Each day when I woke up, the first feeling was Matthew's absence. At work, people talked to me. I heard and didn't hear. I couldn't collect my thoughts. My mind was somewhere else, in a vacuum. Most of the time, I didn't know what I was thinking, except that I wanted Matthew back. It was so hard to embrace reality when I became aware that it was merely wishful thinking. The emptiness engulfed me, from head to toes. I had no way to get rid of these awful feelings despite how hard I tried to rationalize them.

After Mom died of a stroke in April 2006, Dad started traveling the US, visiting places that Mom and he had been. When I learned that Dad would be driving up to Alaska, I told him that I would join him in Anchorage. We would take a five-day trip together the first week of September, and I would plan everything.

I regretted it after informing Dad about my plan.

I asked myself, "Why are you doing this? This could ruin the relationship that you both have. It could end up either you killing him or him killing you, idiot!"

I walked off the plane at the Anchorage airport and there stood Dad. We drove to the bed-and-breakfast that I had booked online. When I came out of my room after settling my bag, in the corridor to the open meeting room, I heard Dad saying, "I came with my daughter-in-law, how about that?" Dad was so proud to introduce me to the group. There were six others seated around a big rectangular table. Two of them were a mother and son, another two were a father and daughter, the last pair was a mother and daughter.

We took a stroll in the tourist areas of Anchorage. I was astounded to find a cluster of Korean restaurants. Dad told me that Anchorage had a sizable Korean community.

I smiled. "See, I learn something new every day. How about having a Korean dinner?"

After we were seated, Dad said, "I was in the Korean War, but I never had Korean food." I asked what he wanted. He said, "You're in charge."

I knew Dad liked oysters. Every Thanksgiving and Christmas he would make oyster stew.

I looked at the waitress. "This is the first time my dad has had Korean food. Could you do me a favor and make the seafood pancake with oyster only?"

The waitress looked at Dad and me. "The pancake mix has already been put together." She paused and looked at Dad again. "I'll ask the cook if he can do that. Just a minute." She headed to the kitchen.

Dad said, "I like seafood."

"Squid is part of the seafood pancake."

"Ooooh, I see."

The waitress presented us with an oyster pancake, BBQ beef ribs, broiled mackerel, cold yam noodles, and nine small dishes with assortments of kimchee and other vegetables. Dad pretty much ate the whole oyster pancake by himself, and then he said to me, "I can't believe you still eat that much."

The trip was delightful. Dad was very agreeable and didn't fight with me at all. He let me arrange lodging, sightseeing, whale watching, and food selection. He didn't even rush me early in the morning like on other trips we'd taken with the entire family.

Dad had promised Jerry, Matthew, Kurt, and Timothy to take them to Disneyland when they were young boys. It was not until 1989 that he fulfilled his promise, with the regret that Jerry was no longer living. Instead, I got to go. During that trip, Dad would say, "Let us boys take a picture," excluding Mom and me. I thought he was rude. I would stick a hand or kick a leg into the picture until he gave up and let Mom and me be in the photos.

Another trip was to the Grand Canyon. He would rush all of us in the early morning to see the sunrise or beat the traffic. The day we were leaving, each driving our separate ways to go home, he knocked at our door at four in the morning. "It's time to hit the road."

Annoyed, I took over the doorknob. "You go. We'll sleep a bit longer and leave after breakfast."

Sixteen months after the Alaska trip, I got a call from Timothy early one evening. "Dad disappeared."

"What happened?"

"Dad has been coughing for a couple weeks. He insisted on not seeing a doctor and drove his truck to Oregon. He's been gone for three days now. I called him, and he hasn't returned any of my calls. I told Kurt, and Dad didn't return Kurt's calls either. I thought he might have contacted you."

"Has this happened before?"

"No, but I know Dad might want to die in Oregon."

"Why?"

"He likes the woods and has no connection with anyone there."

I started calling Dad. I called him every hour for two days in a row. On the third day, my phone rang while I was at the office, at 2:09 p.m. "Dad? Where are you?"

"I'm in Ashland, near the California border." He sounded mischievous.

"Stay there. I can be there in six hours. You'll stay with me until the doctor says that you are okay to go home. Do you hear me?"

"Why make a fuss?"

"We're worried about you, Dad. Timothy told me everything. Don't do this to us."

Silence at the other end of the line, then, "Don't worry, sweetheart. I'm heading home tomorrow morning. I'll call you early evening your time every day until I get home. Deal?"

"You are more than welcome to come here. Stay with me until you feel better," I insisted.

"I'll be okay. I need to go home and take care of the yard."

"Okay, deal. Let me know where you are. I'll call Kurt and Timothy after I finish talking with you."

Six weeks later, my phone rang in the early afternoon again. It was Timothy. "Dad is in an induced coma at the hospital. I thought you might want to know."

I flew out to be with Dad at the hospital. He was covered with only a folded white sheet from his waist down, no machinery or life support hookups. Kurt said that was Dad's wish. Kurt calculated that it took about eight thousand calories in Dad's state to be alive for a day or two. Based on his calculations and the doctor's assumption regarding Dad's development of pneumonia, he would not be able to survive for another forty-eight hours. In other words, Dad could die anytime now.

Kurt and Timothy left the room for me to be alone with Dad. I held this old man's hand, surveyed each of the wrinkles on his face that represented the days and years of sadness and joy. His closed eyes hid the weeping and sorrow week after week and month after month. Now, he was lying there with his half naked aging body, sleeping like a baby.

"Dad, you can go. Go and be free." I squeezed his hand and stayed until two in the morning.

I woke up around eleven o'clock. Kurt was in the living room waiting for me. "Dad died this morning around six o'clock."

"Did he die in a coma?"

"Yes."

"What's next?"

"We'll have a service here and will bring him back to South Bend to be next to Mom in July, when the kids are on summer break."

"What can I do?"

"If you don't mind, Tim and I would like you to clear Dad's personal and financial stuff."

"Sure."

I started with the drawers in his bedroom and then in his study. I flipped through Dad's clothes, put them in piles, sorted out his papers and financial statements.

I was surprised that I didn't have any problem cleaning up Dad's stuff, which wasn't at all the same as with Matthew's. When Dad, Kurt, and Timothy were still with me the first few days after Matthew's death, I told them to take anything they wanted.

Kurt asked, "Could I have the sweaters you knitted for Matthew?"

"Yes, you have to pack them yourself." I could not touch any of them.

"Could I also have the bureau on top of the dresser? I always wanted to have something like that."

The walnut wood bureau was Jerry's. Matthew had kept it from his first wife and never let go of it wherever we moved.

"Yes, but you have to take the contents as well." I couldn't bear to open it.

Timothy, on the other hand, didn't take anything.

I disliked folding clothes. Each time after doing laundry, I made Matthew fold the clothes with me. We had a dresser with ten drawers, five on each side. The left side was Matthew's, and I had the right. He would put his stuff in his drawers and I put mine away. In our entire marriage, I had never opened his drawers. Two months after Matthew died, I opened one of his drawers. Matthew's T-shirts were neatly arranged by color, and old to new. I opened another, all his hats were overlapping by sizes, and his socks by short, medium, and long. I pulled open the third drawer; his flannel work shirts were organized into plaid and solid styles. I dropped down and sat on the carpet, holding the knob of the fourth drawer, breaking into tears. Matthew's drawers were much better organized than mine. I didn't open the fourth drawer.

I went to the phone and called Timothy. "Do you have time to come up in the next few weeks? I need help cleaning up Matthew's belongings. I can pay for your tickets and travel expenses."

Timothy came, and I told him, "You don't need to ask me what to keep or throw away. I leave it all to your discretion."

During the three days of sorting things out, a few times Timothy tried to get my attention then hesitated. The day he left, he told me he had sent books and some of Matthew's artwork to Texas. I nodded and didn't say a word.

I looked up and glanced around Dad's study, which opened to the living room and kitchen. Kurt was standing next to the dining table with his back to me, talking on the phone. "That looks familiar," I thought, then I remembered I'd seen that posture in my living room when Kurt was talking to the insurance agent regarding Matthew's suicide. Kurt was the one who took the responsibility of clearing up Matthew's financial affairs.

I understood why Kurt asked me to help figure out Dad's finances—insurance, investment brokerage, and bank accounts. They both trusted me, and they knew I could get the job done faster than they could. I arranged the legal documents by categories and highlighted the contact information for them.

FAMILY HISTORY

I ALSO FOUND A journal that Dad started in 2007 and wrote in for a period of two years:

I had a few "firsts" in Alaska: first time traveling alone with my daughter-in-law, Vivi; first time staying in a bed-and-breakfast; and the first time eating Korean food, which I don't care for that much.

Vivi is a good kid. After thirteen years, she is still single. I told her, "Don't do this for Matthew. You have your own life; you're young, and you deserve a companion."

She said, "My father said the same thing. I am not doing this for anyone. It's not in my mind, not a priority."

I don't know how to help Vivi to get over her grief. My situation with Rachel was very different. At least I had family near me and my two boys. Vivi has none. She marries eight thousand miles away from home and leaves all the people she knows. Now, she ends up all by herself with sorrow.

Thinking of Vivi and in retrospect, my early thirties were very much like my father's, who did not involve himself with family matters and our daily lives. I was the same; I didn't really know my two older boys and their mother.

I didn't know what the difference would be if I had grown up with my father, who basically was a stranger, a familiar family guest who would visit us four or five times a year and each time stayed for two to three weeks. So I assumed that was the way life is. My mother handled all of us and life events fairly well without my father. In comparison, my work schedule was much better than my father's. I could go home once a month and stay for a week. I never thought my work away from home would cause distress to Rachel, who didn't show any signs of depression or anxiety when I took off back to work. After all these years, I still don't understand why

Rachel did what she did. The only reaction I got was my mother's animosity toward me. I didn't know what I had done to get my mother so angry at me. Perhaps, she blamed me for Rachel's death.

Rachel's two boys were so protected by my mother, who willfully separated them from me. After Rachel's death, I thought my mother would take good care of them, and while I was still young and single, I could make as much money as possible on the lake. I took up other family men's slots and just worked. My schedule changed to going home once every two months. I missed many events in the boys' lives. One Christmas, I was home for a week when the boys were seven and eight years old. We spent Christmas Eve at Berenice's. On the fireplace mantel, I saw three pairs of bronzed copper baby booties, which I didn't remember ever seeing before. I asked Berenice, "Who do these booties belong to? There are three pairs of them?"

Berenice looked at me as if I were joking. "The boys. You've never seen them?"

"No, not that I recall. You made them? Why three pairs?"

"Oh my, Damon! Look inside, each pair has a name and age engraved in it."

I checked. They were Jerry, Matthew, and Alan, all lined up in order of age. Berenice wheeled herself over to me. "Rachel had Jerry's and Matthew's done. When you moved to Mom's house, I kept their booties. Damon, you should spend more time with the boys. Don't follow in our father's footsteps."

Berenice's comment hit me hard. I was not much of a father to Jerry and Matthew. They saw me come and go every other month, and I didn't even once sit down to check their homework or tuck them into bed, which my mother had been doing. Or with Berenice and Henry when the two boys slept over and spent time with Alan. The booties got me thinking, and I changed my work schedule.

I had built up seniority at work and become a second commander on the freighter. I decided to be home at least once every two weeks including a weekend while I looked for an opening at the chemical plant.

I spent time with the boys throwing the football back and forth on the field, fishing at our cabin on the Upper Peninsula, taking rides, and going to the theater, like I was twenty again, going to movies with their mother.

I thought I was doing the right thing for the boys, then I met Erin and a few months later, I married her. Erin was the oldest of five children. Her mother died when she was fourteen. Her father didn't remarry and worked at the factory to support the six of them. She took up motherly duties to take care of her siblings. The youngest was ten years behind her. I thought Erin would be a good fit as my two boys' mother since she had acted like one for so many years. This time, I decided to stay home for good. Henry helped me land a job at the chemical plant. But my mother was not happy with it. She gave me an ultimatum: the boys or my new family, my choice.

Jerry didn't get along with Erin, who sometimes could be too dutiful with good intentions to fill Rachel's place. Jerry was a free spirit. No one had ever told him to follow schedules, do chores, or clean up after himself. My mother did all those daily tasks for them. With Erin in charge of the house, Jerry felt that he no longer had the freedom to do whatever he wanted to do. Jerry was rebellious. He didn't want to live under any house rules set by Erin, who insisted that the boys call her Mom and hung a sign in the kitchen, "If Mama ain't happy, ain't nobody happy."

Erin's presence changed my newly established relationship with Jerry and Matthew. Jerry often went back to my mother, particularly when he had an argument with Erin. Matthew was the one who got caught in the middle. He had his mother's sweet nature that always tried to please everyone. He called Erin Mom. He tried to hold his brother back and stayed home with all of us. He would do all the chores, but each time when Erin found out, she would erase Matthew's efforts and require Jerry to do his part, and then Jerry would just take off and wouldn't come home for days. The conflicts between Erin and Jerry gave me heartaches and put Matthew in the position of betraying his brother or disobeying Erin and me. Poor Matthew, he was only nine years old when faced with the verbal war between my mother and Erin and the runaway episodes with Jerry and the late nights walking alone across the field to home when Erin was furious about him being home late. I didn't know how to handle the feud between Jerry and Erin. I couldn't let either one of them go. I wanted to assure Matthew that he was doing all the right things and he shouldn't feel bad about anything at home. But I didn't think I could ever give him the feelings of security and being loved by parents that a nine-year-old boy should have felt without questioning at all.

Coincidentally, Kurt and Timothy were also thirteen months apart. After Kurt and Timothy were born, Erin was too busy taking care of both babies that eleven-year-old Jerry became less of an issue for her. By then, Jerry was staying with my mother about eighty percent of the time, and Matthew was 50/50 between Grandma's house and home. I didn't have the energy to fight with my mother about them staying with her. Most importantly, the boys were happier with my mother and spent time with Alan at Berenice's house. All my efforts at being a better father to Rachel's boys went down the drain. I had another two boys and a wife to soothe daily and a job that I had to keep up in order to support the family.

As Kurt and Timothy got older, Jerry did soften a bit with Erin. He would take his younger brothers to play in the field, to Grandma and Berenice for treats, but he still stayed away from home. I saw that Matthew smiled more often. He helped Jerry with Kurt and Timothy and did all the heavy lifting, carrying sports gear and taking the younger brothers home so Erin didn't have to worry about their safety.

Kurt and Timothy loved their older brothers. Whenever they got a chance, they were just glued to Jerry for stories and tricks, to Matthew for quick sketches and sweets. My mother and Berenice baked delicious cookies, even Erin hankered after them. Matthew with his sweet nature never forgot to take a few of the cookies to Erin, who said, "Matthew is special to me. He knows how to work with me and respect me." Yet, I never heard Jerry, Matthew, or Erin say "I love you" to each other, despite how much I said to all of them at different times, "I love you."

After Jerry died, Matthew seemed to change into a different person. He didn't talk to me or his brothers. I tried to get him to visit us, but he would always just say he was busy with schoolwork and his part-time job. After he married Shannon, I had no chance to see him at all. Erin didn't like Shannon, which I found ironic since my mother and other family members didn't like Erin, and now it was her turn to not like Matthew's wife. What was wrong with all the women in two generations of my family to cause them to reject another woman? Rachel was the only exception but her life cut short, too short!

After Vivi joined the family, everyone's attitude changed. Berenice and Henry and Alan's family love her, Erin likes her, Kurt and Timothy are delighted to have her as a sister. Even Ernest, who we only visit once a year, said to me, "Matthew's wife is such a joy. She's so energetic and helpful. She would bring a cake or something and visit us every few weeks. Some evenings she'll help get the cows back to the barn when Raymond is late from work. When the cows are too close to the road, she just walks over and asks me what to do to get them back to the field. Matthew is lucky."

I've always thought that we're lucky to have Vivi in the family. Matthew became more engaged after almost ten years of being estranged from us. When we were traveling to Big Bend National Park, Matthew told me, "Vivi said we can't choose our parents and siblings. They're the people who know us from the day we're born. If we don't care about them first, who should we care about? Vivi said I should visit you guys more often, and she would get to know you guys better."

I finally felt that I had my children bonded together after Matthew came back from China. He opened up to me and talked to me once or twice a week. After our trip to Disneyland, I showed him my favorite picture, which was four legs and four hands trying to reach together above the hotel bed and included part of Vivi's head because she was the shortest.

Matthew pointed to Vivi's leg and hand. "That should have been Jerry."

He told me, "Grandma was the only mother Jerry and I knew. Jerry couldn't accept the fact that Erin tried to replace Grandma. Jerry also didn't like the fact that Erin, who you had only known for a few months, took your attention away from us."

Those conversations led me to realize that I owed Jerry and Matthew a better childhood. If I could do it all over again, I would not let my mother have her way in keeping them away from me. I might not have remarried so soon. That had nothing to do with Erin. It was just not the right time for the boys, but I didn't know better. I only thought that the boys needed a mother, never considered that my mother had been the mother for them. Instead, I gained two sons and lost two. I have no words to describe the regrets that I had to make peace with myself. I let them down from the day their mother died to the days they died.

My resentments against my mother came at the expense of my boys' childhood. My mother didn't have an easy life. She raised three children literally all by herself. I was like my absent father to Jerry and Mathew, who were not as lucky as I was. At least I had my mother, a strong, healthy woman, who didn't say "I love you" but showed it in her own harsh mannerisms. Looking back, my mother's anger toward me could have been her projection toward my father, who died two years after retirement in his early sixties when the boys were three and four. The two years my father was home full-time, he was fragile and from time to time he would have Berenice keep the two boys for a while so he could have some quiet time at home. My mother spent daytime at Berenice's and went home to prepare supper for my father. For those two years, she worked like a slave to serve my father and me in terms of taking care of the two boys. My mother became a single mother again after my father died.

When I got remarried, I basically took the boys away from her. No wonder she was mad! But all these years, everyone, including me, thought it was my mother who broke my family apart. Only Jerry denounced how I had separated them from my mother, who didn't welcome Erin and created the rifts between Matthew and me and the rest of the family. I didn't recognize all of this until years after Matthew married Vivi, who influenced my son to be close to me.

I don't know what caused Matthew's depression. He inherited more of his mother's traits—being artistic, sensitive, and sometimes moody, quiet, and sweet to everyone. He attached to Jerry, who acted like a big brother all the way into adulthood. Jerry would tell Matthew what to do, and Matthew just did it to please Jerry. Matthew would follow Jerry everywhere, from college to work and just would not let Jerry out of his sight. I had not seen them fight even in the years when Jerry was unhappy with Erin. Matthew had his way of softening Jerry, while at the same time making peace with Erin. I had no idea how he felt or what he thought about all the chaos while growing up.

I am sad that my son closed himself off from Vivi, who I am so fond of and have come to love for who she is, a kind-hearted, intelligent, reserved, childlike, and quiet young woman. Listening most of the time, she stands her ground firmly and lets me know it. The daughter that I didn't have.

I am just being too much of a coward to tell Vivi all of my regrets and how I feel for her. All these years, she has worked hard and never asked for financial assistance. Every once in a while she calls, and from her voice, I know she is suffering. When she comes for holidays, I can see the loneliness in her eyes. Berenice has said to me many times in different words, "I don't know how long Vivi can hold up like this. She acts cheerful. She hasn't mentioned Matthew, but she doesn't visit the cemetery when she's here. Most of the time, Alan finds her in the white pine grove conversing with the air."

The Alaska trip was pleasant and peaceful. Vivi was very organized. The lodging, eating, outings—everything turned out so smoothly, without a worry, as if Vivi had a magic wand.

I was in the navy stationed in the Pacific during the Korean War. When the water was rough, I got seasick. I was a bit surprised that Vivi acclimated to the sea so naturally and didn't get motion sickness when we were out on a boat with fifteen other tourists for a wildlife cruise outside of Seward.

We boarded the boat with maybe five other families, a few women who were over fifty, and five or six kids from ages four to fifteen. The rest of them were in their thirties or forties. After we saw the glaciers, the wind picked up, and the swells were getting higher and higher. The boat bumped around like a giant globe tossed up and down between the water and air. Most of the tourists stayed put in their seats. Two boys around five to seven years old were still running up and down the stairs, trying to stay on the open deck to spot whales. But their adults weren't doing so well with the waves and couldn't really move. They yelled at the two boys. While the boys plodded back to the seats, the little one swung in between the steps and was about to lose his grip on the railing. The boy's mother was petrified in place. Vivi caught the boy just in time and, bending over, held his hand and balanced him back to his mother. After the boys were safe, someone else was throwing up. Vivi got a hot drink from the staff and gave it to the person. Then someone else needed a hot drink as well. For about fifty minutes, Vivi busied herself back and forth in the cabin handing out drinks and bags, and rescuing children back to their parents. She was the only tourist who wasn't affected by the wailing sea. When the water calmed down and people could move around, they all clapped to thank Vivi, and the staff joined them.

When we debarked, the two boys' parents invited us to dinner. Vivi politely declined.

At dinner I asked Vivi, "You didn't feel sick at all on that tiny boat?"

Vivi smiled. "No, I was fine."

"I was on a big warship in the Pacific, and from time to time I got seasick. How did you do it?"

"I'm a fish." She giggled. "I don't know. I guess I'm used to the sea. I started traveling between Hong Kong and Macau on the South China Sea at age six, four to six times a year. At first, we'd go on a big passenger ship like today's Carnival cruise ships, with several hundred passengers and would travel overnight. Sometimes the night water would throw passengers up and down, left and right. Many people got sick. I just stayed on the outside railing to watch the dark sea as far as I could to look for lights. Later, we traveled by Hydrofoil and Aerofoil boats that cut the travel time down to a bit over an hour. These boats are much smaller, and sometimes I could see the waves pouring over the main hull. For all I know, I can handle waves regardless of their impetus."

The few days we traveled together I got to know Vivi a bit deeper. She has a heart with simple and innocent notions about others. She would give a helping hand whenever it was needed. She treats people with respect, and yet keeps a distance, like a kid that doesn't interact with strange adults. Vivi is particularly friendly with little children. She always lowers herself to the eye level of the child in front of her. She laughs and shows satisfaction at the smell of steaming coffee and tasty food. Yet, she seems constantly preoccupied and searching for something, which I could see in her dazed eyes with a hint of melancholia.

In the evening after dinner, I motioned to Dad's journal. Kurt and Timothy told me that Dad had a habit of writing a diary. They asked, "Is this the only one you found?"

"Yes."

"I don't know where the others are. I'll check the storage to see if he kept them there," Timothy said.

"Have you ever read any of Dad's diaries?"

"No," Kurt and Timothy responded at the same time. "Dad locked them. I remember when Mom asked him what he was writing, he just said 'silly stuff.' I don't think Mom ever read them either." Kurt looked at the journal and then at Timothy, who shrugged without a word.

"I read some of it. Do you want to keep it?" I asked.

"What is it about?" Timothy lifted the journal.

"Dad and me, the trip to Alaska, your grandma, Jerry and Matthew."

Kurt stood up. "I'm not interested in reading it. I have had it out with Dad over his sentiments about my two older brothers, and now they're all dead. You can have it." I saw and heard the resentment from Kurt.

Kurt was always direct, logical, and practical. I know Kurt would never shy away if he wanted or didn't want something. He would openly praise you if he admired you.

Matthew used to say that Kurt was like Jerry but didn't have the same heart regarding others. When Matthew died, I offered the land to Kurt and Timothy.

Kurt said, "I don't want to have anything to do with the land. Don't count me in."

Back then, I should have sensed Kurt's resentment. I thought only the elder two brothers had been affected by the war between Grandma Dori and Dad. Kurt's reactions to the land after Matthew's death signified his discontent, but I didn't discern it at the time.

Kurt and Timothy also were the casualties of the obstinate expressions of love from their grandmother and father. I didn't know Jerry, but from others I gathered that in addition to tidiness, Jerry and Kurt had another characteristic in common. Kurt wanted to protect his mother, who was not welcome in the family, who Grandma had ignored and punished by disowning Dad. Worst of all, was the split among the four brothers. Grandma was polite to Kurt and Timothy but was never close to them like she was with Jerry and Matthew, never exhibited any endearment to them. The only times they could be at her house was with Jerry, who brought them there.

Jerry would say to Grandma, "Kurt and Timothy are my brothers. They're not doing anything wrong. Don't treat them like strangers."

Stranger was the exact word to describe the relationship between Grandma and Kurt and Timothy. They were afraid of Grandma, a stranger who had authority over their older brothers and emotionally crushed their parents, who would never live up to Grandma's idea of being good parents no matter what they did.

As a young child, Kurt didn't understand the tug-of-war among the adults. His sense told him that Grandma didn't want any members of the family except Jerry and Matthew. Yet, strangely enough, Jerry and Matthew had consistently brought them to Grandma, the woman who didn't smile at them, gave them stern looks, and told them what not to do. Kurt estimated that he'd had fewer than twenty exchanges with Grandma in his entire life. In Kurt's mind, Grandma was mean-spirited to Dad and Mom. If it weren't for Jerry and Matthew, Kurt wouldn't have wanted to see that sour old woman at all.

The whole world of Grandma, Jerry, and Matthew fell apart when Grandma and Jerry died within thirteen months of each other. Matthew disappeared. From time to time, eleven-year-old Kurt could hear Dad asking Berenice or Alan about Matthew. Kurt missed both of his older brothers. Jerry had always been there to lift him up when someone at school was bullying him. Matthew would always draw cartoons to smash the bully on flat paper. Whenever Kurt and Timothy wanted ice cream treats and the older brothers were home from college, Jerry would drive all three of them to the ice cream parlor and play putt-putt at the miniature golf garden. A lot of the time Jerry just said, "Let's take a ride," and they'd be gone in no time. Those were the happy days for Kurt: being protected by his brothers, hearing all sorts of stories, learning new tricks, enjoying various sweets, and being wrapped up in their arms without Grandma watching.

In Kurt's life, major events seemed to be associated with the number ten.

When he was ten, Grandma died. He didn't feel sad about her death but felt sad that his two older brothers would still stay away from home. Whenever they were in town, they would stay at Berenice's. Sometimes if he looked hard through the kitchen window, he might see them on Berenice's ramp going in and out of the garage, the sailor's cove.

Ten years after Jerry died, Matthew showed up again with me, his new wife. We would go to Texas for holidays and summer breaks. We took trips together to Big Bend National Park, the Grand Canyon, Disneyland, Arches National Park, Niagara Falls, and ended up at Berenice's house numerous times, all six of the family members. One time, all three brothers and I stayed at Berenice's house while Dad and Mom stayed at Mom's father's house.

Kurt always wondered how it felt to stay at the sailor's cove. The first night at the garage, Timothy just laid out all his stuff on the floor and the long sofa, such that there wouldn't be any space for Kurt. Kurt asked Timothy to clean up and make it tidy just as Matthew was walking in from the house. Timothy looked at Kurt. "Bro, relax. We're on vacation. Tomorrow morning all this stuff will be back in my backpack, no rush..."

Kurt just wouldn't let go. "No, I can't stand this. Move this stuff and leave me some empty space."

Matthew laughed. "Kurt sounds like Jerry." Both Kurt and Timothy looked up. This was the first time they'd ever heard Matthew mention Jerry.

"Jerry was a bit fanatical about tidiness." Matthew started sorting out things on the sofa.

Timothy beamed. "So is Kurt. He sometimes drives me nuts." The two brothers smiled at each other and started to pile up items neatly in their own categories.

Kurt said thank you and helped them put the things in order.

After the space was cleared, Matthew opened the huge refrigerator and took out bottles of craft beer. Each of them took one and looked outside at the darkening sky.

"Jerry and I spent many nights here. Sometimes he would be bitching about me being laid-back, being unorganized, being soft, or being whatever he didn't like."

"Sounds like Kurt to me," Timothy said.

"Are we really like that—Jerry and I, you and Timothy?" Kurt asked.

"It looks like it. Your ways of handling certain things are exactly like Jerry, who would fix it right away, no negotiations."

Timothy laughed. "I feel better. I'm not the only one to be tortured." Timothy raised his bottle and clinked it with Matthew's.

Kurt suspiciously glanced at his brothers. "What else?"

"Jerry wouldn't let anyone hurt either of you guys or me. Protecting us was his mission. He always looked out for me before you were born. After you came along, he did the same thing for both of you. Remember those bullies at school? Jerry scared them all. He would pick up a football and throw the ball right in front of their feet, and pointing at the ball, would shout, 'Don't you ever come near my brothers again.'"

Jerry, big-boned, six foot three, was a well-known football player in school. While in high school, when Matthew was playing too, Jerry was the star and was always in the starting line-up. It was intimidating when Jerry stood in front of younger kids.

141

"I remember," Kurt said. "I miss him."

The three brothers stared at the sky searching for a star that looked like Jerry. The emptiness of his absence hung around the garage. Talking about Jerry brought back the few memories the two younger brothers had of him while growing up. They experienced the loss no less than the adults who were suffering too. The younger two boys had the same fate as the older two brothers, having only each other for comfort, in a parallel that apparently no one else seemed to notice except Matthew, who could not make himself be strong without Jerry, let alone comfort Kurt and Timothy. He decided to walk away, which was similar to Dad's denial. Like father, like son.

During the ten years after Matthew returned to the family, Kurt learned more about Matthew, who still drew and quickly sketched with incredible imagination. Some of his illustrations showed up in the sweaters I knitted for him. Matthew drew the picture on graph paper, and I selected the colors and the size of yarn: obscure aqua question marks stretched across deep pink diamonds. A crimson Indian arrowhead became inverted in an amber field. The starship *Enterprise* with 3D dots in Chinese red flew horizontally starting with charcoal gray into lines of royal blue and sky blue. An exaggerated coffee-brown half upside down anchor hung diagonally in sky blue with ashen white. Colors and shapes abstractedly materialized on other sweaters in gray-blue, pale pink, magenta, bone, cream, pine green, ocean blue, mackerel belly silvery white—I used my knitting needles, precision, and my engineering mind to transfer Matthew's vision onto objects.

One particular sweater deeply impressed Kurt. An ET matchstick figure in cream with big black dot eyes stood in celadon green with the left palm held at shoulder level, the forklike thumb and middle finger forming an irregular square as if it were performing magic. Immediately to the left, barely an inch lower, a firework shooting in red, blue, pink, purple, bright yellow, silver, and gold, spun out in fine symmetrical lines as if it were blossoming right at the moment you looked at it.

"How did you do that?" Kurt asked me when he first saw the sweater on Matthew.

"I ask myself the same question. Every time I finish a sweater, I ask myself, how did I do it? It would seem as if the sweater had been knitted by somebody else. I can't explain to myself how I transform the pattern and colors via the needles. I think the invention of knitting was genius. In a clean knitting, I can just pull apart a knitted object into one single long strand."

"But there are so many colors and the end of that line with a three-dimensional sparkle of fireworks, it's amazing to look at." Kurt touched the sparkling 3D dots.

"The dots are stitches made with a knitting technique to swirl them in a circle. Many knitters can do that. I can carry ten skeins at once, which is rather a tedious task that needs patience and concentration because it's easy to get confused with the colors, and then you can see the mistakes after the shape is formed. Then you need to undo the rows to correct the wrong stitches, sometimes even just one wrong stitch. By the way, it's not a firework."

"What is it?"

I looked at Matthew, who smiled. "Do you see the tiny gold dot just slightly below where the thumb and middle finger are almost touching and about to extend outward? That dot sprouted out various seeds in brilliant colors. Each fine line of color represents the continuing seedlings, and the three-dimensional sparkle is the fruit."

"Wow, I couldn't imagine a seed could be this beautiful on a sweater." Kurt expressed his astonishment.

Matthew saw and communicated with his brothers more often. He would call Kurt and Timothy, asking them to go up north fishing at the cabin. The four of us would set up a couple of tents and go swimming and fishing in the lake. While I was at the cabin preparing food, the three brothers would be drinking craft beer and shooting the breeze, dangling their feet from the pier, an extension of a walkway from the cabin to the lake, which had been built by their grandfather Walter. Kurt discovered that Matthew had a very pessimistic view of the environment. Matthew would cite studies about deforestation and the destruction of other habitats. He mentioned that in Indonesia, in the Amazon, and in Australia, they were cutting down the forests as if they were in a race to shave people's hair. In the urban US, old trees were also coming down at an increasing rate for buildings and other human uses.

"Our green spaces are getting smaller and smaller everywhere, and in record time." Matthew turned his head and looked around as if the immediate landscape were about to disappear with the snap of a finger.

Kurt could see the gloomy picture of the natural world in Matthew's eyes, which were consumed with desperation and fury.

The four of us would go to different microbreweries, which was on the to-do list whenever the brothers traveled together. For Matthew, the tasting would give him some sense of the organic growers' intentions. He was delighted to see that more and more of the new breweries were using domestic, organically-grown hops. Within a five-hundred-mile radius there wasn't enough supply for the local breweries because most hops were grown in Colorado, where mature hop farms provided close to seventy percent of all domestic hops. In the Midwest, only certain local varieties would grow satisfactorily, but there weren't enough established farms to meet the demand. Matthew's farm still had a long way to go before producing a successful harvest, which also bothered him. The joy of working at the farm and the worries of it not producing enough were constantly battling in Matthew's mind. Sometimes he would vocalize it in a matter-of-fact manner that didn't really convey his dim outlook. Kurt saw all of that while spending time with his brother.

For Timothy, Matthew was his idol. He admired Matthew for his humor about the world and his love of nature. Matthew would say, "We have only one earth and one lifetime. We can't just take; we need to put back with respect and nourishment."

Timothy was only nine years old when they planted the vegetable garden in the backyard, where Jerry had so meticulously divided the parcel into green leaves, roots, legumes, and flowers. He also designated who was responsible for the planting and harvesting.

It was then he heard, "Only one earth and one lifetime," which was so stimulating to Timothy, who wished that he could be as articulate as Matthew. On top of that, Matthew's quick sketches gave such pleasure and laughter. Timothy remembered the bullies, who under Matthew's pen, looked like elongated tumbleweeds without any core, kicked by glochids into the air like shooting rockets screaming, "Ouch!"

As a young child, Timothy was timid and clumsy and didn't have confidence in anything that involved himself. He just followed whatever Kurt did and looked up to Jerry and Matthew. Jerry was the bigger version of Kurt, who was so unyielding and staid, everything needed to be done perfectly with no mistakes allowed. Matthew was more relaxed and when things didn't turn out as expected, he would make comics out of disastrous situations. The creative Matthew had provided entertainment and comfort when Timothy was younger, which had helped him to build up his confidence to work through conflicts and be less tense with others, even though he would still try to please everyone, like Matthew did.

Sitting in Dad's house in Texas all these years later, I eyed Dad's journal and resorted to Timothy. "Kurt doesn't want it. You?"

"I don't care. I'll find more of them. One more or one less won't make any difference." Timothy stood up to grab the orange juice.

"In that case, I'll take this journal with me. Any objection?"

"Be my guest," Kurt said, and Timothy nodded.

GROUP COUNSELING

NINE MONTHS AFTER MATTHEW's death, on one of those sleepless nights, I called the twenty-four-hour suicide hotline. I was wailing over the phone, asking questions that no one could answer. The hotline referred me to a counselor. In the following weeks, I saw a volunteer counselor at a church on Saturdays at four o'clock. After a year of counseling, I decided to move to the San Francisco Bay Area, where Matthew had wanted to live among the gigantic redwood trees. I wanted to live there too, close to the Pacific Ocean, where I could see home as a mirage of skyscrapers among greenery in the misty air with a silky cotton-candy sky.

My counselor gave me a contact that he said would be helpful if I wanted to continue counseling after I moved.

After I settled in Berkeley, I called the contact, and she met me one-on-one and told me that group counseling would be helpful for me. I met my group of five other people on a Thursday evening: Doug lost his son; Annie and Liz lost their younger sisters; Jessie lost her father; and Nora lost her fiancé. All of their loved ones had battled one form of depression or another and had committed suicide. With this group, we seemed to have known each other for years. We cried, laughed with tears, had sudden mood swings, and allowed each other to display our state of mind at the moment without any judgment or need for explanation.

Brandon

Doug's son, Brandon, had been obese since elementary school. Throughout the years, Brandon and his family had tried numerous methods to help him lose weight without success. Peers made fun of him into adulthood. At age twenty-five, he was humongous. Doctors had intervened, but he couldn't keep his weight down. Brandon constantly felt desperate about his appearance and increasingly found that nothing could change the way he looked. Gradually, he abandoned himself altogether. He stopped grooming, locked himself in his room for days. Doug could not get Brandon out of his room. The family left food at the door and took the empty dishes away from the door.

One day, Brandon came out of his room clean-shaven and wearing clean clothes. He took a duffel bag with him and drove away. Ten days later, Doug was in the coroner's office of Washoe County, Nevada. Brandon had killed himself in a Reno hotel room. He bought a gun and two days later he put a bullet into his head. He left a note for Doug:

Dad,

Good bye. I don't see that anything good can come out of me. I am just a waste of a human being. I have never been good at anything. In school, no one liked me. I have no friends. They have called me fatty my entire life. If you don't call me Brandon, I almost forget that I have a name.

I am tired of being so heavy, so slow, and so ugly all at once.

Take care,

Brandon

Doug finished reading the note and carefully folded it on top of his right thigh; he leveled the paper with his right palm, traced the folding lines a flip at a time until a smooth square steadily rested on the small flat area on top of his knee. I watched while he lowered his face to focus on folding the paper. His white mustache was shivering as if he wanted to say something, but he did not utter a word. My tears streamed down, and I thought of Dad.

Emily

Annie's younger sister, Emily, a shy individual, had suffered from depression since age thirteen. She didn't think she could be as good as her sister Annie, who was five years older and who had brought honor to their parents by winning competitions playing the violin since fifth grade. Emily had won nothing. She was rather clumsy at almost every single musical instrument that their mother had tried to get her hands on. Annie was also an overachiever academically. From elementary school onwards, she had been top of the class with high scores in most subjects. On the contrary, Emily was just slightly above average. The subject that she constantly battled with was math. Yes, math, which was so easy for Annie that she took calculus for fun at UC Berkeley while Emily only got a B throughout her school years and had worked extra hard to maintain that level.

Emily wanted to prove that she could be as bright as Annie by attending the same university. When she got the notice that UC Berkeley had declined to offer her admission, she looked around at the family. Her father was a well-known heart surgeon, her mother a sensational piano performer, and Annie a future successful environmental lawyer. Emily felt that she was a useless extra, dragging down the family name and their Korean heritage. She jumped off a cliff into the Pacific Ocean, no note.

Annie looked down, focusing on her palms on her lap. "I didn't pay enough attention to Emily. I should have known that she was asking for help when she said, 'What if I can't get into UC Berkeley?' I just thought to cheer her up and assure her by saying, 'Sure you'll get in. You have a 3.8 GPA. That's above most other applicants.' Little did I know..." Tears dropped to her palms while her head was still down.

Karin

Liz's younger sister, Karin, an energetic twenty-year-old stationed in Germany with her husband on a US military base, gave birth to a girl. Seven months later she hanged herself in the bathtub. The doctor said she might have had postpartum depression that somehow no one seemed to notice. For Liz, that was a lie. She couldn't believe that her brother-in-law Rich hadn't seen Karin's symptoms.

Both Liz and Karin were military wives, as they called themselves. They got married right after high school, which I thought was a backward way to live, like it was the late 1940s and 1950s. They were similar to Rachel, Matthew's mother, marrying at a young age. Military wives followed their husbands to whatever base they were assigned. Liz was based in Germany two years before and thought that that base was one of the most isolated bases she had ever been on. She didn't find close friends among the other wives. Liz thought, in exaggeration, that the husbands were just out there performing maintenance, bullshitting, and drinking.

Karin moved with Rich three weeks after they signed the marriage certificate. They didn't have a wedding due to his need to report to the base. Before marrying, she had been a paralegal assistant at a law firm for just about a year when she met Rich through Liz's husband, Karin's brother-in-law.

Liz had warned Karin that military life is very harsh. Having been married for four years herself, Liz had struggled with moving from one place to another so frequently, even though sometimes the moves were only across town. Karin would not have any of it. She was deeply in love with Rich and didn't think she would have the same issues as Liz. In fact, Karin fantasized about living in new towns, new cities, and new countries. "What a great way to explore the world under the American flag," she used to say.

After the birth of her daughter, Karin had expressed to Liz that she was overwhelmed by taking care of an infant without enough sleep and without Rich there to give her a hand. Liz reached out to Rich, who just thought Karin would get used to motherhood; she would be fine. Rich continued to be away from home for twelve to fourteen hours every day, and eventually home become only a place to sleep. He didn't want to face the baby and Karin's irate moods when the child was crying. Rich thought that Karin should have a mothering instinct, which he believed all women should have, like his own mother taking care of him and his brother for all those years without difficulty in different US military bases around the globe. There was no reason that Karin could not adjust to being a mom. After all, she was the one who'd insisted on having a child right away after they got married.

Karin left a note assigning full custody and asking Liz to be the guardian of her daughter, not Rich.

"Had Rachel been in the same obscurity as Karin?" I wondered, my thoughts flashing back to the basement when Rachel put her head into a noose. She didn't seem to be thinking of Matthew and Jerry. But Karin did think of her child and selected Liz over Rich to be responsible for her daughter's upbringing and well-being.

What was in both of these women's minds when they thought death was the only solution to end their suffering? Would it be possible that ending one's own life was a rational choice? I had wanted to not wake up, just sleep into death. I could not bring myself to end my misery. What is the difference in this thinking process? While listening to Karin's story, I noticed my mind floating from being analytical to clinical with a perplexing sense of being far removed.

Liz was angry while telling about Karin's short life. She wept, saying, "Rich killed her. He didn't even fight for his daughter. He just wanted to get away with murder."

Ronald

Jessie's father, Ronald, wrote a lengthy note before he drowned himself in Lake Shasta. Jessie gave a copy of the note to each of us.

Dear All,

Goodbye. I hope you take this note to heart. I want you to know that I am not out of my mind. Life has treated me fairly. I have two grown daughters, who have been the joy of my life. I have a loving wife, who has been my best friend for the past thirty years, and I do not see how I could have had a better life without her. Yet, she is my biggest concern with her Alzheimer's. I believe that Ellen and Jessie will take care of their mother. I am thankful to have their support, and knowing that my departure won't change the care that my wife will receive, I am ready to go.

Fifty-five years is a long time. Some of you may know that my father died at fifty-one and my grandfather died at forty-eight. They both ended their lives, which is what I am about to do. You may wonder why am I ending my own life? Don't. Life is not as glamorous as others portray. Life is pure suffering. Yes, there are joys. But in the span of these fifty-five years, suffering has drained the life out of me.

During the Vietnam War, I saw it all. The blood, the body parts, the sounds of weapons, the smell of explosives, the scattered minds of blind shooting, the unimaginable killing of other human beings has consumed my brain bit by bit in my daily routines, my dreams, and my still moments of being. I don't want to endure it any longer.

If it was not for Ellen and Jessie, I would have gone long ago. To fulfill my duty as a father, I have been struggling daily to live for another day. They both are beautiful and bright and have children of their own, so now I can put down the burden of living. Please don't mistake me, the burden of living is not applied to everyone, it only applies to me, or to my father and grandfather. It's not a coincidence that three generations of males have had the same thoughts about life. My father said his father was tired of living, my father showed me he was tired of living, and I am telling you that I am extremely tired of living. There is nothing for me to continue this life.

If staying alive is a human instinct, then the males in my family for three generations have not had it. I have found it very difficult to face anyone after I killed numerous strangers in Vietnam. All I have been seeing is the blood that keeps dripping from my body, but it never dries out. How could that be possible? To my own surprise, it is other people's blood dripping through my body, not my own. Does this sound crazy to you? If yes, congratulations, you still have hope. For me, that is my reality, that is what happened in my daily life in Vietnam and has never gone away.

Can you imagine the children, lovely and cute children, walking along the vast rice fields with their mothers, and suddenly, American soldiers with weapons emerged and surrounded them? They were scared like little animals; the mothers looked for their children and all of the mothers hugged their children one way or another, but nowhere could they run. I could see the horror in the mothers' eyes and tried to understand why they were so afraid of us. We had not fired a single shot, and we would not harm them. As far as I knew, they were not armed. In the blink of an eye, landmines exploded with flying arms and legs bloodying the surroundings. By the time I realized what had just happened, I saw the mothers' eyes again—they knew, wherever American soldiers appeared, landmines would explode. Their wish was to not see or encounter any American soldiers, just to be in the rice fields, open and immense, and that the American soldiers would stay away from them while they worked in the fields and that they would be home safely by the evening. Little did they know. The Americans would not leave them alone. When they saw American soldiers, their death sentence was set, and they would become the lambs for sacrifice by their fellow countrymen.

Then there was the jungle. Beautiful greenery one minute suddenly turned into a sea of red splashing all over the leaves and branches. I had the same sense as the mothers in the rice field every time I entered a forest. Any moment now, I could be killed or I could kill others to survive. Any sounds would startle, would trigger shooting without targets, would echo groaning, and would cause death, which would be a better ending. But no, many of the enemies and we would be left haunted for days, weeks, months, years, for the rest of our lives.

Being haunted by the color red is not in my vocabulary but in my mind's eye. The veterans' psychologists have not helped in this area, not at all. They may think they do, but in my reality, they may understand, may imagine, may label me with post-traumatic stress disorder, but they could never feel that the color red is a disguised form of evil, could never know that the pretty color could manifest into a watercolor painting in different shades of red slipping through with thin pigments that gradually solidify into a block of bloody red that heavily invades my vision and presses its weight onto me.

I am elated that soon the color red will not be able to find me. This body will no longer experience the dreams, the sounds, the smells, and the scenes of a war zone.

Jessie was full of tears whenever she revealed these things about her father. She didn't know her father had endured this torture for all those years. She knew that her father didn't have many words. While she was growing up, her father would always be there for everything her mother had arranged and said needed to be done. He didn't miss any events like birthdays, piano performances, sport competitions, graduations, holiday gatherings, and the arrival of grandchildren.

"My father was gentle to all of us, helped my mother with chores, and took care of any repairs. I never heard him yelling or cursing. He taught us to be kind and listened to our complaints, but my mother would resolve our problems. I had seen the rare smiles on his sad face. He was often deep in thought."

Jessie looked around at us, "I have always wondered why he looked so sad even when he was smiling. He and my mother never mentioned Vietnam. My sister and I didn't know he was involved in the early part of the war in the sixties."

Patrick

Nora was a slender, five-foot-ten redhead. Her dark brown eyes and beautiful smile could get anyone's attention. She spoke calmly with a deep, seductive voice.

Nora said, "Patrick was a musician and owned a record store. He played in a band and had gigs almost every night around the Bay Area from June to October. I went with him to his gigs. Other times, we just traveled to different places around the world. Last January we were in Nice, and he ran into an old friend. Fitzgerald was his name, and he had taken Patrick on as his apprentice, performing all over Europe for fifteen years.

"After Patrick came back from Nice, whenever there was a new jazz album or new songs wondering about life, he would talk about going back to seasonally tour Europe with Fitzgerald. I asked him what about the store, and he said he could hire someone to manage it.

"Patrick got more and more antsy. He would stay late at the store and would take drugs or smoke dope in the parking lot.

"I couldn't figure out what was bothering him. He was gradually distancing himself from me. He wouldn't tell me when his next gig would be, where he would be. He just said, 'I'll call you.' He got mad when I went to the store without calling first. After a few times, I stopped going to the store because he wasn't there. He did call and meet me occasionally.

"Early one morning, a garbage truck driver found Patrick, strangled with a cord by the fence in the back of the parking lot. Cause of death: asphyxia and hanging, ruled suicide."

Nora looked a bit disappointed and a bit bitter. "We'd been together for three years. I can't believe the way he took off, as if I didn't exist."

Nora upheld herself well among all of us. She cried but with a positive attitude. She kept saying, "I'll be alright."

One Tuesday evening she called and asked if I could spend the weekend with her while her children were with their father. I went Friday after work to her house, which was near the top of a steep dead-end street in Tiburon.

Out on the deck, Nora put some salmon on the grill and poured us both a glass of white wine. "I feel that you and I have more in common than the rest of the group. You lost your husband, I lost my fiancé, and they both died in their early forties." She looked at me as she set the wine bottle down.

I nodded without saying a word. Nora clearly wanted to talk but I wasn't ready to talk about Matthew in detail. After all, we had just met seven times in the group with the counselor to guide us.

Nora sat down, picked up her wine glass, glanced at the sunset, and without any introduction or small talk, she said, "Patrick's parents were drug addicts and had been in and out of rehab and jail. Patrick grew up in one foster home after another for twelve years, in that he only had four years of memorable time from age eight to twelve with the Holley family.

The Holleys had taught him that having an education was the key for him to make a life of his own and become financially independent. He focused on that one single goal and got good grades throughout his school years to survive his brutal childhood. He applied for college and was accepted to San Francisco State. Before college started, he was awarded some grants for a trip to Europe, for graduating from high school. When he met Fitzgerald in Paris, Patrick had such a kindred feeling toward Fitz that he boldly asked if he could tag along.

"Patrick learned the routes in Europe and enjoyed traveling from one bar or restaurant to another. Fitzgerald was a good teacher and had no reservations about introducing Patrick to his connections. Carrying trumpets, saxophones, and guitars from one train station to another during the wee hours, after fifteen years performing side by side with Fitzgerald, at age thirty-three, Patrick just wanted to go home to settle down. But Fitzgerald liked the lifestyle of a vagabond. So, they went their separate ways.

"Ten years later, they met again when Patrick and I went to Nice together. One morning when we'd grabbed our coffees at a little shop near the flower market, we were looking out across the small courtyard and saw this guy sauntering along with a guitar hanging from his shoulder and a saxophone case in one hand. Fitz is tall, late fifties, dark eyes and curly hair. He was surprised to see Patrick in this familiar courtyard. Every January they would stay in Nice for a month or two to avoid the colder parts of Europe and play in local bars and restaurants.

"That evening, Patrick went to see Fitz and left me on my own." Nora took a bite of grilled salmon and looked out at the bay.

She continued, "In the fifteen years traveling and living together, Fitz had become a big brother to Patrick. He showed him the ropes of taking care of himself, how to be streetwise and still kindhearted to others. Patrick had great compassion for people living on the street. Patrick would often give all the cash he had to them, or would buy them meals by asking what they wanted to eat. Fitz was struck by Patrick's sensitivity and vulnerability. After Patrick would give food to a homeless person, Fitz sometimes heard him mutter, 'I could end up like that.' The insecurity had been so deeply ingrained in Patrick that he didn't realize that sometimes he acted as if he had lost everything by abandoning his own belongings, walking away from a relationship, or disappearing for a while in random small towns in Europe. At first, Fitz would frantically look for him. But after a few similar incidents, Fitz just stayed put to wait for his return. Whenever Patrick came back, he looked deflated. He'd hunch his back and avoid eye contact. Occasionally, he would look up to Fitz, searching for guidance.

"When Patrick announced that he was done with Europe, Fitz thought that going back to the States might be a good thing, to hold down Patrick's fears of insecurity."

"How do you know all this?" I asked.

"Fitz told me." Nora sipped her wine. "Patrick left everything to Fitz. He came back and gave me this." Nora held up a beautiful white platinum ring with a rectangular ruby in the center with two proportional diamonds inlaid on each side.

I marveled at the colors of the ruby, and at the same time, I was puzzled.

"Patrick bought this in Zurich when they were touring. He told Fitz that he would give this ring to the woman he married. Fitz said, 'All these years, you're the only woman Patrick referred to as his fiancée. I think you should have this ring.'

"Fitz also thought that Patrick going to Nice to find him was a sign of his troubled mind."

"What was the meeting about?" I asked.

Nora sat up straight to stretch her upper body, attempted to talk but held back before the first word was finished. I could see that she was trying to organize her thoughts and search for the appropriate words. Nora took a deep breath. She stood up and sat down again.

"Patrick told Fitz about the record store in Berkeley that he had started through some of Fitz's connections in LA and how, soon afterward, the store had the exclusive rights in Northern California to sell the newly released albums of certain pop stars and rising artists. Money just flooded in. But Fitz sensed that Patrick had other important things to say. Instead of waiting for Patrick to get to the point, he looked straight into Patrick's eyes and asked, 'Why are you here exactly?'

"'I'm thinking of coming back to travel with you if you are open to it. Or you could come home with me. We can work together and get this music business going. You're like a brother to me. The brother I never had.'

"'What are you afraid of? You've put down roots. You have a good income and a nice-looking fiancée.'

"'I don't know. I feel restless. I don't feel as comfortable with my current life as when I was traveling and seeing the world with you.'

"In hindsight, their conversation did bring to mind some of the long-gone episodes that Fitz had seen in Patrick when he would disappear and come back again. But on this visit, Fitz thought Patrick was in a temporary sentimental mood. He didn't think that Patrick was in any kind of danger."

Nora looked up at the bright stars. She turned her head in my direction and murmured, "I didn't know the Patrick that Fitz described. I thought we were happy together. He was always smiling and liked my kids. He certainly knew how to have fun. We had fun either just the two of us or with my two kids. We even talked about having our own child once we were married. I thought that I could read people, but I didn't see the gloomy and insecure Patrick."

MIXED EMOTIONS

OUR GROUP WENT ON to meet once a month on our own after eight sessions with the counselor. We took turns hosting at each of our homes, some of us for as long as eight years. We became family. Besides our monthly group meetings, some of us exchanged emails, phone calls, and last-minute visits for emotional support. Nora was the most outspoken of all of us. She would vent her frustration and distress at any time. Doug and I were the quietest; we listened most of the time. Annie and Liz were almost the same age and identified with each other. Because of their similar experiences, they often acknowledged similar feelings. Jessie sat there passively, yet would insightfully point out the unspoken feelings of abandonment.

I would never have thought that Matthew, who loved and worshiped me, would abandon me.

I would ask myself, "Is it real that Matthew is gone? Is Matthew real? Is it real that I met Matthew in 1984 on Hainan Island?" I tested this reality again and again. I reread letters, notes, and diaries, and looked at the few photos of us. Cognitively I knew that all of this was true and was part of my history. But the reminiscence of it, the record of it, the talking about it, the feeling of Matthew's existence was so recent that the past seemed not there. I began to have doubts about Matthew's love for me.

"Matthew would not have abandoned me if he truly loved me," I said to the group one Thursday night. "In the past five years I've had two dreams of Matthew that I remember clearly."

I glanced around. "We were on a tour bus to somewhere. We stopped at an open market, like a bazaar. I saw food vendors and arts and crafts in small stalls. I ordered noodles from one of the vendors. The noodles were black. I saw the steam but couldn't smell or tell the taste of them. When we were almost finished eating, the tour bus driver called us to get back on the bus. I was behind Matthew to get on the bus. Before I could put my hand on the handrail, the door shut in front of my face. The bus took off, leaving me standing there.

"In the other dream, we were in a huge shopping mall with spiral ramps in the center. There were a lot of people and all of us were on the spiral ramps to walk up. At first, Matthew and I were next to each other. As we ascended, Matthew was a few steps ahead of me. I tried to catch up but the distance between us widened. I started to feel I might lose sight of him because of all the people around us. I called Matthew, but he didn't seem to hear and continued to walk away from me. I walked up and up for hours looking for Matthew until no one was left at the mall except me, still circling the spiral ramps."

Jessie passed me a tissue, and softly said, "I know that feeling. Sometimes, I don't believe my father would abandon us this way. There was no sign that he preferred death more than us."

Doug lifted up his eyes and looked at me and at the other faces. "I don't think they thought of abandonment. They just couldn't stop the pain within themselves."

Nora was furious. "Of course they did! They were so selfish that they only thought of themselves and inflicted pain on us. We're the ones to deal with the consequences."

Annie and Liz were in tears. They looked at each other and simultaneously said, "Doug is right."

"Nora, I know that feeling of anger," Annie added. "I was angry at my parents and myself. I didn't talk to them for six months after Emily's death."

"I was angry at Rich," Liz said, "and I'm still angry at Rich. He was the closest person to Karin at the time she died. He should have known. How could he not know Karin's feeling of being alone with the baby? How could he not help her to get help?" Tears poured down Liz's face.

I somehow could not identify myself with anger. I still thought that each of us has the right to choose to live or die. But Nora hit the nail on the head—unfortunately, we were the ones impacted by the consequences of suicide.

Ironically, I was angry while Matthew was still alive. I had completely forgotten about the anger part. I was depressed by Matthew's depressive behaviors. I thought that if he was willing to change that, we both would be happier with his illness, which I didn't fully understand. Perhaps this incomprehensible thought was the source of my anger for almost four years. I misidentified his behaviors as if they were his will, his way of showing his contempt. Besides being angry, I was impatient with Matthew, which I also didn't remember until I reread my diary.

Diary One

I am angry. Actually, nothing new about me being angry. I don't know how I have tolerated our situation for this long. I just opened the bank statement. I read it, then took out previous statements to make sure I was reading them correctly. I realized in the past four months, I paid for all the expenses, including rent, utility and phone bills, car payment, monthly grocery, and gas. Matthew didn't share a penny of it. Matthew has been the one taking care of our finances—balancing the checkbook, filing taxes, and managing our expenses. I thought Matthew earned more than me, and since it's his money I haven't checked our account for all these years. We have a joint checking account that each of us puts money into to share the monthly household expenses. I have been using that account to direct-deposit my salary for more than four years, since Matthew has been in and out of work. But now we're both working, and he has not deposited any funds for four months.

We have discussed separation for two months, and he told me that he does not have the money to move out. Looking at the statements, I can tell him to leave now. I will give him all my savings to get himself a place to stay. I don't want to see his "end of the world" face. I just want him to disappear.

I hate myself. How could I allow this to develop to this stage? We've been married for ten years. How have we come to this point? If he doesn't leave, I will. Where will I go? I don't know. If he is still here at the beginning of next month, I definitely will move out.

I was so shocked to read this diary, which was just a few weeks before Matthew's death. Who was I, being so angry and so ruthless to push him to the edge?

I didn't remember that we were talking about separation. I remember that after his first attempted suicide in late January 1992, while staying at the mental health facility to recover, he asked if I would divorce him. The fourth night he was there, his doctor asked me to join a meeting with him and Matthew. The doctor was the facilitator.

"Matthew has something to tell you," the doctor said.

I was still trying to digest the suicide attempt. I didn't have any interest in learning any more news that I might not be able to handle. I just sat there, waiting.

"I've been smoking marijuana," Matthew said.

My eyes were wide open, and I looked at him before bursting out in laughter. "Anything else?"

"No."

The doctor looked at me. "Are you going to divorce him?"

I sat up and squeezed my shoulders backward, turned my head to the left and right in order to release the tension that I had been holding all day long. Laughing again, I said, "I don't know. Let me think about it."

I remembered before we got married, I'd listed three reasons that I would divorce him, and smoking marijuana before retirement was one of the three. Apparently, Matthew was stressed out by not keeping our agreement. At that moment, what Matthew had revealed was the least of my concerns. I was so tired and so beat up by his actions, I couldn't think more than just knowing that I wanted to have a good night's sleep.

While Matthew was recovering from his attempted suicide, I began to notice that I had been angry about Matthew and about our lives. My bad temper was easily stirred. I heard my screaming even when I was by myself. Now a valid reason had been presented to me, and I could walk out of this life and marriage altogether without feeling that I was wrong. Should I?

Letter One

Dear Matthew,

Yesterday I went to Alan's birthday party. I got a chance to chat with David, who will be a father soon. He is a little bit upset about it. He admitted that he and Carolyn have been fighting for months. He knew the fighting is just like waves that come and go. Now, Carolyn is pregnant. David realizes that he can no longer afford to fight or get sick. He has to constantly work and make sure there's enough money to support the family despite the fact that their relationship is not that great. He said, "All of a sudden, everything has changed. An invisible responsibility is on my shoulders. In the past, when I made money, I'd slow down and take a break for a while until the money was running out, and I never made big money anyway. But now, I have to look for jobs and keep myself working all the time, and I start to worry if I don't have a job lined up a month from now. In other words, I need to have a stable income. It's a pressure." Both of them don't want to talk about it in front of everybody. Carolyn knows that David is in an uncomfortable spot. But she can't do anything about it.

I talked separately to both of them. Carolyn is not happy about being pregnant and not eager to carry the baby or be a wife. The reason I'm telling you this is that I'm trying to save our marriage, just like David and Carolyn. They're trying for the sake of the coming baby. Marriage is not a natural thing. We are basically two strangers trying to build a bond. In this century, one out of two marriages ends in divorce. I don't think our relationship is that bad. But I have discovered that I cannot hold my temper when I talk to you. I don't know if it's because of your problems or purely my bad temperament. I can't forget what you did last time for certain things and I predict that they will happen again and I just can't stand your repetitive behavior, which is the main reason I become so angry at you.

I am writing you pages and pages of letters to let you know what I think. I don't like to live alone like now. But I don't want to scream and be angry at you or at our situation. Every time we talk on the phone, we only talk about what is happening in your and my surroundings. We rarely talk about anything else. I am not sure what you think since you won't express yourself either verbally or in writing. As you know, I'm always a thinker. I try to get things straight and try to find solutions. But our marriage, I don't have an answer. I am very tired of my screaming voice. I am very tired of being critical and cynical.

I miss both of us. What should we do?

Vivi

To my surprise, I had found some of my lost memories from 1992 to 1995. Apparently, I was angry for years. I had no recollection of my anger since Matthew's death. I just knew that hardly anyone could make me angry, which might now have been telling me that's because I had used up all my anger on Matthew and our life together. It also told me why, after Matthew died, I seldom got angry, not even with the annoying people I worked with or anyone I knew. I could be sad, disappointed, or worried, but not angry.

This revelation led me to believe all these years that I was feeling guilty. The guilt didn't go away just because I buried the cruel part of myself and still couldn't recall the screaming I mentioned in letters and diaries. I knew that I'd been talking less and less. Perhaps, as my diaries recorded, I was tired of hearing my own voice. It seemed to me that my silence was not solely grief. In a way, I subconsciously punished myself for the behaviors that I had when Matthew was still alive. I wasn't able to lift myself out of the reprimands that I deserved.

One afternoon, I got a phone call from Doug's second wife, who had made it clear that only she could initiate contact with us, telling me that Doug was in deep trouble. He was trying to drink himself to death, and his driver's license had been suspended. I informed others in the group, and we came up with a plan.

Annie's office was close to where Doug worked. She'd wait for him to get off work and we'd all meet at Annie's house since her roommates were out of town. Annie, Jessie, and I lived in Berkeley. While Annie was picking up Doug, Jessie and I would prepare supper for all six of us. Liz lived in Alameda. She was trying to get a last-minute babysitter. Nora would join us from the North Bay, fighting the traffic to cross the San Rafael Bridge.

By the time we sat Doug down, he was crying, the first time I'd heard him bawling like a little boy.

"I failed Brandon," he said through his sobs.

Annie, Jessie, Liz, and I just sat there, ready to listen.

"I should have known about obesity. I didn't give a thought to it when Brandon's mother mentioned that he was a bit heavy when he was nine. By the time he was thirteen, I realized he was heavy by comparing him with my coworkers at the electrical plant. They were big but they were adults. I also noticed the quantity of food that Brandon was eating."

Nora rushed in and apologized for being late.

Doug smiled at her through his tears. "I started to research, contacted professionals for advice, and even consented to let Brandon have an operation, but it was all too late. I didn't know Brandon was so depressed and that food addiction was so hard to kick."

I handed him a tissue, and he blew his nose. "Thank you for getting me here." He composed himself. "You all are wonderful. I am the oldest but you all are taking care of me." He started weeping again.

Nora was the second oldest. She touched Doug's hand. "I can feel your pain. I used to take drugs with Patrick. I tried many times to kick the habit but it's just not easy." She searched our faces to see if we had anything to say. We just indicated that we were listening.

"I went cold turkey after Patrick died. The silver lining of his death is that I don't have a free supplier anymore. I couldn't afford the expensive habit, not to mention the damage to the lives around me. I have a teenage daughter and an eight-year-old son; I need to think about them." Nora lowered her head, put her face close to Doug's, which forced Doug to look up. "You can kick the drinking habit too. You still have a daughter to raise."

We were surprised that Nora had broken a rule the counselor had set forth for us, and yet not surprised that she was so bold and so candid with Doug in front of us. We were glad that she spelled it out. Only Nora could provide this answer to Doug's wife's prayer.

Privately, I could not shake the feeling of being guilty. I identified with Doug's difficulty in forgiving himself. I hadn't thought of forgiveness as one of the elements that I experienced with Matthew's death. I didn't know whether there was something or someone to forgive, particularly myself. Watching Doug, I realized that I'd been punishing myself without knowing it. I should not have been so bloody honest in responding to Matthew's inquiry about death. I should have clearly seen his distress. I should have understood his thinking. I should have been more compassionate with him being ill. I just kept thinking that if I could have stopped that day from happening, Matthew might still be alive.

Letter Two

Dear Matthew,

It's Thanksgiving, and Dad wanted me to be home with "the boys." When I arrived at the airport, Timothy, Kurt, and Dana were there to pick me up. I knew Timothy would be there, but was surprised to see Kurt and Dana. I thought they would have better things to do. A warm feeling came over me.

We were a bit sad at dinner, and I wished that you were here. I didn't know if I could handle this, but Dad, Mom, Timothy, Kurt, and Dana were with me, being sad and being supportive.

It is your family, and now it is mine. Eleven years of being a member in the family is a long time. Your folks are good people. We may not have the same values about life or the same topics to talk about. But I feel at home. I feel their warmth toward me. I have felt this all along but you were there, the credit was yours.

This is my first time being alone with them. I really appreciate their warm family hospitality.

Vivi

Letter Three

It's your birthday, which I am thankful for, but not your death. I really wish that I could come to the point of accepting what happened. When I think of you,

I wouldn't be filled with only sorrow. I know that time will eventually come. But I am impatient! I want it now!

I have been part of this family for eleven years, and I don't want to hide my emotions. I want it all out in front of your family. I wonder if they feel the same. I see that each of us are aching, missing you at the house without a word, not a single word. I feel the tenderness from everyone without a word, not a single word. I want to shake Dad with all the questions. But I don't have the heart to disturb his apparent peacefulness of having everyone under the same roof.

Took a long walk on Challenge T near here. A lot of tall trees surrounded me.

I asked, "What are these trees?" You used to tell me the names of the trees or said you didn't know. I then turned around, expecting an answer from you and caught myself standing alone there in the semi-cool air.

I feel sad today watching your brothers and the relationship between Kurt and Dana. I know we all have trouble in our marriage at one point or the other, and you were right—we had a better relationship than others. I don't feel that there's affection between Kurt and Dana. I don't even know if they love each other. It seems that Kurt loves everyone in the family except Dana and me. I don't have trouble about him not loving me, but Dana, his wife? By the same token, I don't see much affection from Dana either. I begin to think you and I were perfectionists. We both were seeking love from each other and we valued that by giving, yielding, and accepting. I believe we were in love most of the time until the obsessive behaviors and depression took over. We both were lost in the illness that tore us apart.

I am still suffering from whatever you left behind. I miss you a great deal especially in these few days. Would you visit me in my dreams?

Vivi

I have been talking to Matthew since he died. I know he is gone. But it seems possible that he'll just show up at the door saying "I'm home" as usual. I just do not believe he's gone. He couldn't have dematerialized at the snap of a finger.

Letter Four

Dear Matthew,

I think of you. I still don't know why I didn't get your message on the day of your departure. You obviously said "goodbye" to me. I responded, "Keep up your spirits." I didn't think you really meant it, even though you never said "goodbye" to me before. Perhaps I was really tired of your illness. I was being insensitive about your state of mind. I was too busy being concerned with my own well-being. I tried to save myself from your depression. I didn't react consciously. Yet, I believe subconsciously I was protecting myself by turning a blind eye to you. I reacted to our circumstances naturally and it killed both of us.

I feel dreadful when I think of you. I really really really wish that you were here. I find myself empty. You used to tell me things and give me feedback. Now, no one tells me anything. I talk to the air and ask, "What is wrong with me?" What's wrong is I have lost you.

Vivi

Letter Five

Dear Matthew,

I watched Sleepless in Seattle *again a couple nights ago. Remember when Tom Hanks says, "I'm gonna get out of bed every morning and tell myself to breathe?"*

Yes, yes, yes, I have done that for more than three thousand days!!!!!

I am still reminding myself: "You will be OK. Get up and go out to smell the fresh air."

Your death is a very deep wound, which I'm gradually recognizing bit by bit. There are many things I've recently become aware of, such as, overall, I have no regrets about our marriage despite how painful it was at times. I thought I regretted and resented it from time to time. It was because I couldn't remember our spontaneous outings, from midnight movies in the city to driving overnight to catch the sunrise in Niagara Falls. I could not remember the harmoniousness of our marriage. For four years, we struggled with your illness. I was blinded by our emotional ups and downs. For another ten years, I've tried to pacify my pain with grief, sadness, guilt, resentments, and other feelings that are interwoven with each other.

I am still trying to find my way to full acceptance, to peace, to seeing the glory of life in front of me.

Vivi

I had naively thought that although Matthew had tried to kill himself once, he would not try it again. I was so convinced of that notion and was being completely mindless. Similarly, Doug took for granted that Brandon was a growing boy and that it was natural for him to eat whatever he wanted. Between Doug and me, we both silently continued blaming ourselves for contributing to the death of our loved ones.

Doug could not get out of his grief. Eventually he disconnected from us even though we constantly reached out to him. After six years of knowing him, on another bright summer afternoon in the Bay Area, Doug's second wife called. "Doug died of heart failure this morning." She spoke in a monotone.

Annie has a daughter and a son, Liz and Jessie each have a daughter, and Nora had moved with her two kids to Florida a year before Doug died. Four of us went to Doug's funeral. Doug's college-age daughter, Katie, was teary-eyed and greeted us with warmth. Brandon's mother was not there. Doug's second wife stood a distance from us as if we had the plague. According to the program, Doug was sixty-three, an electrician, had two children from his first marriage, and was survived by a daughter, his ex-wife, and his second wife.

Katie asked if she could have coffee with us after the service. We all nodded. We met at Claremont Avenue, on the Oakland/Berkeley border.

Katie held out an envelope. "My dad left this for you all."

We looked at Katie and each other. None of us took the envelope. We sat there and silently kept our eyes fixed on Katie's hand. Katie was taken aback by our reactions. She put down the envelope and picked up her coffee. Personally, I didn't want to know what was in the envelope. I didn't want any surprises or disturbances as we were already disturbed enough by Doug's passing.

Annie picked up the envelope and asked Katie, "Do you know what it is?"

"I think it's a letter. I don't know what it says." Katie sighed.

Annie flipped it over and read the front of it, "All our names are here." She slightly shook the letter. Still, the three of us didn't say a word. I assumed Liz and Jessie had the same thought as mine.

Annie looked at the names again and again. She tilted her head, sought our consent by glancing at our faces, and then said, "Katie, do you want to know the contents of this letter?"

"In a way, I do. I know my dad was grateful for your support but only left a note to all of you, not to anyone else, not even my mom. I wonder how much influence you all had on him."

Annie addressed us, "Would it be okay for Katie to read this to all of us?" We nodded.

I added, "Should we call Nora?"

"Good idea." Annie dialed, no answer.

Dear All,

I started writing this letter a few months after Brandon's death. I didn't know who I was writing to. I could not share this with Brandon's mother, and Katie was still a bit too young to understand my state of mind.

I am sorry to cause you pain for my departure. I want you to know that I am blessed by all of you for being there when I had no words to describe my feelings. I tried very hard to forgive myself, but I could not. Only you will understand. You have gone through as much pain as I have. But you all are resilient. I thought I was too, but I am just an old man and am too tired to change.

I didn't only fail Brandon. I have failed myself as well. Being a father and not protecting my son is unforgivable, no matter how you look at it. I don't think I am being too harsh on myself. I was there, watched him grow up, and was cognitively ignorant about his being and health, just unspeakable.

Jessie, I know your father's feeling, being tired of living. I am too. I don't think depression did this to me. I just don't want to wake up anymore. But I could not bring myself to end it.

I have been a drinker for my entire adult life, which may have contributed to my negligence of Brandon. The only peace I can feel is when alcohol fills in my brain. My only way out is to drink.

Now, I am gone. I want you to know that nothing is more precious than you, your own well-being. You all have the scars and wounds in your hearts. No one else can mend them for you. You may not be able to mend them yourself but you can, while still young and vibrant, learn to coexist with them.

I know expectation is the weapon that's killing my spirit. Please do not let it happen to you.

I will be at peace with myself when you read this letter.

Take care,

Doug

Katie sobbed, put down the letter, "He didn't think about the fact that I have lost a brother. Dad excluded me."

None of us had words to comfort Katie. Parents sometimes have their own bias toward their children. They may have a preference for one child over the other. Doug focused on his own guilt concerning Brandon and forgot about Katie.

Doug knew all along that expectations kill. My counselor once said to me, "You have very high expectations for yourself and others. In your mind, Matthew's death is your failure. You are having difficulty justifying yourself."

Expectation is just like chess—you can make certain wrong moves such that when they meet a particular threshold, the game is over, no matter how brilliant your subsequent moves might be.

Expectation is like quantum mechanics—particle movement is predictable with hidden variables, despite Einstein's, Podolsky's, Rosen's, Heisenberg's, and Bell's contradictory arguments throughout the twentieth century. But no one knows exactly when there will be off-beat momentum: therefore, movement is predictably unpredictable, and so are the consequences of our expectations.

Here was Katie, another soul who had been forgotten by her father in the midst of losing her brother. Callousness had played a trick on Doug and left Katie to pick up the pieces.

There in the coffee shop, all these thoughts were like lapping waves, spurting, rushing, flooding, and I couldn't stop the shaking of my body. I lowered my head, crying like a lost child. I wanted to hide myself in a hole. I heard and didn't hear my counselor, but Doug's words pierced my heart.

"Doug, you spoke the unspoken. I don't know how to get out of this rut," I whispered, still sobbing.

It had been eight years since Matthew died, and I had the same thoughts as Doug. Every night I prayed to not wake up the next morning—just let me sleep and be gone.

GUILT

MY DAILY ACTIVITIES AND the people I encountered occasionally reminded me of something that flashed quickly and was then forgotten, nothing significant. My memories were selective. I remembered the bad of Matthew but didn't remember my misbehaviors or other elements that might have contributed to the shadow of Matthew's death shrouding me.

I hadn't suspected that expectation was one of the culprits of my miserable sentencing.

I remembered one evening we arrived home at the same time. Matthew got out of his truck and then walked back to the driver's seat, "I forgot to get bread."

I looked at him, sarcastically mocking. "When was the last time you *remembered* to buy bread?" I pulled out a loaf of bread from my grocery bag.

Two weeks later, I came home with another loaf of bread. Matthew looked disappointed. He picked up the loaf and opened the freezer. I saw there were already two loaves.

I became frustrated. "How am I supposed to know that you've remembered to buy bread?" I saw consternation in Matthew, and I felt disappointed with myself. I walked out to the garden to breathe.

Matthew's indifference and withdrawal were so obvious to everyone. We didn't work in the garden every day, but when we were in the garden on the weekend, he often disappeared into the white pine grove while I was watering, weeding, and cleaning. He stopped balancing the checkbook or taking the initiative to do the laundry. I had to ask him to fold clothes with me or the heap of clean clothes would stay there for days to the point he didn't have his favorite shirt to wear. He didn't run with me in the early morning at the high school track anymore. He sometimes didn't eat and stayed in the bedroom for the rest of the evening. I took up all the household chores and ran errands. My patience wore thinner day by day. Resentment was like an avalanche that could be triggered by anything, at any time. The silence between us had widened. Under the same roof, Matthew was aggressively passive, holding himself in a shell while I just didn't believe in the seriousness of his illness and reacted with my bad nature. I was lost in his illness.

The challenges and lasting effects of chronic depressive disorder had become the calamity that continued to live with me.

Diary Two

Watched a French movie, Ponette, about a four-year-old girl's grief at losing her mother in a car accident. The last phrase in the movie: "She told me to learn to be happy." I could not stop crying, my tears like a fountain. I didn't try to stop. For all these years, I've stopped using the word "happy" because I seem to not know the feeling of it. I have not learned well. I was so swallowed by grief that for years I had forgotten my own existence. Now, I am gradually moving away from grieving, yet, every time death is the subject, I draw back to the grieving process again, repetitively. I have not used the word "healing" because I don't know if I will ever get there or if I have already passed beyond without knowing it. One thing I do know: I have not concluded my emotional turmoil over Matthew's death, over the loss of my love, over being abandoned, over my years of being trapped in a depression that originally was not my own but has become mine, and over not knowing how to make this life a bit easier and happier.

Diary Three: A Note to Matthew

I was looking for you while I walked in the Financial District. I did that when I was in my early twenties after Zi Meng died of hepatitis B. I knew I was searching for you with very different feelings. I was hoping that among the people I saw or met, there must be someone who could replace you. So far, I have not had any luck. In a way, I am relieved. I don't want anyone to replace you. But I long for someone who would appreciate me as much as I would appreciate him. You definitely are not accepting me in our hopeless situation. I still miss you. I still imagine that we would, after all this time, eventually meet again and start to know each other better. Could you tell me why you have occupied my heart so fully?

Diary Four: Continuing Note to Matthew

I was swimming and watching the sunset. I thought of you. I wish that you were home for Thanksgiving.

I miss you. At the same time, our unfinished/finished linking has continued. Don't ask me why I feel this way, even though it seems that I am waiting for Godot, like in Samuel Beckett's play. I still feel that some years from now, we will be together again. I have a sense that the way I thought of you is the same way you thought of me. How strange? How should I tell you my complaints for eleven years; you have not really communicated with me? But I know, on Thanksgiving Day, I am in your thoughts. I only hope that you are happy where you are and not paying too great a price for what you are doing. We would not be younger than yesterday, but my heart is still yours.

Diary Five: Continuing Note to Matthew

Recently, you have been clearly in front of my eyes. Your smiling face and your movements have vividly distracted my mind. I miss you terribly. I write you notes that mainly remind myself: I exist! I don't expect your response but am hoping for one. Your silence has given me one more strike with absolute discouragement. How much pride could I give up for you? How could I continue talking to a wall? I have done this for eleven years. I remember the day before you were cremated, I kissed your forehead and said, "Someday I will forget you."

Perhaps writing to you will help me to put you out of my life. I know that out there are other people who I may be attracted to. But I have not given you up. For whatever reasons, you are still in my bleeding heart. I don't consider your coldness is being equal to hopelessness, but I know it is, and you are being rude!

I had heard two of me constantly debating and arguing with my writing and talking to Matthew and my relentless staying in the shadow of guilt.

My evil twin had tried very hard to persuade me, "You couldn't stop what Matthew wanted to do. You are taking too much ownership for his action."

"If I could prevent that day from happening, he might still be alive today."

"I've heard you saying that for eleven years, but there is no if. 'If' never happened. Why are you continually beating yourself up?"

"I am guilty of not totally understanding his state of mind. I could have been more supportive instead of being frustrated and angry with him."

"How could anyone totally understand another's state of mind? Do you know being a caregiver of a loved one is the most difficult job on earth?"

I was shocked and looked at my evil twin. "I was not a caregiver. Matthew didn't need me to take care of him. He did everything himself."

"Ah, what did you do on those days when he didn't eat? What did you do on those days he couldn't get out of bed? What did you do on those days he locked himself in the bedroom?"

I was speechless. I had not considered myself a caregiver. Matthew could walk and talk and perform the activities of daily living. I only looked at the daily physical functioning, and I completely neglected the fact that I was also involved with the care of his declining mental health, which contributed to his behaviors such as lack of response, emotional isolation, loss of interest in normal activities, low energy, lethargy, and all others that I don't have the names for.

I couldn't respond to these questions. My evil twin looked at me. "Love yourself a little. Treat yourself as kindly as you have treated others."

I burst out in tears and cracked a dry laugh. "I am kind to myself. I just haven't fully mastered living peacefully with the hole in my heart."

I emailed Chris.

"Dear Chris, what should I do? I don't seem to know. I am having a hard time remembering things that were important to Matthew and things that he told me. I walked on the field looking for clues, and I found none."

"Dear Vivi, to be alive and sane is a blessing. Life is fragile, yet, we must be thankful and humble for we are still thinking of making this life a bit easier, a bit happier, and a bit better."

"Dear Chris, I am not humble enough to view the beauty of life, but I am fully aware that being alive is a blessing. Every morning when I wake up, I tell myself that it's a new day, live it fully regardless of what will happen. It is just not easy..."

"Dear Vivi, I think, therefore, I exist. It is invigorating to hear from you, always food for thought."

"Dear Chris, Matthew and the farm should only happen in movies. I want to switch movies and do not want to play this role anymore. I just want to escape from earth, and if I could, I would only take my soul."

"Dear Vivi, if you disappear from earth, then who is going to save the earth? If I am still alive, I may bury you with the earth. But this will only, and definitely, happen in the coming millennium. At least you still own a piece of green in the bottom of your heart. This is really a luxury to many people on this earth."

I could not help laughing and crying at the same time. Chris had become my confidant. Even though we were an ocean apart, I had no fear of discussing my views of the world, humanities, politics, and anything with him even though we didn't always agree with each other's perspective.

"Dear Chris, For Zi Meng, I could only present him a white rose and recite the poem from *Dream of the Red Chamber*. I do wish you'll be alive and bury whatever form I will be in with the earth.

"Could we go back to the Tang Dynasty? Once we go back, we can do all the drinking, poetry, and crying anytime we want. I've never been there but have missed it terribly."

"Dear Vivi, you are really a poet. An accomplished poet as good as me, if not better. Smile for those who are still alive and struggling."

A few days before Christmas, I went to London and stayed with Chris for a week. Before I went, I wrote to Chris:

"I do not want to meet anyone in your life. I only want to see you, and I don't need to stay at your place."

Chris wrote back:

"You will stay at my place. No one else will disturb you."

Chris, as usual, gave me the key to his flat. He lived in a two-bedroom flat on top of a hill near Islington. Once I settled in, I picked up his thesis and started reading. He'd spent the last seven years with three-quarters of his time devoted to study and writing this PhD thesis. The supervisor in charge of his study didn't like his progress and had given him an ultimatum to complete and defend his thesis by the end of the coming year.

Chris said, "Good thing you're here. I can use your literary sensibility." He pointed at the thesis in my hands. I looked at him with an indistinct smile. Ah, literature, a twinge for the contents of it seemed a distant memory that was so recent, so familiar, and so irrelevant, which all dropped in as if a typhoon had just arrived, picked me up to two floors high and dropped me down hard, leaving me with scratches and bruises, but no broken bones. I hadn't had a literary discussion in over fifteen years. I didn't know if I still had the critical thinking to comment on Chris's doctoral dissertation.

Chris worked part-time. When he was at home, sometimes I would just take walks by myself in the nearby park and have tea at the pub right at the foot of his apartment complex. Chris gave me all the space and solitude that I did not deliberately seek. Yet, I was grateful for his thoughtfulness. He left on Christmas Eve to house-sit for a friend. On Christmas Day, London was totally dead, no public transit, no commerce, no people around except people like me, who had no family to visit, no place to call home. I walked to a church before noon under the gray sky through a strong, chilly wind. I looked up; white dots were reluctantly coming at me. I looked down; feathery snowflakes, few and far between, cowardly landed. The unwilling snowfall didn't seem to be one of the "worst storms to hit London," as it had been portrayed on the news last night. I just walked round and round in front of the church entrance under the brisk breeze. I didn't intend to go in. I heard Christmas music, choirs, and a hypnotic solo voice full of emotion praising the almighty. By the time the sermon started, I turned around, headed back to the apartment.

We talked very little. I was there in Chris's living room, reading, looking for words in his poems to see if the dancer was still in his heart, reading, searching for me in his poems, and reading, tracing for any signs of our youth together— none. Chris had published a few poems here and there after moving to London. In recent years, his poems had been deeply involved with Hong Kong politics, immigrants' lives in London, and advocacy of democracy in Hong Kong and social equality for new Londoners. The early years of tenderness, haggard and splendid melancholy seemed to have hardened his heart, and the voice denouncing the Hong Kong government and accusing local governments' disregard for the economic disparity among immigrants was forbidding.

My mind drifted in and out of our time in Hong Kong, working with the group at the office for the young writers' publication, chatting, laughing, all throwing pillows at each other. At Chris's request, I had organized friends and family members to attend concerts and plays to support the less popular musicians and actors, which I thought Uncle Mike would have been delighted to see me doing. I embraced performing arts and literature so enthusiastically. I thought of the times in Chris's apartment listening to operas and classical music, his recitals, my piano playing. I remembered drinking red wine in the quietness of the late evenings; the times Matthew and I visited him in both Hong Kong and London; telling Matthew about our silliness, craziness, and our passion for literature and the universe; my yearning for Chris's letters, all of this seemed surreal to me. If Chris were not there, I would have thought I had made all this up, entirely my imagination of another life, where I would want to stay for eternity.

A few weeks later, I received a letter. Chris wrote:

"Here is a picture I took when we were in Soho. I called your name and you turned. Look how elegant you are with the black-and-white woolen hat on top of your blue-black hair and a long black coat, standing in the middle of a tourist street breathing the chill air. Your eyes, full of vicissitude, so desolate, pain me. I miss your laughter, your smiling face with all its wit when I was acting like an idiot. I want that you back. You have a full life in front of you. Be well, be kind to yourself."

My eyes were fixed on the last few words. My evil twin had told me to be kind to myself, and now so had Chris, who could see the harshness of unforgiveness in me.

FINDING THE WAY

AFTER MOVING TO BERKELEY, I worked at a nonprofit serving people with developmental disabilities. Basically, I created a small profitable business inside a nonprofit by contracting with the counties' regional rehabilitation centers. I provided independent living skills training to all of my clients. Based on each of my clients' needs, I designed training curriculum, hired trainers, and set weekly hours. I counseled and met each of them individually once a week in addition to meeting with social workers and reviewing each client's progress with their respective trainers. I worked endlessly, advocating for my clients in getting all the support they needed. But I still didn't want to get up in the morning. I dragged myself out of bed every day and arrived an hour late to work.

The second week of January, one evening at work, I thought I was the only person in the office. I ran into my CEO, who used a wheelchair and was right behind me when I picked up the monthly invoices to the counties on the printer.

He held a cup of water and rested it on his thigh. "It's eight thirty. Why are you still here?"

"I have a confession to make, and an apology," I replied.

He looked up at me and waited.

"I'm sorry that I have been late to work for all these years. I am just making up the hours."

I had been puzzling from time to time over the eight years why no one had ever talked to me about being late to work. Now I was the one to bring it up and didn't know how well it would be received without any explanation.

He looked at me with soft eyes. "But I also know that you have been working more than eight hours a day all these years. Accounting has informed me monthly that you are the only person to get the counties to systematically pay us on time. You have done an excellent job keeping the cash flowing in. You're a godsend."

I just stared at him and the papers in my hand.

"The social workers told me that you've trained the clients so well that they have many fewer issues with your clients."

"Thank you. Good to know."

"Go home." He wheeled himself back to his office.

Godsend again? Was I dreaming at this hour when the CEO suddenly appeared and knew what I had been doing? I had been so goal-driven that I only cared about my clients' needs, and I had been shutting down the world outside of my work. I only knew about other staff members' work by attending monthly staff meetings, or if we had mutual clients, but sometimes I wasn't there because I had to monitor trainers, visit clients, or attend meetings at the counties' offices.

My clients had different developmental disabilities of varying severity. Some of them couldn't talk, some of them didn't talk, some of them used wheelchairs, and some of them had more than one disability. By observing them individually, I learned their ways of communicating, their ways of receiving information, and their ways of learning. I had to convey each person's abilities, responses, and progress to the trainers and coach them all.

Some of the clients were capable of performing essential daily activities. For those clients, I requested that they meet me at my office, which was one of the skills that they had to perform one hundred percent in order for them to continue obtaining the full support from the Rehab Center. Every once in a while, one or a few of them would get warnings from me when they didn't show up at their appointments with me or with the social workers.

At the beginning, I had one repeat offender, David, who would show up late or the next day. David could talk but I needed to work very hard with him to get a phrase or a few sentences out of him. He never looked up or made eye contact with me. He would come in and sit down, keeping his eyes on the carpet. Nodding, shaking his head, or pointing were the ways he communicated. I tried giving him a pad to write or draw on. He looked at the pad and shook his head. I put on music; he just sat still without any movement. I turned off the light, he pointed to the window and said, "The shade is down."

Aha! I realized that David was in tune with his surroundings, even though he never looked up or looked around.

"Do you like any sports?" I asked him casually while turning on the light.

"Tennis."

"Have you been playing?"

"No racket." David kept staring at the carpet.

"If I lent you a racket, would you play?"

He nodded.

Holly, David's trainer, a newly graduated physical therapist, was energetic and eager to facilitate exercises to strengthen bodies and souls. I met with Holly and discussed how we could bring the best communication skills out of David, who had autism and most of the time didn't talk.

"David likes to play tennis," I told Holly.

"Really." Holly settled herself in my office.

"Do you play tennis?"

"I can play."

"Here is my thinking: if you play tennis with him, that might help him to express himself more often. What do you think?"

"We can give it a try. Each time we meet, we go to the laundromat, go grocery shopping, clean his room, run through his budget for the week, mark all his appointments, and check his public transit passes. He doesn't show any interest in doing any of these things. If he likes to play tennis, that could be an incentive for him to take the initiative of running errands on his own to save time to play with me."

I was thinking along the same lines. "Let's give it a three-month trial."

I pulled out David's weekly training hours and designated two hours a day and three days a week to playing tennis and gave a tennis racket to Holly for David.

Six weeks later, David no longer showed up at different times and didn't miss our appointments. One day I knew he would be playing with Holly and decided to drop by his residential hotel room before their game. His door was open, and I walked right into his room. As I expected, he was cleaning the room. He raised his head and said, "Hi." That was the first greeting he'd initiated. I was thrilled with his progress and smiled wildly.

I watched them playing tennis. I had never seen David be so open. He expressed triumph at hitting hard on Holly, and lamentation at missing opportunities to take control of the game.

David was the model of success in my program. But another client proved the failure of the program and me. Shirley, deaf, the mother of an eight-year-old hearing daughter and the wife of a deaf man, didn't seem to comprehend social etiquette and relationship boundaries. She had no trouble performing activities of daily living, but she would argue with anyone if she didn't get her way. She came to my office three or four times a week. When I visited her home, the husband and daughter would report Shirley's unruly behavior, such as taking items and eating fruits in a supermarket without paying, lying on the seat of a public transit vehicle, making loud noises in the library, and many more daily nuisances that all involved social interactions. I discussed these behaviors with her social worker, and we put her in a classroom and other forms of training, to no avail.

One morning Shirley came in around eleven instead of two in the afternoon, which surprised me. She sat in front of me quietly, which was a bit unusual.

"What's up?" I signed.

She made a sad face. "I cannot do anything right."

"Who tells you that?"

"My husband took my daughter to his mother's house."

"He may just want them to spend time together."

"They have been gone for three days."

While I tried to think how to comfort her, she took out a pocketknife and was about to slit her throat. I caught the knife right in front of her throat and my knuckles hit her lower jaw. Her eyes rolled back, showing the whites, and her head tilted backward. I yelled for help while struggling with her for the knife. Four colleagues rushed into my office and two of them helped to pull the knife down. Shirley was about five foot two and a hundred pounds. My colleagues were able to pin her to the chair. Soon after, the paramedics restrained her hands in front of her body and took her to the county hospital for observation.

There was a cut between my thumb and index finger. I didn't even feel it until my coworker brought the first aid kit and instructed me to sit down. The whole episode happened so fast, my entire focus was on taking the knife away, and my mind had gone blank. While my coworker tended to my wound, our in-house psychologist, Amy, hurried in to check on me. Thirty minutes later, I hauled myself into her office.

"How's your hand?"

"It's okay." I shrugged.

"How do you feel?"

"I feel fine."

"What happened?"

"Come on, Amy, you are not investigating this."

"No, I'm not, but I could try to help you if I knew what happened."

"I'm okay. I don't think it's necessary to have a counseling session right now. Give me some time to absorb the whole incident. If I need counseling, you will be the first one to see me."

Amy looked at me. She knew that I only communicated with others relating to work matters. I was also trained as a counselor, and no one knew my personal life. The connection we had at work was cordial and respectful of each other's space.

"Sometimes it's easier to seek assistance from others. I'm here if you want to talk."

"Thanks, I appreciate it."

I took off from work right after talking to Amy. I just could not concentrate. The whole afternoon at home, I kept revisiting the less than ten-minute interaction with Shirley, who had never exhibited any intention of harming herself or others.

Shirley was clever and cunning. She had a cheery nature and loved to gossip. But some wiring in her brain didn't function as expected, such that a mental health professional could not give a name to her behavioral issues; she didn't fully fit any one type of human behavioral category. Despite daily complaints about her, the fact that she had managed her life up to this point was due to her own merit.

I kept wondering if I had missed any signs in the past few days. I found none. I started writing my report to the county at home, and I just felt that something was aching, something was tugging my heartstrings.

As dusk was falling, I planned to cook dinner. I held an onion in my hand. Instantly, I had a flashback of holding an onion in my hand and not knowing what to do with it. That was in 1995, a few months after Matthew's death. In a split second, I dropped into a chair. I recognized why I was aching.

In my life, I have literally saved two lives; I was there for Tony when he attempted to jump out of a fifth-floor hotel window, and I was there for Shirley when she tried to slit her own throat. But I was not there for Matthew, the man I loved, lived with, and saw every day. I could not save him. How's that for being a godsend? My ache at not being able to save Matthew was held deep down in me so that sometimes I didn't even know it existed.

"Are you going to sit there mourning again?" My evil twin just popped up. I couldn't remember when she'd visited me last since I'd been buried in my work and hadn't been paying attention to time.

"Why can't I move on?"

"You have."

"If that's true, why would you say I'm mourning again?"

"You are. You move on by not really facing your inner struggles."

"You're silly. I don't understand what you're saying."

"Come on, Sis. Protective mechanisms are a way to shield yourself. You've known that all along, being a counselor."

"I don't think you're right on that. Why do I do that?"

"Because you're still lingering on 'if that day had not happened.'"

"But it did happen. It has been over ten years. I know that Matthew won't come back for real."

"Yes and no. You still love him."

"I can't feel him, I can't touch him, I don't know if I'm still loving him."

"You are in love with a ghost."

"Ha, you're right. What's the harm in being in love with a ghost?"

"The harm is that you are living like a turtle under its shell. But whenever there's a shaking up, you become a mess again. Like today."

"I am trying to find my way. Give me some slack."

"Slack is not what you need. You need to be compassionate, kinder to yourself."

"I have been taking care of myself. I exercise. I have joined a basketball team. I eat healthily, and I meet up with friends regularly."

"Who are those friends?"

"My teammates."

"You see them regularly because you have to practice your sport. Besides, remember what Jenny said the other day. She said, 'I still don't know you.' None of your teammates know you."

"That doesn't mean I'm not kind to myself."

"You act like a robot. Do you know that?"

"Nothing wrong with that."

"How do you feel?"

I had not asked myself this question for a long time. After Matthew died, I stopped many of our routines, like Sunday morning pancake breakfast. I have never been a morning person. On the weekends, I love to sleep in until ten or eleven o'clock.

Matthew used to bring a cup of steaming coffee to bed right below my nose and sing, "Good morning, good morning, good morning to you. Good morning, good morning, and how do you do?" to get me out of bed. Then he would make pancakes.

I stopped going to film festivals and movie premieres. I stopped running. I stopped hiking. I stopped making dumplings. I stopped knitting. I stopped using the word *happy*. I stopped loving Christmas. I stopped other activities that we both used to do together. What I had now was basketball practice four times a week, reading thirty minutes each way on BART to and from work, doing chores on the weekends, and work, work, work day and night. Basically, the only people I encountered every day were either my colleagues and clients or my basketball teammates.

Nonetheless, I still slept in on the weekends.

I could not answer my evil twin's question: How do I feel?

She looked at me. "Do you know, you've had 'Stay Away from Me' written across your forehead for over ten years?"

"Really?" I knew I had built a wall and set up strict boundaries. My colleagues and teammates didn't know that Matthew had once existed, and certainly not a marriage. Some had asked about my last name. I just said it was from my adoptive father; I selectively told a fact rather than a lie.

"And when was the last time you made any friends?"

"You are absurd. My teammates are my friends. You can't discount them."

"You know what I mean. Besides practices, you don't hang out with them. You go to movies by yourself, eat out by yourself, and travel by yourself. Do you really enjoy doing things by yourself?"

"I like to go to movies by myself. I wouldn't compromise just for the sake of having companions to go out with, if they're people I don't care to spend time with."

After I said that, I realized I didn't even know them. Colleagues and teammates were there by default. I had not thought of wanting to know them. When did I turn ice-like and isolated? I wasn't like that before. When Matthew and I first met, helping him to get around the island was something I didn't think about. I just automatically took the responsibility upon myself.

Who am I today?

"Now you're thinking. Think hard. Goodnight." My evil twin was gone while I was still sitting there holding an onion.

I understood my evil twin's perspective. It wasn't my fault that Matthew made his decision. I wasn't responsible for his death. But I didn't feel that way.

I had been pondering all these eleven years, "If I had been able to stop that day from happening, Matthew might still be alive." Cognitively, I did not blame myself. Mentally and emotionally, I was guilty of not being fully supportive of his conditions and requesting that he move out while his mind was in a fragile state a few weeks before he died. I wasn't angry at him for what he did. Rather, I was angry at myself for what I did and what I didn't do. Anger with guilt had transformed to something deluding, the feelings of which I could no longer identify with practical psychology. I had withdrawn from the world; as my evil twin pointed out, I was living like a turtle under its shell. Work was a big part of the shell, where I put all my energy into planning and advocating for my clients. It had served me well for eight years, but now I had to evaluate my auto-polite mode: Was it really helping and benefiting all of us? Shirley's attempt was a wakeup call. She ended up in a mental institution. Her husband divorced her, and he and their daughter moved to another town.

I had been so consumed with reports, research, and resources for my handful of clients that I hadn't done any cultivation of my personal life. I enforced the separation of my personal and professional lives by setting strict boundaries at work, where no one dared to ask me personal questions. I checked my contacts and found none I could talk to regarding my state of mind. Not even the members of the group, who were busy raising families. I shouldn't intrude in their lives with my own deficits. My family, Chris, Ethan, and Bora were thousands of miles away. I couldn't burden them more than I already had. Berenice, Alan, Dad, Kurt, and Timothy had had their share of pain, and I wouldn't have even known how to start with them, as Dad had shown me all these years that he believed denial would cure and time would cause the cherished feelings of loving Matthew to fade away. With them, reminiscence was the only surviving piece that all of Matthew's family had held on tightly to.

Loss of womanhood was one of my deficits. I left home in my late twenties, and I missed the opportunity of building bonds with women my age.

"I am going back to square one. What should I do now?" I asked my evil twin.

I knew she was upset with me, but she would never abandon me even when she kept her silence or stayed away as long as she could hold up.

"I don't know how to change. Help!"

"Talk to a shrink," my evil twin casually threw this phrase out.

"I have not seen a shrink for more than six years. I don't want to start all over again."

"You need to start somewhere. You want changes but don't take action. How can others help you?" my twin yelled.

I remembered that was my thought with Matthew before his diagnosis. It was me who made him see a shrink, and then there was the outcome of his illness. The psychiatrist told me the onset could have been there for years before the official diagnosis. That was a painful process, and it took almost two years to get to the point that he needed to be medicated. During the first two years, Matthew worried that after his twenty sessions of counseling we would not be able to afford any continuing treatments. Therefore, he shouldn't even start.

"You don't want the feelings that you're experiencing now, do you?" I asked, lowering my head while Matthew's head rested on the dining table.

"I don't." He looked at me sideways.

"Let's take the first step, and we'll find a way to deal with the rest." I put my hand on his arm and tried to get him to sit up.

By the time the counseling sessions were exhausted, the psychologist transferred Matthew into a regular patient, as if he were treating Matthew for cancer. By then, Matthew had quit his job at the college and was working at the farm.

Fretting about money had increasingly weighed down our lives. Matthew thought his illness would cost all our assets, and there was no guarantee that he'd get better.

My job covered health insurance for both of us, with copayments. I had not thought that asymptomatic mental disturbance was a health issue. For me, mood changes were just daily occurrences—I would feel happy, frustrated, sad, angry, loving, lonely, whatever. I could regulate it by myself without a doctor or medical care. Matthew's symptoms gave me a firsthand understanding of mental illness, and I also learned that mental health counseling was limited to twenty sessions per year. Any additional sessions needed to be approved by a subject matter expert and classified as an extra cost when a patient became chronically ill and needed long-term treatment. All of the requirements and expenses revealed the discriminatory structure of our healthcare system. I began to wonder, in what ways would society accept mental illness as a common disease?

One evening we were out for dinner and a movie. On the way to the theater, there was a young homeless man asking for money. I handed him the leftovers from our dinner.

Matthew entreated, "What if I wound up like him?"

At the time, I thought it was impossible. He had family here and a lot of people would support him. And he was not that sick. He just needed to do better at managing his mood swings with the help of his psychologist and psychiatrist, that's all. How naïve I was, a would-be mental health counselor.

"You wouldn't. We are all here to support you." I looked up at him. Our eyes locked. I continued, "On the contrary, I could easily become one. I have no one here except you by marriage." I spoke my mind.

"I'm sorry. I haven't bought you a house. And I still owe you a diamond ring." Matthew sounded defeated.

"No, I don't care about those. I only want you to get well." I put my hand into the crook of his elbow.

Matthew had given up most of his assets when he divorced his first wife. The land was the only asset left, which Matthew had been strong enough to deny Shannon. For Matthew, the land belonged to Jerry and him, and he had already sold part of it when he married Shannon. Instead, he sold the house and gave the proceeds, with all the cash he had as an additional settlement, to Shannon for a peaceful dissolution.

Matthew had never asked Dad for financial support. When he married me, he needed to provide financial support documents to the US Immigration Service in order for me to migrate to the US. Dad gladly obliged and acted as my sponsor and lent Matthew twenty thousand dollars for other expenses relating to the divorce and new marriage. All these things had been eating Matthew alive when he was sick and couldn't earn much of a living. He felt that he was dragging me into economic disadvantage and that my quality of life was going down the drain. For me, I had never thought finances would be part of his disappointments. I always thought that we didn't need much money to live on and we could earn our living as long as we were on the same page about where our lives were heading.

When I married Matthew, when I signed the marriage certificate, I thought, "This is it, it's for life."

I hadn't had second thoughts about our marriage. Even when I asked him to move out, I wasn't thinking of a divorce. I thought that we needed our own space to breathe and that separation might do us good, at least to temporarily take me away from his depression.

Matthew's illness continued to deteriorate and my mental health was also imbalanced by his disorder. We become more passive-aggressive toward each other, even with tiny non-issues in our daily lives, which had become unbearable and tormenting. Animosity built up daily.

One day, I asked Matthew why he treated me like an enemy.

He responded, "What makes you think I treat you like an enemy?"

"You don't talk to me."

"When did silence between us start to mean I'm treating you like an enemy?"

"Our silence has changed. I see you but I cannot feel you."

"You mean I don't exist?"

"I want to know how you feel, and how I can be helpful." I felt chastened by his literary sense.

"I wish you had a magic pill to help me and get me out of here." He pointed at his head with a faint smile. I saw pain in his gloomy eyes.

I was bone-tired by this type of communication. We were talking in circles, going nowhere. Matthew had not raised his voice or shown anger. Nevertheless, his round and round talking was worse than my silent treatment, which used to motivate him to sort conflicts out. Our roles had changed. I became the one who needed to think deep to convey precise meanings. Sometimes, I was tongue-tied. I didn't even know the accurate words or descriptions to present to Matthew regarding our relationship and life together. We both were sick in heart and mind. I wanted to not see, hear, feel, or continue the utterly illusive reality.

ROOTS

I DECIDED TO QUIT my job. Four months after Shirley's incident, late one evening when I knew the CEO would have just finished a meeting with the board, I went to his office and handed him my resignation letter. He looked at me with concern. "I don't want to accept your resignation. Would you consider taking a week off to think this over?"

"No, I've already decided."

"What are you going to do? Do you already have a job lined up?"

"No, I will become unemployed."

"Then why are you rushing?"

"I've been thinking of resigning for four months, and it's time for me to go."

"Are you still upset about what Shirley did?"

"No, but her action was a wakeup call for me. I don't think I am being effective."

"That's not true. You are very efficient and effective in what you do."

"I'm worn out. I have my own mental health maintenance to do."

"Would seeing Amy or a counselor from your health provider help?"

"Counseling maybe. But I need to stay away from this environment to help me really face my own issues." I lowered my eyes, not wanting to explain further.

"I see." My CEO looked at my letter and looked up at me. He held out the letter. "I'll hire you again if you change your mind."

I was unemployed for the first time in my entire career in the US. The first two weeks, I slept in until after ten o'clock. I knew I needed eight hours' sleep, and I always set my alarm to wake me in the morning for work. But I was surprised at the accuracy of my own body clock. I stayed up late at night and no longer set the alarm, but I would automatically wake up after a full eight hours of sleep.

My day would pass quickly. After breakfast, it was already noon. I read the news, checked email, took care of bills, ran errands. Then it was time for basketball practice. After practice, I prepared dinner, and after dinner, I listened to Hong Kong radio programs via the internet while cleaning up the kitchen. Then it was time for bed again. I found that I had not talked to anyone. By the time I spoke the first word to my teammates, I heard my hoarse voice. I started saying hello to myself in front of the mirror in the morning when I washed to make sure my vocal cords would do a fine job in the afternoon when I went to practice. On days we didn't practice, I basically didn't say a word.

"Now what should I do?" I asked my evil twin.

"Are you enjoying your time off?"

"Yes, but I think I'm ready to go back to work."

"It has only been two weeks. You haven't started the healing process and you want to run away from it again?"

"No, no, don't mistake me. I'm not running away from it. I think I'm fine. I just need to stay away from mental health services and find a new career."

"You mean you want to stay away from your own mental health."

"How can I convince you that I'm fine?" I asked with a subdued voice.

My evil twin left without responding.

From the first time when Dad told me, "Just deny it. If you deny it long enough, you will believe he is just far away from home," I had already decided that turning away from the fact would not do me any good. I thought I had faced reality and worked on my grieving. I thought I was doing a good job. But part of me would tell myself that I wasn't dealing with my emotions.

I remembered reading Elisabeth Kübler-Ross's book on the five stages of grief, a guiding tool that didn't necessarily fit my situation. I just needed something to reference. I reviewed and reminded myself of the series of five emotions: denial, anger, bargaining, depression, and acceptance. I was neither in denial nor angry at Matthew. Bargaining was a bit unclear for me. "If I could" had held me for all these years. Yes, I was depressed before and after Matthew's death, and could still be in depression. Regarding acceptance, I wasn't sure how to interpret it. I thought I had accepted Matthew's death. Yet, I hadn't accepted being "not guilty" nor the baggage of "if I could," both of those emotions I was having a tremendously hard time overcoming.

I took out the letters, notes, and my own diary to search for the missing memories. I laid them out on the living room table and floor. I read one then picked up another, inserting papers or cards relating to a certain time period. This took my full attention, and other things were put aside. I no longer had a regular schedule. I forgot about practice, read into the wee hours, ate whenever I felt hungry, only washed dirty dishes when there were no clean ones left.

"Look at you. What's the matter with you?" My evil twin dropped in at ten o'clock.

"What do you mean?"

"Your place is so disorganized. Papers, journals, and letters are scattered all over. Dirty dishes are stacking up in the kitchen."

"Ann will be here Friday; she'll clear all that up."

"You weren't like that. You used to consider making the place tidier before Ann came to clean."

"I know, but I'm busy. I'll add an extra amount in addition to her cleaning services. By the way, you're the one telling me to get help. I'm in the process of doing that."

My evil twin shook her head. "You are being extreme."

"Look, let me have my way to deal with this, okay? I need to find out who I was, who I am, and who I will be."

She pointed at the diaries and other records. "Have all these been helpful?"

"Don't know yet. I read through 1985 to 1995. I couldn't find much on 1994, then jumped to 1998. I'm still searching."

"Don't forget the Chinese saying, 'Doctors cure others but can't cure themselves.'"

I looked at my evil twin, wondering if that was what I was doing, trying to cure myself.

In the middle of looking for 1994, I found my UCSF folders. In them, I came across a paper—*The Other Side of Sadness* by George Bonanno—that described psychological resilience. Simply put, it's the ability to mentally or emotionally cope with a crisis or to return to a pre-crisis status quickly. I didn't see that it had much to do with my situation.

"I would not call a single suicide a crisis. Rather, I see the difference if it were a terrorist suicide bombing—the event itself would create a crisis. What do you think, Sis?" I spoke aloud in the air. No answer.

I continued to read the paper, which stated that a person will utilize their mental capability to evaluate "personal assets" and protect oneself from the potential negative effects of stressors. In other words, "psychological resilience exists in people who develop psychological and behavioral capabilities that allow them to remain calm during crises/chaos and to move on from the incident without long-term negative consequences."

"Ha, that sounds right for how I reacted and felt in Shirley's incident, but it's completely inapplicable to Matthew's case," I said to myself.

On the other hand, this study told me that I could use psychological resilience to protect myself externally, not internally, not my inner self, which meant that deep down in me there was something that I still couldn't untangle from its cord—Matthew's death, the only matter in which my ability to access psychological resilience had become useless.

Before starting to research what I could do for a new career, I had to take a trip back to the land. Connor had completed his ten-year contract and renewed the second contract for five years. And now, in the third year of the new term, Connor's wife had a stroke, which changed everything. She had tremendous difficulty uttering a word, her speech was blurry. Besides this communication deficit, she couldn't control her body movements and was strapped into a wheelchair to keep her body upright. Connor became her caregiver 24/7. They decided to move to a town in Pennsylvania where one-third of the population was Amish and where Sam had attended college at Penn State University.

I needed to find someone else to farm the land. Otherwise, it would revert back to residential status by the township's tax code.

After I boarded the connecting flight to South Band, I took a window seat since I was the only passenger in my row. As the plane was descending, I felt warmth and coolness on my face. It was my tears. I don't recall if I was thinking of anything in particular, but after Matthew died, I had taken this trip many times, and tearing had happened a few times on this last leg of the flight for no apparent reason. Perhaps it being Matthew's hometown, Matthew's soil, and Matthew's resting place brought me to tears.

I picked up a rental car and drove directly to Berenice's. Henry was out on the front lawn waiting for me. He always welcomed me in this way. He gave me a big, long hug, rested his arm on my shoulder, took my bag, and walked me up to the front door to greet Berenice. Berenice's health had been declining, but that didn't stop her from laughing. She looked at me sideways and extended her bony hand to take mine.

"Sit down, let me look at you," she said while directing my hand to the seat on her left, her better eye.

"How are you doing, Aunt Berenice?"

"I'm fine. I am so glad you're here. Look, Aunt Jodie baked you some morning buns, and she'll be here in the next hour or so."

Jodie and Berenice had learned what I like. The boys liked Jodie's berry pies; Matthew liked blueberry; Alan, cherry; Kurt, strawberry; and Timothy, raspberry. But I didn't like pies. I would eat her morning buns for breakfast.

Sitting in Berenice's kitchen brought back many scenes as if I were in a movie again. The aroma of fresh baked gingersnap cookies and cinnamon from the morning buns made me feel like I was in a wonderland where children were cheerfully playing with each other and adults seriously working together in harmony. Berenice was instrumental in this concinnity of elevating and binding together family members despite her disability and losses.

"Matthew loved Aunt Berenice, but still, he left her," I thought to myself.

"How is your family?" Berenice's fingers still held mine.

"My father is in and out of the hospital two, three times a week. Looks like he is taking up camp in the hospital permanently."

"Oh, I am sorry to hear that. What kind of illness, may I ask?"

"He has a benign tumor in between the rib cage and his left lung. He also has emphysema."

"Oh my, can it be operated on?"

"The doctor does not recommend it. My father was a smoker and had half of his lung removed when he was in his early forties. The doctor said my father might not survive the anesthesia. Eventually, he won't be able to breathe on his own. Now, he carries an oxygen cylinder with him everywhere he goes"

"That is tough. I am sorry for your father and your family to have to bear this."

"Thank you. My mother has been his caregiver. He won't allow anyone else to help him or clean him, not even the nurse."

Berenice looked at Henry and me. "Men are stubborn."

Henry scratched his forehead and looked at the floor. I felt funny about this. Why should he be lumped in with my father's selfish behaviors?

Berenice continued, "How's everybody else besides your father?"

"Everyone is doing well. My siblings and I feel that my father has taken our mother away."

"Long-term illness is hard to live with—" Berenice stopped in the middle of her sentence. "Do you want anything to eat?"

"Yes, let's have teatime. I'll make coffee. Do you want some?" Berenice only drank coffee, and Henry didn't drink coffee, only iced tea.

"Oh, sure, I'll have coffee, and I baked a fresh batch of gingersnaps, if you want some, but I know you won't." Berenice chuckled.

I could see Matthew come in and walk straight to the ceramic owl cookie jar that was constantly stocked with gingersnaps and chocolate sugar cookies, Berenice's famous cookies that no one ever rejected except me. He would take the lid off and put it next to the owl's face, and without looking, stick his hand in to take a cookie. This was a game that Jerry, Matthew, and Alan played, to see what kind they got. Actually, I thought they could tell by touch what kind they had taken, but no one ever said that out loud. After getting a cookie, Matthew would lean back on the corner counter and start munching on the cookie while listening or talking to Berenice. When the cookie was half gone, he would take the milk from the refrigerator, pour it into a glass, and finish it with the rest of the cookie.

I could see contentment on his attractive, smiling face. I wanted to touch that face, when suddenly I heard Berenice asking, "Do you still remember where the coffee filters are?" My hand was in midair in front of the corner cabinet where Matthew used to stand.

"Yes," I said as I turned to the sink and opened the counter drawer for the coffee filter. I recalled part of a letter that Matthew wrote to me the first month I lived in this house:

Dear girl,

…Have you learned to bake cookies? Actually, I don't care if you know how to make cookies. I like your food, Chinese, Hong Kong, or others, I like your cooking…

Love Matthew

I never learned to make cookies because I thought there would always be a supply from Berenice. I never baked a single cookie for Matthew.

Berenice was right. In addition to pies and cookies, I didn't eat muffins or most other sweet foods. But I loved a good fresh donut from the mom-and-pop store down the road. They made only one batch every morning and sold out by eleven o'clock. Whenever I was in town, the owner would save me one. I never failed to accept such hospitality and enjoyed every single bite of those donuts.

Matthew was puzzled by my sense of taste. He didn't get why I wouldn't eat most sweets, like chocolates and ice cream, but I would eat a donut. Sunday was his pancake day. Saturday was my donut day.

While I was eating it, I would say, "Mmm, as good as the fresh bread I got every day when I lived with Grandma."

"Did you get bread at the bakery every day?" Matthew asked.

"No, fresh bread was delivered to my grandma's house twice a day, six thirty in the morning and three in the afternoon."

"Wow, that must have cost a fortune." He looked at me with his smiling eyes.

"No, that was the custom in Macau, the way people got fresh baked goods. If people were living in those four-story apartment buildings, they just lowered a basket from a window, and the delivery person would place the bread in the basket."

Matthew looked at me, his face a question mark. "Really?"

I only nodded. I didn't give any thought to what I had just told him; I didn't detect that he didn't take my words seriously until about five years later when we got a chance to see an advance preview of the movie *Song of the Exile*, by Hong Kong director Ann Hui, presented by East Asian Languages and Cultures at the university.

While we were walking out of the performance hall, Matthew held my hand with delight. "I thought you were exaggerating about the fresh bread you used to get every day while living with Grandma. But all these years I've seen your pickiness about bread, and watching tonight's movie, I apprehend that you are really true to your words."

"Huh?" I searched his face, and at that moment I had no idea what he was talking about.

"The scene where the woman lowered her basket from the second floor to receive her bread, just like you told me…"

"Ah," I laughed and bumped myself into him. "You didn't believe me."

He pulled me close into a side hug. "I do. I just thought you were fantasizing about your fresh bread."

"So, now you also believe my rock chocolate and plain ice cream on top of iced coffee, right?"

He looked down and smiled. "Yeah, I do."

I lived with Grandma in Macau from second grade until I finished junior high. I grew up with twenty other children within a five-year age range in the community. Grandma was a community leader and strictly disciplined us about how we should conduct ourselves.

When I was seven, I could already recite the poem "Pity the Peasants" by Li Shen: "Do you know, each grain in your bowl, is from farmers' arduous work with beads of sweat under the burning sun each noon?" My classmates learned it in third grade, but Grandma had taught us this poem and recited it before every meal like a prayer. She would not allow us to waste any food.

On all the twenty-four holidays in the Chinese lunisolar calendar, Grandma would prepare seasonal tributes to the community members for that particular solar day, and community members would also individually celebrate the day. One of the solar days was the ghost festival, which I liked the most because on that evening, I could see fires in every street and every corner in our neighborhood. I liked to stare at the fires, imagining the flames and smoke rising up and maybe bringing the ghosts to their resting place instead of them floating in the fourth dimension with no place to put their feet down. Neighbors would burn paper images of money, houses, cars, and any materials that we use daily in our mortal life to make sure that there would be enough wealth to send off their deceased loved ones. Besides burning paper, people also scattered real coins and sometimes bills. Other children would rush to pick up the money. But my siblings and I would just watch, never picking up any money on the ground even if it were right in front of our toes. Grandma had warned us in the morning that that money was not for living souls; we needed to pay our respect to the dead. The neighbors always commented to Grandma on our good behavior.

Our house was a magnet for other children because Grandma was grooming my older brother (two years older than me) to be the future leader of the community. She allowed my brother to plan barbecues and soccer, ping pong, and Chinese chess games in the summer, and we would watch World Cup soccer live at our house, all of us staying up until three or four o'clock in the morning.

When I was in junior high, I got my allowance and no longer needed to rush home for teatime, which was at three thirty. After being in boarding school for a year, each day before I got home to Grandma's, I would stop by the small local store to pick up my treat for the day, a piece of dark chocolate. The store owner ran an honor system. In a clear jar were chunks of chocolate in different shapes, as if chiseled from a boulder. I would pick one and decide how much it was worth and drop my money into a small open box next to the jar. The owner never questioned me since my family had an excellent reputation and I had the badge of being trustworthy and having good manners. After my chocolate treat, I would walk a few stores down to the neighboring café and pick up my iced coffee with a scoop of ice cream on top. On those summer days, with close to one hundred percent humidity and high temperatures, the white ice cream rounded on top of the indigo iced coffee was delectable!

The café also had a do-it-yourself station for toast on the front porch, where three tiny charcoal braziers were lined up like a buffet table facing the street. At both ends of the braziers were arranged a box of sliced breads of different shapes, sweetened condensed milk, coarse sugar, butter, bamboo plates, and utensils. People would put one or two slices of bread, depending on how big they were, into a wire toasting frame and hold the frame over the brazier to brown the bread to their liking. When the bread was toasted, customers could select any or all of the condiments for their toast. I would make toast and spread a big slab of butter on the days when I had basketball practice. Eying the cow fat seep through the hot bread on one hand and a glass of iced coffee topped with ice cream on the other, I knew I was so fortunate to enjoy those treats, sitting on a bench in front of the café and observing the hustle and bustle throughout my early adolescence.

But when I went back to Hong Kong, living with my parents, my appetite for dark chocolate and ice cream with iced coffee vanished overnight. From then on, I painstakingly chose from a limited selection of certain sweets, and a crisp fresh donut became a permanent favorite.

In Indiana, my liking of donuts was made known to the whole town. I asked the store owner how he made them. One time he and his wife gave us a tour of his small donut-making facility, adjacent to the store. They only used potato flour, which was a major contributor to the crisp texture. They also made small batches and changed the oil every day. They sold the used oil to bio-truckers since their store was located near the exit of an interstate route.

"Sweetie!" Jodie came in through the kitchen door and extended her hands. I gave her a big hug. Jodie was two years younger than Berenice. She had always adored Matthew and dreamt of him being her daughter's husband. She would tell me how charming and handsome Matthew had been. Her daughter, Camila, was the same age as Matthew but somehow had never been close to any of the three boys. They knew each other from a distance. After Matthew died, Camila and I became better friends than Alan and Camila had ever been. Camila loved plants and worked at nurseries for her entire career. She knew her mother's wish, but she had a different feeling about Matthew.

Camila told me, "Matthew was funny and smart. He always seemed to know everything, from local plants to the world. I didn't see how I could match his brain.

He was my idol. The closest togetherness we ever had was in the woods in back of our house. We were nine or ten. One summer weekend Berenice and Henry brought all three boys to our place to have a barbecue in our backyard. Jerry and Alan were throwing the football with my older brother. Matthew wanted to show me the different trees and a secret in the woods. We went into the ten-acre woods that were part of our backyard. He pointed out the pines, red cedars, green ashes, and said he would grow more of them and protect them. While we were walking, he collected dried leaves and placed them in a sunny spot. Then he took out a magnifying glass. Soon, I saw white smoke and a tiny fire starting on the pile of dried leaves. I thought it was magic. Then my younger brother called our names. We put out the flame and walked back to the house. My brother asked what was burning. Matthew told him that we were barbecuing a squirrel and it was yummy. My brother took it seriously and told my mother we had killed and eaten a squirrel in the woods. My mother laughed so hard and patted Matthew's shoulder. 'You rascal.'

I liked Matthew with his harmless humor and dreamer's spirit. He made my mother laugh too. As we grew, our interactions diminished. When he went to college, I rarely saw him. Before you came along, the last time I saw him was at Jerry's funeral."

"How are you, Aunt Jodie?" I released my thoughts of Camila and my hug.

"I'm doing well, still walking three miles every day, playing bridge four nights a week at the church, and going out with Berenice to the mall and grocery shopping." She stood there and looked me up and down. "You're thinner. Do you eat?"

"Yes, I eat like a horse, at least that's what my teammates are saying to everyone."

"You don't look like that horse. You're too thin. Let us feed you up before you head back to California."

I have been blessed to have Berenice and Jodie as a mother and an aunt. From the beginning, Jodie was there through the entire family's tragedies. She knew Rachel through Berenice. She told me that she thought Rachel was beautiful and intelligent, and that Damon just couldn't match her. Jodie didn't like Dad that much. She thought Dad was too playful and lacked commitment and responsibility. Rachel's death convinced her further about Dad. She wouldn't show up at Berenice's whenever she heard that Dad would be there to visit. But she loved both Jerry and Matthew, particularly Matthew, who in her eyes was tenderhearted with a sweet, gentle nature toward every living thing. Jodie said that if she were the same age as Matthew, she would have pursued him, a dream of romantic love that she didn't think she had in her marriage.

Feeding me was Berenice's and Jodie's agenda from day one, when I arrived and only munched on iceberg lettuce. Whenever I stayed with Berenice, she would cook up a storm of beef pot roast, chicken breast cutlets, ham, or pork chops and watch me eat until I cleared my plate. The amount of meat that I'd have in a weeklong visit was almost equal to what I'd consume in a year in California.

Matthew loved to tease me at holiday meals. "I saw you eating a lot tonight. You really like the Thanksgiving meal, don't you?"

"Yes, I do, except the salad, which is not a salad at all, no fresh produce involved."

Matthew laughed. "Yes, that's a Midwesterner's salad, made with Jell-O and canned fruits and topped with marshmallows."

"I was so looking forward to having some fresh greens to balance the meal, and that Jell-O thing was just comical."

"Yeah, we eat a lot of that crap with cooked-to-death vegetables and meat. Now you understand why I ate everything offered to me in China. It couldn't have been worse than what I had here."

True, Matthew ate anything—no legs, two legs, four legs, wings. As comical as the Jell-O was to me, Matthew's first meal at my parents' house was no less hysterical, yet it was at that meal that Matthew won my parents' hearts.

Two days before we headed to city hall for our marriage, Matthew had arrived in Hong Kong from South Bend and rushed to meet my parents at their home. After the initial greetings, my mother brought out a big bowl of chicken feet soup and put it on the dining table. I was stunned.

I led my mother by the hand into the kitchen. "Ma, what are you doing?"

"I just made him soup."

"Ma, you know what I'm asking. Why are you making it difficult?"

"Well, he wants to marry my daughter. He'd better learn to eat Chinese food."

"We've never had this soup at home ourselves."

"Now we have."

I was frustrated with my mother; I hadn't thought she would do such a thing. It was too late for me to stop her, and it wouldn't be a good idea to argue with her in front of Matthew.

196

I thought the soup should taste good. There were a lot of good ingredients—pork tenderloin, chicken feet, dried red dates, goji berries, raw peanuts, black-eyed peas, and fresh ginger. But I didn't know how Matthew would take the chicken feet.

I brought a ceramic soup spoon, a pair of guest chopsticks, and a saucer for bones to the dining table.

Matthew looked at me and asked, "How should I eat this?"

"It's soup. Just the way you normally eat." I didn't tell him what the ingredients under the broth were. But he certainly saw the chicken feet and some red dates.

He dug right in. My parents and I sat there watching him. He gnawed the chicken feet bones clean and neatly placed them on the bone saucer. He ate all the other ingredients with a smile on his face and looked up every once in a while. Then he picked up the bowl to drink the rest of the broth. The bowl was as clean as if it had just come out of the dishwasher.

He held the bowl and looked at my mother. "That was delicious. Could I have some more?"

My mother's smile widened. She clapped her hands and said, "Of course, but let's have the main courses and then I'll get you another bowl of soup."

My mother turned to my father, who was also smiling with satisfaction, and speaking in Cantonese, said, "He couldn't have been pretending, could he?"

"No, I can see his enjoyment. He's a trooper," my father responded.

I was sitting there, amazed at what I'd just witnessed and at my parents' comments. I winked at Matthew, and he winked back. He didn't ask me what my parents said, but I knew he already knew that he had passed the test. We never talked about the chicken feet soup, but whenever we went out for dim sum, Matthew would order chicken feet steamed with black bean chili sauce.

Throughout our marriage, I seldom made traditional Cantonese soups, although I loved them. I knew how to enjoy them but didn't know how to make them. At home, there was always either my parents, sisters, or sisters-in-law to make soup for me. Whenever I went home, from the time I landed in Hong Kong to the time I took off, my second sister-in-law always had soup for me.

"No wonder people are getting bigger and bigger." I smiled at the memory of how Matthew had passed my mother's trial and of my longing for Cantonese soups.

"But you like the food though, right?"

"They taste good, and I don't eat them every day."

"I know, I love to see you eating so freely. I always love your cooking, your way of handling fresh produce." He clasped me into his big coat with half of his body while we were walking toward the land after our Thanksgiving feast.

"I cannot imagine what I would look like if I ate like this every day."

He made a puffer face with his two hands bent into brackets in front of his torso, lowered his upper body to a hunched back, and picked up his feet one slow step at a time. I watched the goofy Matthew and erupted in laughter.

The holiday meal was a collage of processed food and a few fresh ingredients. Turkey stuffing from a box, gravy from a bag, cranberry sauce and mashed sweet potatoes from cans, frozen green bean casserole mixed with a can of Campbell's cream of mushroom soup and then topped with generous splashes of canned fried onions, oyster stew layered with saltine crackers, heavy cream, and milk with chunks of butter in each layer, plus Jodie's buttermilk biscuits, parmesan chive dinner rolls, and pies. The whole meal was loaded with sugar, salt, fat, and MSG, the umami flavor abundant in every dish. At the end of the meal, while others were having pecan and pumpkin pies with ice cream for dessert, I chewed on a few pieces of iceberg lettuce to clean my palate.

I stayed in the same bedroom where the overdone, retouched professional photos of Jerry, Matthew, and Alan in their twenties were still hanging in the same place across from the bed. I looked at them, touched them, but didn't recognize any of them. The artificial colors on their cheeks were too feminine, their smiles like an elastic band stretched into a straight line. The eyes were the only thing that gave life to these waxen images. I have questioned for years why people would want pictures of themselves like these. If I could make a decision in this house, I would take them out. In a way, these photos upset me. The Matthew in the photo was not the Matthew I knew, the Matthew I loved, and whenever I was there, the pictures on the wall were a forceful reminder that two brothers were dead, leaving a cousin who was as devastated as the rest of us in this house.

The next morning, I walked over to the farm before breakfast. The black locust trees were crooked and new shoots completely encircled each one. Connor, Alan, and I had known from the time they were three years old that Matthew had been wrong. He thought the locust trees would grow straight and in ten years we could harvest them as poles. He didn't know that black locusts produce offspring everywhere the wind blows. Connor had been cutting the invasive shoots for over ten years, but he left five months ago. The farm was growing into disarray again. But on this late summer day, the fragrance from the white flowers that were in full bloom on the black locust trees swept through the air. As I walked on the path of the curving driveway, I was fully covered by the whiteness with a sweet scent sailing across my face at every step. As I approached the white pine grove, I held my breath. I hadn't visited for almost two years; the white pines took me by surprise. I knew that white pines grow slowly the first ten years. At ten to twenty years, the growth rate speeds up. They were planted as twelve- to eighteen-inch seedlings and had been standing there fifteen years. I could not have imagined they would be this tall and magnificent. In front of me was a forest, not just trees here and there. The display was for Matthew, who should have seen this splendid scenery.

"There you are." I heard Alan walking toward me. "Sorry I couldn't get to Mom's house last night." He stood next to me.

"This is amazing." I smiled at him.

"Isn't it? This is more like the plan Matthew had envisioned."

"Yes, unlike the black locusts."

Alan burst out laughing. "You're right about that. But the scent of honey at this time of year, nothing can beat that."

"I suppose. What should I do with them?"

"I need to think about it, or you can take all of them out."

"Then what? Take another ten years to grow another row of trees?"

"Yeah, it's not ideal but a decision needs to be made. Otherwise, you'll have to have another Connor to cut them every year, with no good results."

I looked at Alan. He spoke my heart. I had been thinking about the locust trees all these years. I knew they would be a long-term issue, I just didn't have the energy to resolve the current and recurring problem year after year. Connor's departure impelled me to see this.

"I know. I need to find someone who is willing to farm this place."

"Vivi, would you sell the land to me?" Alan looked me in the eyes.

I was a bit taken aback by this inquiry. For over a decade, some real estate companies had sent me letters expressing their interest in buying the land. I had saved the letters but hadn't given them any thought. Now Alan was the one asking me for the land, face to face. I wasn't prepared to give an answer.

Alan walked a step closer to the entrance of the white pine grove. "This is an enchanting place. It could be because the trees are Matthew's children or because of our childhood here. I just could not see someone else occupying this piece of land."

I had been paying taxes every year without any return but had not thought of selling it. Dad had suggested that I sell the land since I didn't intend to move back to the farm, but I hadn't been able to let go of the only physical connection I still had with Matthew. Once the land was sold, I would be a complete outsider.

"Alan, thank you for asking. I have not thought about selling it. Give me some time to think it over, okay?"

"Sure. As my boys have gradually become adults, I've been thinking of building a house just next to the property line, parallel with these guys." He pointed at the white pine grove. "In a few years, we can all live on the same parcel that's now owned by Mom and you."

Actually, Alan would be a better steward of the land than me. And it would stay in the family for at least one more generation. I had had a discussion regarding the land with Timothy, who told me that Grandma Dori would prefer Alan to live on that land rather than Kurt or him. I found that believable, given the stories that I have heard over the years, but I didn't take her desire into consideration because I didn't know her. She was just as fictional as any story I had ever heard. What Matthew wanted was what mattered. Matthew would want me to carry his torch, but I was not as dedicated as he was. That made me feel I owed him something. It could be the guilt I had felt over his death, the dream that we once had, or an unspoken promise that had not been fulfilled; I just couldn't pinpoint it. My life had its own will, and I couldn't make it compromise with Matthew's wishes. These were the torments I had been in for over a decade. All this, just running round and round in my head, and I just couldn't really face it while I was standing in front of the white pine grove with Alan next to me.

"Let's get some breakfast." Alan broke the silence, sensing my quandary.

"I'll be right there," I said as I walked into the grove.

A cool dampness swiped my body. It was still early morning, but by the afternoon this canopy trapping the humid air would be most welcome; now, it was a bit chilly. I looked up and saw sunlight starting to penetrate the east corner, with vertical beams streaming through all the green overhead. I couldn't see the tops of the trees. They were too high for me.

Matthew had planted them from the boundary inward to form an octagon, intending to build log benches and wooden tables on the four boundary corners with wide paths. Inside the octagon, there would be cross paths from north to south and east to west.

As the trees grew, they did not turn out exactly like the drawing on the blueprint. Yet, it was amazing to see the appearance of an octagon within a square space, all formed by white pine trees. Standing at the central point of the cross paths, I couldn't see the end of the paths in the four directions. The trees stood magnificently all around me. The sun's rays shone brighter and brighter, small star shapes of the rays luminating here and there, as if there were thousands of ornamental light bulbs knotted into a fishing net cast over the treetops for a carnival. I kept looking up and turning to chase the sparkles; my reality brought me back to the years of growing up, living along the sea, racing with the sunrise in the early morning, running uphill to school. That me had no sadness, no memories of unforgiveness, no experiences of death. How pleasant it was to trail the golden illuminance as I ran to the top of the forty-five-degree slope then turned right for about two hundred meters to the school gate.

I opened my hands, closed my eyes, turned round and round, searched for the sounds of water hitting the rocks, a foghorn, a motor roaring. I wanted to catch up with that girl who always held fast to her uncle's visits because he brought the sunlight, full of vitality, full of brightness, full of brilliancy. He also brought laughter, sweet smiles, and attentiveness to his niece's curiosity of the world.

I opened my eyes, there in the grove. I had the chill air with the sun's rays surrounding me, and all the experiences, the weights, the sorrows came back like a tsunami without visible waves or the audible velocity. It seemed that the past decade hadn't happened. There was no time gap. It all felt recent and raw.

Who had I become? I so desired answers, so desired a way to move forward, so desired a miracle to put all that had happened back into one piece and stall time.

I walked back to the house. Jodie, Alan, Henry, and Berenice were having breakfast. I poured a glass of orange juice, picked up a chair from the dining room, and joined them at the corner of the table just next to Berenice's wheelchair.

"Do you want a morning bun? Jodie just baked them this morning." Berenice offered me one.

I put it on the plate. On the table were scrambled eggs, bacon, sausages, pancakes (Alan's favorite), hash browns, white bread toast, morning buns, and a big bowl of fresh strawberries.

"I'd like some bacon."

"Wow, that's new. I only remember you eating rabbit food." Alan smiled and put two slices of bacon on my plate.

"I eat meat. You can ask Aunt Berenice."

"He's pulling your leg." Berenice glanced at Alan and me. We both just smiled at each other.

"What's your plan for today?" Alan asked.

"Not much, just relaxing and buying fish for tonight's dinner," I replied.

"Ah, Henry's feast of fish," Jodie joked with Henry.

"Yep, I can't wait." Henry winked at me.

Henry loved all kinds of seafood. Berenice didn't. She would only consume one or two bites of shrimp cocktail on the cruises they took every year. Berenice could cook up a storm with any other ingredients, but not seafood.

Matthew was like Berenice regarding seafood when we first met. He said Grandma Dori would make a casserole with canned salmon. He hated it, and it had traumatized him about seafood. The only fresh seafood the family ever made was the oyster stew during the holiday season, which still had too much of a fishy smell. When I introduced fresh steamed fish with ginger and scallions, Matthew loved it. From then on, he would eat any seafood, either homemade or from restaurants. He would brag about my fish when we visited Berenice and Henry. The bragging put me on the spot, and Henry joined Matthew in eating the fish and shellfish I cooked, which became a ritual whenever I visited.

After breakfast, Henry and I were ready to go shopping.

"Alan, will you stay for dinner? Aunt Berenice and Aunt Jodie will have chicken. You can have chicken, if you want?" I asked.

"Thanks, sounds great, but I need to check with Sandy first. I'll let you know when you come back."

The only time Henry and I would spend time alone is when we shopped for fish. He didn't talk very much when Berenice and Jodie were there. Even with me, we talked very little. Occasionally, when we'd find orange roughy, perch, and walleye, the fish he normally ate while working on the Great Lakes, he would talk about life on the boat.

"I miss working on the lake," he would say.

"I understand, just like I miss the ocean."

"I thought you were close to the water. Aren't you?"

"Yes, I am. The marina is about two miles away. Still, it's not the same. I used to hear the waves and foghorn, which were my lullabies."

"I know what it feels like. I loved to sleep at the bottom of the freighter. I could hear and feel the buoyancy. That helped me sleep deeper."

I nodded, looking out the window.

"Have you thought of moving back to Hong Kong?"

"Sometimes."

"And?" He looked at me.

"I don't know. I just feel I don't belong. I left decades ago, missed the chance to build my adulthood there. I'm more like a visitor, like here; I'm a foreigner, just a visitor."

"No, you aren't a visitor. We are your family; we're here for you." He tapped my hand.

I smiled at Henry. Good old Uncle Henry. I knew they loved me. Yet, I wouldn't tell them how my days went, wouldn't share my emotional and mental rollercoaster for all these years, and how I wished things had turned out differently. I couldn't say any of these thoughts to anyone anywhere. I felt that there was no one there to lend me a shoulder, to give me a hand. It was as if I were constantly floating on the water and couldn't find dry land.

The connection between us was Matthew, who was like a magnet pulling us all together even after his death. But his magnetic energy was hidden behind everyone's masks. Whenever someone mentioned him, only the memories of happiness would survive the conversation. I didn't know I could act that way, but I certainly had acted that way. A few times I tried to break the "happiness" reminiscences, but I couldn't open my month with the words that I wanted to say when I saw frail Berenice, denial Dad, and distancing Kurt and Timothy. None of us had the courage to communicate the pain that was deeply implanted in our souls with each other.

We purchased fresh walleyes and four jars of shucked oysters. After we got back to the house, I told Berenice that I'd make my version of oyster stew. "We don't need to wait for the holidays," I said.

When Alan learned that oyster stew was on the menu, he phoned Sandy and asked her to bring a salad and join us for dinner at Berenice's. Alan's three boys were in their twenties. Jerry (named after Matthew's brother) was twenty-four, Jay (Mr. No) was twenty-two, and Jason had just turned twenty a week before my visit.

"Are the boys coming for dinner?" Berenice asked.

"I don't know. They're hanging out with their friends in different places. I wouldn't count on them."

"Fine, we have hamburgers in the fridge. If they show up, they can have that."

"Mom, don't worry about them. They can get pizza or something." Alan just wanted Berenice's hands off his children's eating. Berenice acted like Grandma

Dori, very controlling of what the boys did and ate. Under Berenice's roof, "the boys" was the term for all the children and grandchildren, which she used even after they'd become adults. Jerry had completed his master's a year ago and was working as a city planner with the county. Jay was working for a landscaping company while going to community college. Jason would be a college senior in the fall, and he wanted to be a firefighter.

Among the three boys, Jerry had a much closer relationship with Matthew in comparison to his two younger brothers. At the farm, we had a green 1959 Ford long-bed pickup with a personalized license plate: 59 Angel. The first few years of working at the farm, the Ford would be running from north to south to transport tree seedlings and other farming materials back and forth. From the road, people could see the green truck was working hard. Jerry would walk over to the farm from Berenice's house after the school bus dropped him off. He watched Matthew, and sometimes Matthew would ask him for a hand. When that happened, Jerry was so excited and eager to work side by side with Matthew, who would teach him about putting up wire fences for beans and peas, fixing the manual hydraulic pump to get water from the well, sieving piles of dried compost into fine dark matter, and then adding that humus to the vegetable rows, and he would sit among the hay on the bed of 59 Angel while Matthew drove it to the other side of the farm.

One afternoon in late summer, while I was harvesting tomatoes, I saw 59 Angel moving toward the north entrance, which let out onto the main road. The driver was Jerry. He moved the pickup steadily and smoothly, made a U-turn right at the entrance rather than turning onto the road. After he turned, I saw Alan drive into Berenice's driveway and park at the end of the path that was in a horizontal line from where I stood. Alan saw Jerry driving the truck. He walked over and stood next to me. Together we saw Jerry make another U-turn and drive toward us. Alan flagged the truck down. Jerry got out of the truck, and before Alan could say anything, Jerry was running and jumping to tell Alan, "Uncle Matthew is teaching me to drive 59 Angel. She's beautiful! She listens to me, and she works well with me!"

I coated the walleye fillets with egg batter mixed with fresh ginger juice, fresh thyme, ground white pepper, and paprika, then rolled them lightly in almond meal before sautéing them. Right before I served dinner, Jerry walked in. "Hi, Aunt Vivi." He waved his hand and greeted the rest of the family members and Jodie.

"Hello, Jerry," I said. "You're just in time for dinner. Would you care for chicken or fish?"

"What kind of fish?"

"Walleye, Grandpa's favorite," I replied.

"I would try that."

I served the walleyes with a salsa. I heated up some olive oil, added fresh grated garlic, diced shallots, and smashed capers. With the smell of garlic and shallot just rising, I turned off the stove, tossed in abundant chopped fresh parsley and lemon zest, sprinkled salt and pepper, and then put the mixture in a serving bowl. Henry loved the fish with a spoonful of parsley condiment, and so did Jerry, who rarely had fresh fish at home.

Alan did not care for fish so much but went for the oyster stew. Berenice, Jodie, and Sandy were happy with the crispy-skin chicken thighs.

"I normally wouldn't eat the skin, but this is so good. How do you make it so crispy?" Sandy asked after a few bites of the chicken.

"I just place them skin-side down in an oiled cold Dutch oven, turn the stove on medium heat, and let them sizzle for about thirteen minutes without disturbing them. Once I turn them over, I put them in the preheated oven at 425 for another fifteen to eighteen minutes."

"Wow, that's easy. They are so tasty." Sandy smiled, and Berenice and Jodie nodded their heads in agreement.

After dinner, Sandy and Jodie cleaned up and Berenice kept them company. Jerry headed out to meet with friends. Henry, as usual, sat in his armchair next to the window in the corner of the dining room, reading his newspapers. Alan and I walked to the rock pile with a thermos of tea.

We sat on the largest surface of a boulder, looking at the western sky to get the last gleams of sunset.

"Remember these rocks? Matthew, Glenn, and I hauled them with the Ford, 59 Angel."

"I remember. You guys got them from a distant relative's abandoned farm, right?"

"The relative was Grandma Dori's cousin. His family doesn't live here anymore."

"How did Matthew get the permission for the rocks?"

"You know Matthew, whatever he needed on the farm, he first tried to find from recycled and reusable materials. He talked to Uncle John, who gave Matthew the cousin's son's contact info. The family was elated that Matthew wanted to take the rocks away."

"Yeah, Matthew was big on sustainability and nature conservation." I sipped the tea.

"I can see that right here. See all the trees are growing big and strong." Alan surveyed the land.

"How have you dealt with Matthew's death?" I didn't plan to ask that question but it slipped out.

"Oh, gosh, I was so mad at him. Even now, from time to time I'm still mad at him. How could he do such a thing to all of us? Particularly to my son Jerry."

"Do you know why?" I was hoping that Alan could give me a definitive answer.

"I don't know. Mom kept saying, 'On the day he came back from the mental health facility, he promised me he wouldn't do it again.' I don't know what was in his mind, what got him so desperate. Do you know?"

"I have tried to figure it out. I thought he had already tried once and that he really would not do it again. His promise to your mom was a guarantee to me. But we were so overconfident…" I looked down at my cup of tea, wondering if the tea leaves could tell me the truth.

"Do you know besides my mom, Uncle Damon, you, and me, who got hurt the most? My son Jerry."

I was a bit surprised. "I had no idea."

"By the time Jerry became a teenager, he'd been spending after school time with Matthew for almost three years. Besides me, Matthew was the other adult male who taught him life skills and dreams for the future. He has a special attachment to Matthew."

"I understand. I remember Matthew let Jerry drive the Angel."

"On that day when I came back from work, seeing the Angel coming from a distance, realizing that the driver was Jerry, I was indignant with Matthew. He took away my privilege of teaching my son to drive. I should have been the one doing that. But now when I think of that day, remembering Jerry's gallantry and joy, I smile. At least he left the memories of those good times in Jerry's heart."

Yes, how could one forget an unforgettable uncle? I had one. I knew how Jerry felt, the feeling of being cheated, the feeling of missing him, the feeling of wanting to hold onto the lively interaction, and all of that was wrapped in an edgeless sea, which, no matter how hard I tried, I still could not find my way to a solid ground. Those feelings would not go away; they stay for life.

"How is Jerry doing?" I came back to the present.

"He's doing okay. He has been seeing a counselor for eleven years. Wow, time flies."

I looked up to the sky, searching for stars without responding to Alan.

"Actually, it was Jerry's suggestion that I should buy the land. He has asked me many times what will happen to the land in the future. He wouldn't want to see someone else own this place. I want to do this for my son, who treasures the land as much as I do. First, I lost my cousin Jerry, then part of me died with Matthew. Feeling my son's pain is similar to mine. I just want to keep Matthew's spirit alive in this piece of land. Every time I sit here, I am comforted by this thought of seeing the three of us at nine or ten, this timeless place..." Alan stopped, waiting for my reaction.

"I see. I need time to think it over. I hope by now, you also know that this land has special meaning to me. I am not ready to let go of it." I wrapped my hands around the cup, gripping it tightly.

Besides wanting to reassure Jerry, Alan has his own grief. When he said, "Part of me died with Matthew," my heart palpitated. "I'm not the only one to feel that way," I said to myself. I still didn't know how many parts of me had died. Memories, perspectives on life and the world, mental capacity, and emotional intelligence were all entwined into this equation, like a ball of multiple strands of yarn that, after all these years, I still could not untangle.

Alan lost two cousins who were brothers to him.

I tried to imagine how I would handle it if any of my brothers or sisters, my playmates and buddies from earliest childhood left me alone to witness life and changes on this earth. Uncle Mike's death was difficult for me to accept. I still didn't know where his grave was. My parents didn't know how to help me and believed that by sending me to boarding school, where I would be surrounded by my peers, soon I would overcome my grief at losing Uncle Mike. Somehow, I could feel the pain that Alan and young Jerry had been carrying all these years. Their pain was partially mine.

"Should I sell the land to Alan now?" I asked myself again and again.

ALMOST FORGOTTEN

THE NEXT DAY, I LEFT the house without having breakfast with Berenice and Henry. I told them I was going to get my donut. I picked up not only one donut, but half a dozen and two cups of coffee. Then I went to the cemetery.

It was a beautiful Sunday morning. The sun was out. I saw that all the surfaces of the three tombs were clean. The geraniums were in full bloom, bright red bedding in front of Jerry. Matthew's "The Tree Man" was behind Jerry's because only ashes are buried there.

"Matthew, I brought you coffee and donuts." I walked around Jerry and leaned against a maple trunk diagonally next to Matthew. The coffee smelled so good in this open and quiet place. I bit into a donut, with a smile. "It's still as good as my daily fresh bread in Macau." I took a sip of my coffee and finished the last bite of the first donut.

"Two things I need to tell you. First, Alan wants to buy the farm. Second, I didn't know Jerry had great difficulty in dealing with your death. Alan just told me yesterday, the first time we talked about our feelings without cautiously worrying about the outcomes. Alan is still angry that you didn't keep your promise. Look what you did to all of us, particularly young Jerry."

I looked at Matthew's tomb. To my surprise, I saw two small bundles of red sticks stuck into the ground about an inch above the soil, along the edge of the lower part of the plaque.

I leaned toward the sticks, picked up a couple of them. They were brittle, which indicated they had been there for at least a few months. They were incense sticks. Burning incense in front of a tomb is a Chinese tradition when descendants visit and pay respect to the deceased.

"Who would do this besides me?" I asked myself, turning the sticks to look for any marks.

"Vivi?" I heard a woman's voice above me.

I looked up. There was a middle-aged woman with light blonde hair wearing thin gold-rimmed eyeglasses standing in front of Jerry with sunlight glaring behind her head.

"Pardon me, do I know you?"

"Shannon. We met at the Xi'an Film Studio in Xi'an, when Matthew and you visited me."

I was totally surprised. My memory of her was of a medium-built woman without glasses. But now she was almost twice as wide.

"You put these here?" I extended my hand upward with the incense sticks.

"Yes, on Matthew's birthday last November."

"Thank you. I appreciate your efforts."

"Vivi, I wanted to say I was sorry when I received the news, but I was still in China and never got around to contacting you."

"No worries." I held out the remaining cup of coffee. "I got an extra cup of coffee and some donuts. Do you want them?"

She took the coffee. "I assume it's for Matthew." She took a sip.

"Yes. How did you know that Matthew is here?"

"Glenn told me. But I could have guessed because Jerry and his mom are here."

I looked at her. I didn't know her at all. I'd only met her once when she was working on a translation project for a movie.

"Did Matthew tell you about me?"

"No, and I didn't ask."

"Matthew told me you never asked him about his marriage. Were you not curious at all?"

"No, I wasn't interested in his past relationships. And I'm not in the habit of asking personal questions."

"Yes, you're good about that, Matthew said."

A silence fell.

"Do you remember the green scarf that you knitted for Matthew? I cut it to pieces when Matthew insisted on a divorce."

"I know. Matthew told me. I knitted him a blue one after what you did."

"I didn't want a divorce. Did you know that?"

"No, Matthew didn't tell me that. He just told me he gave you all the cash to settle the dissolution."

"What else did he tell, may I ask?"

"When we first met, he said you were having an affair with a Chinese PhD candidate, who was also married. I remember he was there at the Xi'an Film Studio when we met. Was that true?"

"At that time, it was just a fling. I didn't realize Matthew took it so hard."

I looked at Shannon with an amused expression and pondered, "Ha, sexually involved with a married man and she thought it was okay for her own marriage. What kind of reasoning is that?"

"I know it sounds crazy. Come to think of it, Matthew had the right to a divorce. I wasn't prepared for him to initiate the process and act so quickly. I was angry that he no longer loved me."

"Did you love him?"

"I don't remember." She looked at me and continued, "First, I had my eye on Jerry, but he wasn't interested in me. Then came Matthew, who was much sweeter, with a good sense of humor, very easygoing, being artistic and a dreamer, really single-minded. He didn't second-guess anyone and treated people equally. He was a husband type, and I didn't mind marrying him. For eight years of our marriage, he didn't stop me from spending money. He took care of me and our finances. But I underestimated Matthew's tolerance of my freedom to do wild things." She looked at me again.

I didn't know how to respond to her story. I looked back to her eyes. "But you are here. What compels you to burn incense and come back again?"

"Matthew had tremendous respect for Chinese culture. He thought every mundane traditional ritual represented certain wisdoms. I thought he would appreciate that I burned incense for him. That's what the Chinese do, isn't it?"

"Yes, but neither of you are Chinese."

"Ah, I lived in China for fifteen years. I also have learned to value some rituals. I do it for Matthew, who made my life easier. He was more Chinese than most of the white people I met there. I had never seen Matthew at his happiest in this country. He belonged to China. Burning incense is the least I can do. I'm also on my way to see my folks, so I stopped by."

I agreed with Shannon's assessments. I concurred that Matthew was much happier in China. In fact, he wanted to live in China. I had thought that if we had stayed in China, he might still be happily alive, safe and sound.

"Why are you telling me all this?" I asked.

"I didn't plan to. It just happened that I found you here. Glenn said you hardly ever visit the cemetery even when you're in town. What brings you here?"

I looked at her, wondering, "Are we switching roles? I'm the surviving spouse, and it's natural that I visit my late husband's grave." Instead, I asked Shannon, "Do I need a reason to be here?"

She shook her head, smiling. "No. Matthew told me that you're subtle. I can see that now."

"Did you often communicate?"

"Only when I was still in China. From time to time, we had phone calls here and there. After you married him, I still had his credit card that I was using. He wanted me to stop using it. At first, I just wanted to make it difficult for him. After a few months, my anger subsided because he didn't cancel the credit card. Then I stopped using it. After you left China, he was shopping in Xi'an before heading back here. He didn't see me. He just visited other old friends at the university and left me a note, which was the last note I had from him."

I nodded, looking down at The Tree Man.

"Do you want to know what he wrote?"

"If you want to tell me."

Shannon walked over, picked up a donut. "You really are who Matthew described. He wrote, 'Thanks that you stopped using the credit card. My dad paid off the balances. Vivi has not asked about money or anything related to my past. She keeps the way of the Tao with her own modifications, doesn't want to intrude, and doesn't want to involuntarily know something that she doesn't need to know.' Matthew really admired 'your way.'"

"If people want to tell me their stories, they'll initiate the telling. My mother said that I was a fool to behave this way after she asked a lot of questions about Matthew and I had no answers." I turned and faced Shannon.

"Fool, maybe. But you won the hearts of Matthew's family. Glenn told me they adore you." Shannon finished her donut, dug into her bag, and held out a package of incense and a book of matches.

"Here," she said, turning to leave.

I took the items. "Thank you. I'm glad we got a chance to chat about Matthew."

She looked back at me. "He was a good man, a gentle soul."

We waved goodbye. I watched her walk away, gradually diminishing on my horizon. I tore open the package. There were ten small bunches bundled individually. I took out one bunch. Two-thirds of the top were yellowish with velvet-like paste cladded onto red sticks about twelve inches long. The matches apparently came from a bar. Matthew had a habit of collecting matches from every pub or microbrewery. "Who influenced who in this habit?" I wondered while turning over the matchbook. From years of observing Matthew, I knew the reason he collected them. Once he said, "The cover of a book of matches sometimes is fascinating. Some of them are so graphic, and some are so artistic." I still had one with an image of a woman's naked body with long curly hair, vivid teats, hips, and long legs in only dots and skinny lines.

I lit a match and put it under the bunch of incense. Soon the white smoke and an earthy scent floated in the air. I stuck them on the lower edge of The Tree Man. I stood up and paced back and forth.

"Matthew, you are lucky to have both of us here to see you. I like Shannon. She keeps her own pride yet knows her place and where to stand." I mumbled, "I don't know what to do with the land. I just know that the land should stay within the family and Alan would be the perfect person to own it. I thought I would be okay selling it to him. But I am having a hard time letting go. Something is aching. Could you tell me what it is?" I kicked the leaves that had dropped from the maple tree. I looked up, realized it was late August. Some of the leaves had started turning yellowish brown.

I looked back at The Tree Man, absentmindedly asking, "Isn't it a bit too early for the leaves to turn colors?"

The next day I drove to the high school track. Students were still on summer break and wouldn't be returning for another week. I walked to the gate, which surprisingly was unlocked. I went in sideways. The field was newly mown. The cut-grass smell was still fresh. From the outer lanes inward, I walked in a straight line diagonally across all the lanes, from one staggered-start line to the next, six, five, four, three, two, one. I liked running because I only needed a pair of running shoes, which are easy to carry, and I could run anywhere at any time, not having to depend on any equipment or facilities. I liked to knit for the same reason. I could pack knitting needles and yarn in my backpack and knit anytime I wanted.

I ran on this track for almost four years. I liked to run in the outer lane, as opposed to Matthew, who ran in the inner lane. Matthew was not an enthusiastic runner. He preferred physical exhaustion from farm work. During the first year we moved back and lived at Uncle John's house, we were just four-tenths of a mile from the track. I would run in the early morning before school started while

Matthew was home preparing for the day of work at the farm. One winter, I was about to finish the last lap of a 10K and was running toward the entrance gate. I stepped on a small stone that had no reason to be in the field. My left ankle twisted outward, and I fell. The pain shot up to my brain in no time. I sat on the ground and held my left calf with both hands to allow the pain to subside. Soon, along with the pain, I felt cold. It was in the low twenties, Fahrenheit. I looked around. No one was in sight. I tried to stand up, but my left leg would not take the weight. I could not even put it on the ground, which was icy. I decided to use my hands to get myself out of the field. Once I was on the pavement, I might be lucky enough to get someone's attention. I straightened my left leg, my hands on each side of my hips, and lifted my upper body at the same time jumping my right leg forward. This seemingly simple maneuver took different muscles to coordinate with a lot of energy required to achieve a small forward movement. But I still felt cold, particularly my palms on the icy ground. By the time I had inched out of the gate, I was trembling and my teeth were uncontrollably chattering. The sun was just beginning to shine on my part of the earth. The sunrays reflecting on the white ground made my surroundings light up as if thousands of spotlights were turning on one at a time to guide my way, only I wanted them closer to keep me warm. I moved closer to the curb in hopes of getting passing cars to spot me while I continued testing my muscular endurance.

In my mind, I kept repeating "consistency and discipline," which was the phrase my coach lodged in my head when I was on a marathon-related team in high school. I tried to envision that home was just around the corner, one more move would be one step closer. The cold gradually numbed my palms, and I was having blurred vision.

A shadow hovered on my left side. I turned and there was 59 Angel. Matthew ran out and picked me up. He put a hat on me and covered me with the Pendleton Native American wool blanket that came with 59 Angel when we bought her. The owner said it was 59 Angel's guardian angel. The cold thwarted my voice. Matthew drove to the closest emergency room. The doctor and nurse cut away my clothing that limited the movement of my body and wrapped me with extremely lightweight ready-heat blankets. A nurse fed me hot chocolate, which was a lifesaver and the best hot chocolate I ever had. After my body was warm enough and I was able to talk, the doctor checked on my ankle. The X-rays indicated that I had a hairline fracture at the distal end of the fibula. I was on crutches for six weeks.

Matthew said, "You scared the life out of me. I thought you would die when I picked you up."

I could only swing his hand with a coquettish grin. "I knew you would come to get me."

"What if I weren't here?"

"What do you mean?"

"I could be away, or if I die."

"No, you cannot die before me." I held up my pinky, eyeing Matthew for his. Matthew, with a doting smile, raised his pinky. I hooked his into mine. "Deal."

He purchased a cell phone with a Velcro accessory to fasten on my upper arm. He programmed all our nearby relatives' phone numbers and gave me an ultimatum that whenever I went out alone, particularly running, I had to attach the phone to my arm. Aside from giving me the phone, Matthew started to run with me.

Now, on this day in August, I put on my running shoes. While tying my shoelaces in the sixth lane, I looked up at the field that stretched in full view in front of me.

I hadn't run on this track for years; would I walk out of here safe and sound without Matthew?

I tried to shake the thought and examined my cell phone to ensure it was tight on my left upper arm. When I completed the fourteenth lap, I started to breathe heavily in company with an incessantly intense burning sensation from my lungs to my throat.

"I'm getting old," I told myself.

"You are not," my evil twin's voice dropped in.

"Breathe slowly. Consistency and discipline. Eleven more laps to go. You will get to your 10K."

I strategically slowed my pace, picked my lower legs up higher in a bouncing and jumping stride. I looked straight ahead, both arms symmetrically moving back and forth at ninety degrees, perpendicular to the floating rib on each side of my torso. By the nineteenth lap, I felt like I was flying. Each step was very lightly touching the ground and automatically lifting up to the air as if I were running on clouds, no solid surface to feel. Yet, gravity remained for my landing. I didn't want to stop at 10K. I could keep running on my runner's high.

"Don't overdo it," my evil twin warned me.

I slowed my pace, gradually transitioning to fast walking. There was no one else on the track. I walked a full lap to cool down.

"Good job, girl. I am so proud of you."

"I have the cell phone with me." I raised my left arm in triumph.

"Keep running, let go of me and let yourself free."

"Let go of me." I had never thought that I was holding Matthew back. At the moment, as I was cooling down after running 10K, flashbacks of watching the fires during the ghost festival came back to life: I, as a nine-year-old, watching the fires and asking, "Would the burning of artificial wealth help to secure a resting place for the ghosts?"

I stopped walking and asked myself, "Have I inadvertently interfered with Matthew's passage to a resting place?"

"No, he meant to get on with your life; you have stalled long enough," my evil twin said out loud. She continued, "Please, don't corner yourself in your head again."

I had been fixated on the thought "I contributed to Matthew's death," which took a long trek for me to discover, from being a fearless child tumbling along with life's happenings and who constantly asked *why* and had blind faith that I'd procure the answers, to now, still struggling with questions without answers.

Life's happenings have their own agenda regardless of whether I agree. I tried to adapt to living without Matthew. Still, I was not living. I was scrambling along to fight my twist of fate. Perhaps guilt over Matthew's death was my incarnation that had dragged me all these years to be struck in a rut. But with my own intellect and experiences, there were indications that I was not alone on this planet in feeling this way. Most of us never meet, never cross each other's path. But depression and death are universal.

The evening before I headed back to the Bay Area, after dinner I walked over to the land again. Through the winding driveway, the white flowers of the black locusts were gracefully flickering in the descending sun, their saccharine aroma saturating the air. I felt like I was walking in a wedding procession. When I approached the rock pile, little birds were singing and flying around the wild sumacs, which were dramatically striking with narrow pyramidal fruit clusters exhibiting a velvety crimson. In the marsh area, a few ducks were drilling on the mud. The rest of the cover-crop field in hues of verdigris blended with golden cream and sporadic medium-orchid in varied heights waved softly, beckoning me to touch. The greenish earthy scent of white pines was intoxicating at the hour of sunset. I entered the grove seeing shredded lights and shadows among the tree trucks. "Seraphic." I exhaled.

I felt the encompassing giants with their stillness on the vast expanse of quietude. I closed my eyes, walking warily on the soil, swaying my hands to scan my surroundings. I lightly thumped on a trunk, my equanimity permitting me to hug it, to place my face on its bark. "Should I let go of you?"

ANOTHER JOURNEY

I GOT A JOB eleven months after I left mental health services. Still working for a nonprofit, acting as a strategic planning analyst to evaluate risk and control for an environmental protection agency, a new career thanks to my architectural design education and hands-on experience in growing trees and sustainable agriculture. The agency was full of talented people of diverse backgrounds and ages. Keith, one of my teammates, previously a forest ranger, worked closely with me to evaluate reforestation of montane forests north and northeast of Santa Rosa that had gone through a few fires since 2002. As we drove into the vicinity, naked black stalks were clustered in one place and others were scattered on both sides of the road. I could spot the dark circles on the ground and the destruction that was prolonged mile after mile. "I have seen this before." I registered the scene in my mind.

The first time I saw a burnt forest was the devastation of the 1988 fires in Yellowstone National Park when we drove across the country in 1990. The ghostlike black stalks stood their ground in a stretch from Wyoming to Montana.

The second time, I witnessed it right across a fire zone.

Early one summer morning, Matthew got a call. After the call, he got out of bed, changed his clothes, and asked me to pack a lunch.

"What was the call about?"

"There was a lighting fire fifteen miles south of here. The department asked me to help prevent the fire from jumping over to the community adjoining a golf course. I need to call my crew. Could you pack food and water for six people?"

"Sure, and I want to go with you."

Matthew turned to face me. "The area will be hot and dangerous."

"I know. I can help with the tools and feed you guys."

Ten minutes later, we were on our way to the affected site. The woods on the other side of the burning area were separated by a shallow basin at least fifteen feet wide with an eight-foot-high chain-link fence along the golf course property line. The space was clouded with smoke through which could be seen the ghastly black and orange. Across the fence in the distance, the skeleton trees stood densely clustered with charred cores and limbs producing steaming ashes, and the sounds of shrieking, sizzling bark echoed. I shuddered as if the world were about to end.

Matthew gathered us in a circle.

"Vivi will be the runner for supplies. The rest of us are going to work in two groups. Connor and I will climb the trees. Two of you belay and spot one of us. Remember, don't touch any trees. Only listen to it and get my attention before taking any action."

I identified electrical outlets and brought in a spare generator and other equipment. I made sure the batteries for the chainsaws, drills, and other small electrical tools were fully charged, and I continued to charge the backup batteries. The residential area was south of the golf course. Matthew and Connor began north and south and worked in opposite directions to mark trees that needed to be cut down, and they met in the middle. While the trees were being cut, I used a hedge trimmer to shear the low-growing vegetation along the fence. As our work progressed, more volunteers merged on both sides of the fence, clearing grasses and shrubs to avert the fires from advancing.

"Any tree doctors here?" a firefighter yelled from the other side of the fence.

"Yo!" Matthew raised his hand and walked toward the fence.

"Over there, a tree is producing a clicking and hissing sound." The firefighter pointed to the northeast corner.

Matthew, his team, and I went over to the tree.

A tall silver maple stood in front of us. Matthew looked up and around, told all of us to stand back, changed to a pair of heat resistant gloves, circled the trunk while scrutinizing up and down, and assiduously placed the lower part of his left palm on the smooth, gray surface. Immediately, he backed away from the tree.

"It's burning inside." He looked at us.

"I have no experience putting out a fire in a tree that looks normal like this one. What should I do?" the firefighter asked. Matthew trod the soil back and forth with his boots, took out a small spade from his tool belt, lowered himself to the ground, and poked the soot.

"Do you have hoses connected to water?" He looked up sideways at the firefighter.

"Yes, we can have a fire engine park close to here."

"Here is what we can do. We'll dig a shallow trench around the tree, create a dripline to soak the area, and erect a barrier at least forty feet in diameter to stop people coming near, post someone to watch it for the next forty-eight hours, and hope that the tree will stop burning. Once the burning stops, we can remove it."

"Is it possible the tree could fall?"

"Yes, that's why we need to have a barrier around the tree at least forty feet in diameter to block access. The watcher needs to understand the blowing wind and be alert when the wind direction changes to protect him- or herself from a potentially falling tree that's burning inside. The good news is that this is a young tree and I think it's less than thirty feet high. If it falls, the ambit of destruction should be less than a full-grown tree would cause."

The firefighter gave him a thumbs-up and said, "Will do."

"Okay, let's get to work. Jimmy and Jake, you take turns watching and walking around the silver maple while others dig the trench. Could I have four to five people to help dig?" Matthew asked the firefighter.

"Sure, I'll put them at your disposal." The firefighter went to get the firetruck and people.

With Matthew's leadership and directions and more volunteers, we cut down sixty-five percent of the marked trees in twelve hours before dusk fell around nine o'clock. The fires on the other side were still torching the communities but had not crossed over.

My mind came back to the present. While driving along with Keith, I wanted to ask Matthew, "How did we get to the point that the fires could leap from this upper hill across to the lower slope of this mountainside town?" With the presence of wraiths ushering us, I asked but didn't expect an answer.

"Global warming." Keith moved his head left and right to keep his eyes in the shadows while driving.

I was surprised to hear Keith's response. I didn't give any thought to the fact that other people weren't aware of my habit of talking to Matthew. Keith must have thought I was talking to him about our current work together.

I gave a quick assessment: "The upper hill is a bit easier to replant. But houses are built on the lower slope and potential fires are still an imminent danger in this area."

"Yes, people are the problem for this as well." Keith glanced at me with approval.

"In what way?" I asked.

"We have lost lives in these fires. But some residents wouldn't think of moving out of this area. Some because of financial infeasibility. Others just want to be the hermits that rule this forest terrain," he said as we stepped out of the car.

We walked along the lower slope. A few houses were still standing. Others were either burned to the ground or uninhabitable.

"Is this all federal land?" I pointed my index finger in a semicircle around the scorched landscape.

"Yep. And that's another obstacle to sound forest management."

"How so?"

"Forest Service invests very little in forest management. Lack of resources, ample bureaucracies with copious schools of thought and political divergence—all of this has already created a perfect storm of inefficiency, not to mention environmental catastrophe."

"How eloquent," I think. "I guess our organization is part of this turbulence?"

"In a way, yes. You and I are included. I am hoping that with us as a third party to give some practical suggestions to the federal and state decision makers, we can get something done in the near future."

As my work progressed with more visits to the wildlands and to the reclusive residents, I realized that categorizing wildfires was not as simple as I had previously thought. Global warming leading to climate change was one of the factors; inefficient forest management was another; political disagreements and non-standardized policies were others. Human error was the most often cited factor. But we neglected the residents, the most isolated ones, whose only way of life had been living in the mountain terrain for several generations.

It took me more than nine months to get to know Brian and his extended family of three generations. Brian, his father Jack, brother Tom, and Tom's son Scott lived in the mountain ranges within three hundred miles of San Francisco. Brian and Jack lived in Sierra County, and Tom and Scott lived in the foothills of the Sierra Nevada. All of their houses had burned down in different fires.

We were sitting at a picnic table near the newly installed electric grill, thirty steps away from his front door. I asked Brian, "Why do you continue living in the mountains?"

"The mountains are our anchor."

"In what way?"

"My father was born and grew up here. My brother and I were born and grew up here. We've known this environment our entire lives. The forests were my companions growing up. They're solid. No matter how my days go, they are always there for me. Solitary walks in the woods soothe me, just feel right. I can't imagine living without them."

"How did it feel when your house burned down?"

Brian swept his left cheek with his fingers, scanned our surroundings, and turned back to face me. "It was very hard. In only a few hours, everything I was familiar with turned to ash and smoke."

He looked up to the sky, then continued, "Ninety percent of the structure was completely blackened inside and out, or burned completely to the ground. We couldn't salvage any one whole item that belonged to my wife, my daughters, or me. We basically started all over again with just some memories of things that once existed in our lives. We got a trailer and lived on my father's property for three years before moving into this house. The girls had a very hard time adjusting to the new school to begin with and then returning to the old one later. You know, at ten and eleven years old, you get disconnected from your friends and then three years later, you come back but the friendships may not be there or have already shifted to a different level. But they're young, and they're resilient. In the past year, they seem to have a better experience of living in this danger zone again. As teenagers now, they're beginning to appreciate this environment more than ever. My wife has learned to let go of our daughters' childhood stuff that now only exists in her memories of those first days of school and other first-time moments. She's even changed her buying habits. She doesn't buy things that aren't practical for the girls or for our lives, which is a good change for me." He chuckled.

"How about you?"

"Me? I feel like I've lost something. I can't explain exactly, but it's here." He taps his chest. "I thought it would always be there. When I was growing up, my brother and I were so free to ride our mountain bikes or roam the hills with the fresh smell of trees and plants, hearing animals howling, insects calling, and birds singing, and seeing the colorful small crawling creatures. Fires were not in my thoughts at all. Now, look around—only a few places have not been touched by the fires, which are getting too close, very personal..."

"Did the loss of your house change your feelings about living here?"

"No, not really. But I noticed that I'm more nervous about fires. I even built this house with only electricity. And whenever I come home and see my wife cooking with closed windows, I immediately open them whether the exhaust hood is on or not. I keep telling my wife to make sure there's open air when she's cooking, as if she were using combustion natural gas. In that respect, I am always alert to my surroundings. My wife says I'm a bit paranoid." He chuckled again.

"I understand the anxiety of it. The forests are diminishing. With the growth of the human population and the changes in the weather patterns, these mountain forests may not be as solid as we thought."

"I know. That's all the more reason to stay. They provide so much for me as a human being. I want to be here to guard them."

"Aren't you afraid of the fires?"

"Sure I'm afraid, but that's nature. There's nothing we can do to stop it except try to protect ourselves and our livelihood."

"As the fires happen more often, have you thought about the safety of your family?"

"Of course, safety for my wife and two daughters is my number one priority. But there are other dangers out there that I am not familiar with. At least I know how to fight fire and how to lead my family to safety."

"What if you can't fight it off?" I didn't want to push but I needed to get to the bottom of this.

"That's life, that's my destination, and that is nature calling me if that happened."

"How about your wife and two daughters. Do they think the same as you do?"

"They're with me. My wife is a college graduate. She knows city life but chooses to live in this remote place. My daughters are learning about the world in school and via the internet. They know there are other lifestyles. As for now, they are preparing themselves to live differently in the future, when this environment no longer accepts us as cohabitants."

Brian was an adjunct lecturer at a community college and taught energy efficiency in building. He also worked on contracts with the utility company and state agencies to audit home energy efficiency. His reason for living in the mountains was to be where his family roots were. Yet, the way he conducted his life was complicated by driving long distances to and from work. It made me wonder about the contradictory thinking of the human mind. Specifically, "when this environment no longer accepts us as cohabitants" profoundly lingered in mine.

Matthew had thought that way. He wanted to be a steward for the trees, for the earth. He studied and became a tree doctor, spent his entire life working with trees and their health, educating people to respect trees, for they existed before many of us. We, on the contrary, being dominant rulers, do not think that someday we will have exhausted nature's gifts to the extent that the repercussions eventually hurt ourselves. Being ignorant, we continue to harvest for profit, and cut down trees to satisfy our needs for space and convenience. The failure of stopping the tendency of human greed stampeded Matthew's mind to the point that he had no hope in saving the trees, to retain our cohabitant status with nature.

Letter Six

Dear Matthew,

I feel the pain that you had when the ancient white pine tree was cut down by the order of the court. I have known all along that people are gradually killing trees for the purpose of having more space for themselves. With increasing evidence, climate change has added to the selfish human efforts to destroy our environment. I see the burning forest again. I feel the bleeding and howling from the dying trees, which are frightening. What kind of life will we all experience with the ever-increasing fires?

The irony of what I am doing now is that I'm beginning to understand your desperation. I know you had mental health issues. But I didn't know the agony of feeling nature being deliberately ruined daily for human benefit until now. It's piercing the core of my being. How can I make this better going forward?

I don't know if my efforts will make a difference. But I have to do what I can to make peace with Mother Earth. This time, I am no longer a standby. I am in the mission of trying to restore and replant trees that were here before and that will be here after me.

Vivi

The mountain area where I was involved was huge, with an unevenly subdivided population. The wildland–urban interface is a more prevailing issue than the fires themselves. Policies and enforcement in this area would not be efficient. With the foehn wind, droughts, and human exploitation, figuring out how to communicate and implement fire prevention, vegetation planting, fire prediction, and rescue planning in the local communities will be the key to gaining stakeholders' support.

I visited Brian, Jack, Tom, and Scott more often. I asked for their help in gathering their local communities, wanting to hear their thoughts, their concerns, and their ideas for preventing fires, which, according to historical data, were getting deadlier every year.

At first, the communities didn't like my proposal of cutting down trees that encircled or were otherwise too close to individual residential units. I pulled historical fire data, created models for planting trees more incrementally, and performed simulations of post-fire predictions to persuade them to back me up on removing trees that were too close to individual residences. With Brian's professional knowledge and support, I also proposed that each community should have a team leader or point person who would dedicate time to organizing fire prevention plans. These plans would be implemented by each of the residents, and evacuation contingency plans would be communicated to related parties, all of which the community members consented to without further argument.

Taking down trees is a huge undertaking, it is a matter of being respectful and being responsible. Sometimes I asked myself, "Am I doing the right thing, cutting down some of these trees?" Each time, scientific studies, data, and common sense told me that it was the lesser of two evils.

Matthew hadn't hesitated to cut down the trees when he led a crew fighting the lightning-strike fires. He checked the clusters and individual trees, watched the winds, calculated the distance between the burning area to the south side of the communities, talked to the captain to ask for his expertise regarding the burning trend. With his thorough evaluation, crew members and volunteers followed instructions. Matthew knew the actions would be beneficial in the long-term despite the fact that he would not normally want to remove those old and young trees. In a split second, I saw in his eyes that an agonizing decision needed to be made. With his knowledge, he didn't vacillate. He executed with resolution, which was the charismatic Matthew I had seen emerge again and again when there were either emergencies or difficult situations involving nature and human life.

Residents within the wildland–urban interface are often widely dispersed from each other. Not all of them wanted to go along with the plans that my company recommended. But most of them realized that although those plans weren't perfect, they would reduce the risks that the community faced every day, particularly in the windy season.

By the time we got stakeholders' consent, more fires had erupted, more structures were destroyed, and more lives were taken.

"We cannot win," I said to Keith.

"This is not a battle. It's an ongoing life saga." He looked at me.

"Sometimes, I don't see the point in continuing what we are doing." I felt defeated by the newly started fires.

"Let's look at it this way: we are living in fire country. Wildfires have become part of our lives. If we don't do what we've been doing, the outcomes could be worse."

"You are optimistic."

"That is the only way we can survive in today's environment. I fought forest fires for twenty years. I have seen the various patterns of fires from Southern to Northern California and the Pacific Northwest. The fires have horrified me, but at the same time I am captivated by their beauty combined with deadly destructive force that is mingled with love and hate, with no alternative for us to pick."

"May I ask why you quit firefighting?"

"Ah, my body is giving up. In this case, the fires have won the battle, beating my physical strength. Nonetheless, I am still in firefighting."

"Where are we heading with this? I mean, how can we feel good about what we're doing?"

"We may not feel good in our lifetime." Keith looked me in the eyes. "For me, there must be a way to get us to suppress the frequency of wildfires. I know it sounds cliché. But I have faith in it. With people like Brian, you, and me, we have the power to motivate others to find better solutions to our dilemma, which is not going away."

I admired Keith. I wished that I could be as optimistic as he was. I seemed attracted to dead-end plights again and again. From mental health to wildland fire prevention, I didn't see any light at the end of the tunnel. I found myself falling into a rabbit hole, stuck with no way out. Was that how Matthew felt?

In our years of farming, I should have known that Matthew's mental health was declining, but I didn't. His hard work on the land masked his feeling of desperation, a feeling that nothing could change for a better tomorrow, which would come with the same old feeling of hopelessness. I thought he wasn't trying hard enough. If he had been disciplined and forced himself to do daily exercises, focused on the tasks at hand instead of thinking and worrying about the future, and concentrated on drawing cartoons, he would not have had time to swirl in the misery of depression. My subjective view of his state of mind disabled my trait of using keen rationality to comprehend the fact that depression had basically impaired Matthew's ability to behave as his authentic self.

I was at a crossroads once again. "How do I make my life free of 'no hope' endeavors?" I could not see a clear picture of the roads in front of me. I could easily continue to do risk assessment and control in wildland fire prevention. But how to reconcile with the bitter feelings I had about the recurrent fires was the million-dollar question that had been swimming in my head.

"Reconcile, I have too many loose ends to reconcile in life. Where to start?"

"You are doing it," my evil twin confirmed.

"I don't feel it."

"Sometimes feelings do not arrive at the same time as doing."

"You are philosophical."

"No, see how far you have come. At least, you have not given up on finding a way to live with your pain."

"I am tired. I don't want to find a way anymore."

"I know, it is tiresome. Still, you have to carry on."

"For what purpose?"

"Being alive is a merit by itself. Don't underestimate it."

"It is life that's overestimating my tolerance."

"How do you measure tolerance? If averting a fire will make you feel good, does that mean your tolerance has increased? Or if a fire kills more trees and people, does that mean your tolerance has decreased?" My evil twin hurled all these questions at me.

In a flash, I saw that my tolerance of suffering in life meant different things as different life events unfolded.

I studied Sanskrit in my youth literary group that was led by Zi Meng, who introduced *samsāra*, the realm of rebirth, which is basically an endless cycle in which the odyssey is perceived to be disappointing and tormenting.

In one of the series lectures Zi Meng asked, if we could choose our next lives, what would they be?

"I want to be a flying pig living in the Milky Way looking down on earth." I raised my hand and expressed my desire.

"Reasons for being a pig?"

"Pigs are considered to be intelligent. I want to be a bystander, look down on earth, and watch people's lives. I don't want to be a human again because I don't like the feelings that come with it."

"What good is it to be reborn?" I asked Zi Meng, after the lecture. We walked to the shore and sat on the rocks that were facing the sheltered Tolo Harbor to wait for the sunset.

He looked straight in the water. "I don't know. In fact, I don't even know if rebirth really happens. But I choose to be convinced that it exists, that I want rebirth, which gives me a sense of hope that I may be able to do better in my next life."

"But the doctrine indicates that the rebirth cycle is considered to be *duhkha*, unsatisfactory and painful. If the suffering is too doleful to bear and my current life ends with such tragedy, I cannot imagine my next life will be better. As the doctrine emphasizes that the cycle of rebirth is still woeful, how can I expect the misfortune won't reoccur in my next life?"

"It depends on what kind of karma one has cultivated. If I generate enough good karma, the outlook of my next life may be different."

"This life is already hard. Can't we just focus on the present? Why do I have to think about the next life?"

"Your current life is dictated by your previous life, in which you may not have thought about karma. What you do in your current life with karma in mind will impact your next life, so you don't have to think about it."

This recollection about karma reminded me that the sufficiency of being human for only one lifetime was an idea that had been sown in me during my years with Zi Meng and the young writers group. This enlightenment could have come from the influence of studying Buddhism or simply my experience of losing Uncle Mike.

Perhaps in this life I was paying the debt of what I did in my previous life. Would my payments in this life be enough to make my next life less haunting, more comforting?

Alan called, wanting a definite answer about the land.

"If I sell it to you, what would you do with the land?"

"I plan to grow hops, pick up where Matthew left off."

"I can partner with you on growing hops."

"Are you going to move back?"

I stopped. I hadn't thought of moving back.

"Vivi, I can hire anyone to do the job. But I need a committed person who lives here and is dedicated to the farm. You have been gone for over a decade. I don't see how you would fit into the picture…"

What Alan said was true. At the same time, I finally registered that he didn't want me to be the owner of the land. He wanted to carry out Matthew's dream without me, for which I didn't blame him.

I inherited the land by marriage. Alan had the family blood and was the only person who lived next to the land. He would be the most appropriate person to have the preemptive right to bring the land back into the family. He should have the preemptive right to bring the land back into the family instead of part of it being owned by a foreigner, a woman who didn't belong to it.

"If I sell it to you, could I come to visit?" I asked after a short silence.

"Of course you could. You always have a bed here, no matter what."

A month later, after talking to Timothy and requesting his honest input, after four years of debating, I decided to sell the land to Alan.

Letter Seven

Dear Matthew,

I have hung onto the land long enough. It is time to let it return to your family. The good news is that Alan will take good care of it. At least the land will stay in the family through Jerry's generation, if not longer.

I still have the aching feeling of letting it go. Letting the land go means I am letting the essence of you go. But why is it so hard on me?

Vivi

Letter Eight

Dear Matthew,

Remember the day I sent you to the incinerator, before you were pushed through the French door to the heat, I kissed your forehead, saying that someday I would forget you?

I was wrong. I cannot forget you. Whenever I encounter a troubled soul, I think of you.

This morning, I went to the laundromat to wash my comforter. When I walked in the laundromat, a homeless man in his thirties asked for money. I told him that I didn't have cash. After I put the clean comforter in the trunk, I walked up to this man and asked him if I could buy him lunch. He said sure. I asked what he wanted since he was sitting on the ground facing a restaurant. He told me what he wanted, and I placed the order with the cashier in the deli area. While I was waiting for the food outside the restaurant door, the man asked, "If you don't have money, how could you do the wash?"

"I used a credit card to load money onto the laundromat card. No cash exchanged."

A young woman stopped in front of the man, handed him a bag.

He asked what it was. The young woman replied and the man said, "Thank you. I have a stomach ulcer. I can't have that."

The young woman walked away with the bag.

When I handed him the bag of food and drink that he wanted, he opened the bag and smelled but didn't rush to eat.

This young man looked up and said to me, "God loves you."

I was just walking away. I turned back to him. "God loves you too."

In my memory, this was the first time I've said "God loves you too."

I felt that this young man needed a lift, so I used his language.

I only offered food, which is one of the entitlements that we all deserve. But the way he expressed his gratitude, citing God's love, gave hints that spiritually or mentally, he was struggling.

I wanted him to know: "I see you; I hear you; I feel you; 我懂."

Vivi